"What the devil..."

Dexter shouted in alarm ....
howling, an ambulance roared out of the
Georgetown hospital driveway and swerved in front
of the cab. The cabdriver braked immediately and
swung around in his seat, aiming a gun straight at
Liz's head.

"Either of you move and she gets it," he said.

The two doors closest to the sidewalk were
wrenched open. "He has a gun!" Liz screamed in
warning.

It was all she said. A leather-gloved hand was
clamped over her mouth and she was hauled from
the cab. Her captor pulled her arms behind her back
and thrust her onto the floor of the ambulance. The
doors were barely slammed behind her when the
ambulance shot into the narrow street.

The fist pressing her down relaxed its pressure. "You
can sit up now, *dorogoya*."

Liz lifted her head, too stunned to move the rest of
her body.

He smiled the warm, familiar smile she knew so
well. "Hello, Lizushka. Welcome to Washington."

Dear Reader:

We are delighted to bring you this daring series from Silhouette.

Intrigue — *where resourceful, beautiful women flirt with danger and risk everything for irresistible, often treacherous men.*

Intrigue — *where the stories are full of heart-stopping suspense and mystery lurks around every corner.*

You won't be able to resist **Intrigue**'s *exciting mix of danger, deception... and desire.*

Please write and let us know what you think of our selection of **Intrigue** *novels. We'd like to hear from you.*

Jane Nicholls
Silhouette Books
PO Box 236
Thornton Road
Croydon
Surrey
CR9 3RU

Free Fall

JASMINE CRESSWELL

SILHOUETTE

Intrigue

All the characters in this book have no existence outside the imagination of the author, and have no relation whatsoever to anyone bearing the same name or names. They are not even distantly inspired by any individual known or unknown to the author, and all the incidents are pure invention.

*First published in Great Britain in 1995
by Silhouette Books, Eton House, 18-24 Paradise Road,
Richmond, Surrey TW9 1SR*

© Jasmine Cresswell 1989

Silhouette, Silhouette Intrigue and Colophon are
Trade Marks of Harlequin Enterprises B.V.

ISBN 0 373 22105 3

46-9507

Made and printed in Great Britain

To Fiona and Stephen, with love

Chapter One

Liz saw the crowd outside her apartment building as soon as she turned the corner from the bus stop. Her mouth went dry and her stomach lurched in horrified recognition. Her hands cradled her waist.

"Oh no! Please, no!"

She wasn't sure if she spoke aloud. Blood drummed in her ears, cutting off sound. Inside her silent world, the lights of the squad cars flashed with hypnotic brilliance, glazing the falling snow with orange glitter. One, two, three. Three whirling lights. Three blue-and-white Denver police cars.

Last time, in Seattle, they'd only sent two.

Liz read the neat copperplate inscription on the door of the car nearest her: To Serve and Protect. A great motto, much favored by police departments. It looked so much better than To Harass and Intimidate.

Her gaze raced feverishly over the neon-lit scene. Two dozen spectators, three squad cars, a half-dozen cops—but no ambulance.

No ambulance, and no paramedics. Hope flared briefly. Maybe this time there never had been an ambulance. Maybe the police were here to investigate a burglary. Liz started running.

She saw the chalk outline on the pavement as soon as she'd elbowed her way through the crowd. The spring snow wasn't settling, and the chalk shone white and clean in the evening darkness, a wet gingerbread figure sketched on asphalt. A child's drawing, except for the blood.

Fear clawed at her throat. Liz swayed, grasping the police barricade for support. Dear God, it had happened again.

"You sure missed a horrible sight," commented the woman next to her. "They only moved the body ten minutes ago. The side of her face was smashed right in from where she fell. Terrible tragedy." The conventional words of grief didn't succeed in masking the relish in the woman's voice.

Liz fought to control the sickness welling up inside her. "Was it a young wo—? Do they know who it was?"

"A girl from one of the apartments. Look, you can see the open window up there on the top floor. That's where she fell from. Or jumped."

Liz didn't look up; she didn't need to. Her stomach gave another warning heave, and she pushed through the barricade, barely making it to the corner of her apartment building before she vomited.

When she finally stopped retching, she straightened to discover herself surrounded by three uniformed police officers. One of them—a sergeant—held out a wad of tissues. She wiped her mouth. The policemen watched, their eyes hard.

"The victim a friend of yours, Miss?" The inquiry was polite but cold.

"Maybe.... I think so.... I don't know.... I live here."

"Terrible for you to come home to all this." The sergeant's voice had warmed, now that he knew she wasn't just an overcurious bystander with a weak stomach. "Which apartment is yours? I'll see that the officer guarding the entrance lets you in."

She glanced up, finally allowing herself to look at the open window, a big bay in the center of the sixth floor. It was hers, of course. Hers and Karen Zeit's. She had known all along that it would be.

"I live in 6B," she said flatly, returning her gaze to the ball of soiled tissues.

She felt the policemen exchange glances. She closed her eyes, shoving the tissues into the pocket of her jacket and wrapping her arms more tightly around her body. She was shivering, she realized, and the little clicking noise resonating inside her head had to be the chattering of her teeth.

"You'd better come along inside and get warm."

She forced herself to look at the sergeant. "What's happened to Karen?"

"There's been an accident," he replied, his voice gruff. His two younger colleagues shuffled their feet and stared over her shoulder. They were worried, poor things. Worried about how a law-abiding citizen was going to take this shocking intrusion of violence into her life. It wasn't true that cops had no emotions. Liz had found that out in Seattle. The first time, when Brian died, they'd all been very sympathetic.

This time, once they knew the truth, they weren't likely to waste much time on sympathy. Some bright-eyed cop, eager for promotion, would check with the authorities in Seattle, and Liz would instantaneously be transformed from victim into suspect. Being a suspect was no fun at all. She'd found that out when Jill killed herself, only four short weeks after Brian.

She needed to know the worst about Karen, to have the horror confirmed. "Is my roommate dead?" she asked brusquely.

The sergeant made soothing noises, avoiding her eyes. He put a hand beneath her elbow, guiding her toward the rear entrance of the apartment building. "I think we should talk about this inside, where it's a bit warmer. Lousy weather for May, isn't it? But that's Denver for you. Swimsuit temperatures one day and a blizzard the next. If you'll follow me, I'll ask the apartment manager to make you a cup of coffee.''

Liz allowed herself to be led in through the service lobby and down to the basement where the superintendent had his apartment. She sat meekly at the appointed table and waited in silence while one of the policemen brought her a cup of coffee.

Dear God, Karen is dead. Dead. The awful word echoed in a bleak rhythm with her chattering teeth.

The policemen didn't ask how she wanted her coffee served, and presented it already laced with milk and sugar. The oily liquid tasted revolting enough to jerk her into renewed awareness of her surroundings. The sergeant had disappeared, to be replaced by a tall man, wearing a raincoat that was a fraction too tight. A homicide detective: she'd learned to recognize the breed. She wondered how long he'd been standing on the other side of the Formica-topped table, staring at her.

"I'm Lieutenant Rodriguez," he said, flashing a badge and a small smile. Three months ago, she would have found the smile reassuring. Now she knew better. She blinked her eyelids, the only part of her that seemed capable of movement.

"I'm sorry you had to find out about your roommate this way."

"She's dead," Liz said flatly. "Isn't she?"

"I'm afraid so. If it's any consolation, Miss Meacham, I'm sure your roommate died instantly."

Instantly. Ten seconds after she hit the ground? Twenty? A minute? Liz blinked again, then glanced at the lieutenant. He doesn't look Hispanic, she thought. She stirred her mud-gray coffee, wondering how he knew her name. Perhaps the superintendent had told him. She could have asked, but it was too difficult to form the question. Shock always seemed to reduce her brain to a scattershot incoherence of half thoughts. Maybe she should carry a sign: Sharing an Apartment with Liz Meacham is Terminally Hazardous to Your Health. Horrifyingly, she found that she wanted to laugh.

She took another sip of coffee, swallowing the laughter along with the disgusting brew. The lieutenant's chair scraped over the thin carpet as he sat down. Gradually she became aware of the acrid smell of stale cigarette smoke. Her senses, numb ever since she turned the corner from the bus stop, were beginning to function once again. The cigarette smoke, now that she could smell it, made her stomach roil. All in all, it might have been better if her body had stayed numb.

"There's a few questions I need to ask you, Miss Meacham. I'm sorry, but there's nobody else we can ask."

Liz avoided the lieutenant's eyes. She stared into the kitchen, where she could see the police sergeant talking on the phone. The apartment manager was at the sink, filling his percolator. She shuddered, then dragged her gaze back to the lieutenant.

"Have you told Karen's parents yet? They live somewhere near Detroit, in one of the suburbs. I guess their phone number is on the bulletin board in Karen's bedroom."

"We found it, and we're working on notifying the parents. Have you shared an apartment with the deceased for long, Miss Meacham?"

The deceased. Karen probably hadn't been dead more than a couple of hours, and already she had been transformed from a human being to an item of official jargon. Liz wished she could switch off her awareness of Karen's humanity as easily as the detective. She ran her index finger around the rim of her mug. "I moved in with Karen six weeks ago."

"I see. And did you know her before that, Miss Meacham?"

"No. I only moved to Denver recently." Liz spoke rapidly, giving the lieutenant no time to interject awkward questions. "I met Karen at a party a couple of days after I arrived in town. She was looking for a roommate, and I was looking for somewhere to live. We were glad to find each other."

The lieutenant wrote painstakingly in his notebook. Unlike TV cops, who never seemed to take notes about anything, Liz had learned that real-life policemen wrote everything down. The lieutenant turned the page. Did it take that long to write "Deceased met roommate at a party"?

"Just for the record, Miss Meacham, would you tell us where you lived before you moved in with the deceased?"

Liz's fingers closed around her mug. So there it was, the question she had been dreading. The innocuous-sounding question she had known would come up sooner or later. She wished it hadn't come up quite so soon.

She cleared her throat. "I lived in Seattle."

Lieutenant Rodriguez was not a fool. He obviously heard the tension in her voice, although she'd tried hard to smooth it out. Damn it, she wasn't responsible for Karen's decision to jump out of their apartment window. She wasn't some freakish, latter-day version of Typhoid Mary. Despite what had happened to Brian and then to Jill, the rational part of Liz's brain still insisted that suicide was one of the few deadly diseases you couldn't catch from your roommate.

"Seattle is a big city, Miss Meacham. Could we have an address, please? Just for the record, of course."

Of course, she thought with silent irony. Nevertheless, she gave him what he was asking for. "755 West Arbor Avenue. Apartment 14D."

Jill's address. No point in saying she'd lived there less than a month before Jill had been found splattered on the pavement outside their living-room window. No point in explaining that Brian had committed suicide a month before Liz moved in with Jill. On the other hand, there was no point in lying. Her name alone would be enough to pull up all the facts on the Seattle police computers.

"Do you know where the deceased was employed, Miss Meacham?"

She should have been more alert to Karen's moods, Liz berated herself. Karen had seemed uptight these past few days, ever since Liz had returned from Mexico. But Liz had deliberately refrained from inquiring, deliberately kept her distance. Since Brian died, she hadn't wanted too much emotional closeness—

"Miss Meacham?"

With considerable effort, Liz focused her attention on the detective. "I'm sorry, I didn't hear your question."

"The deceased, Karen Zeit. Do you know where she was employed?"

"She worked for Dexter Rand. She was the senior secretary in his Denver office."

Lieutenant Rodriguez finally showed a degree of surprise. "Dexter Rand? You mean the senator?"

"Yes." Liz didn't—couldn't—elaborate on the stark response.

"Oh, brother, the media are going to love this," the lieutenant muttered under his breath, scribbling in his notebook. "Was the deceased interested in politics?"

"Not that I know of. I think she just enjoyed the hectic pace of Dexter's office."

Something in her voice must have betrayed her. Or perhaps it was her slip in using Dexter's first name. The lieutenant looked up quickly. "Nothing personal in their relationship?"

"Not that I know of."

"Would you have known?"

The look Liz gave him was cool. "Probably not."

The lieutenant changed the subject. "And you, Miss Meacham? Where do you work?"

"I'm in charge of market research at Peperito's. You probably know them. They're headquartered near the airport."

"Peperito's? The Mexican-food company?"

"Yes."

The lieutenant smiled, a genuine smile this time. "My wife always buys their *salsa*. She says it's the best."

"Thanks. We really work hard to keep up the quality. We import all the spices from Mexico."

"Is that so?" The lieutenant flipped through his notes, his moment of informality over. "Well, back to the matter at hand. Did the deceased give any indication that she was depressed, Miss Meacham? Did she have any reason to take her own life? Any arguments with men friends . . . colleagues . . . the senator . . . that sort of thing?"

"I don't know much about Karen's personal life," Liz said. "I travel a lot with my job and I don't suppose Karen and I spent ten evenings together in six weeks. I just came back from an extended business trip to Mexico."

"Is that why you shared an apartment, because of the travel? You and Miss Zeit could both have afforded your own place, I guess. Rents in Denver aren't that high."

"It was one of the reasons. I need to keep expenses down. My mother's in a private nursing home." Liz clasped her hands on the table and stared at her thumbs. Her nail polish was chipped, she realized. Karen would never have left the office with chipped nail polish. Karen had been the most immaculately groomed woman Liz had ever met.

Too immaculate to contemplate ending her life smashed to smithereens on a driveway overlooked by two large trash Dumpsters.

The thought sprang unbidden to the forefront of Liz's mind, then lodged there, obstinately refusing to go away. "Are you sure it was suicide?" she asked the lieutenant. "Couldn't it have been an accident or—or something?"

Why in the world had she said that? Good God, was she actually trying to suggest to the police that Karen's death might not be suicide? Hadn't she had enough trouble as a murder suspect in Seattle? Liz clamped her lips tightly shut, before she could make any more disastrous suggestions.

Rodriguez, thank heaven, didn't pick up on any undertones to her question. He shrugged. "An accident's not likely. There's a kitchen chair pulled up to the living-room window and an open bottle of Scotch standing next to the chair. The bathroom sink has aspirin spilled into it. I guess she might have taken aspirin for a headache, then decided to clean the windows and drink neat Scotch at the same time." The lieutenant's tone suggested that after several years on the city police force, he'd learned to accept any act of human folly as possible. "I'd say everything points to a straightforward suicide, except she didn't leave a note, and suicides usually do. The autopsy will tell us more."

Brian and Jill hadn't left notes, either. Brian had shot himself in front of an open window. Then, four scant weeks later, Jill had filled herself with prescription tranquilizers and pushed herself out headfirst from the fourteenth floor of their Seattle apartment. How many more variations could be worked on the theme of suicide victims spread-eagled on the sidewalk?

Three bloody, crumpled blobs, waiting to greet Liz, waiting to torment her with the knowledge that she had been totally insensitive to their problems, totally insensitive to the edge of desperation that must have crept into their lives.

Unless they hadn't committed suicide.

Brian's suicide had seemed tragic but within the bounds of possibility, given his recurring black moods. Jill's sui-

cide a few weeks later had seemed a terrible, malignant coincidence. But Karen's suicide strained the limits of Liz's
credulity. Three roommates tumbling to their deaths within
three months just didn't make any kind of sense.

Unless they had been murdered.

Liz sprang up from the table, hearing her chair crash behind her as she groped blindly toward the bathroom. She
stumbled into a closet and a bedroom before she found the
right door. The light was on. The room was empty. She
leaned over the sink and turned on the hot water full force.
She heaved for a few seconds but, thank God, she didn't
throw up. Her stomach had nothing left to vomit except
two sips of coffee.

She was still sluicing her cheeks in zombielike repetition
when the lieutenant appeared in the doorway.

"Feeling better?" he asked.

Liz raised her head from the sink. "I feel one hundred
percent lousy."

"We'd like to ask a few more questions."

"No." She shook her head. The police were going to find
out about her past sooner or later, but tonight she was too
tired and too scared to face up to any more of Lieutenant
Rodriguez. "I want to go to a hotel," she said abruptly.

"If you wait another half hour until the technicians have
finished upstairs, you can go into your apartment and pack
a suitcase."

"I don't want to go into my apartment." Liz fought to
keep her voice calm. "I can't hang around any longer. I'll
buy a toothbrush at the drugstore. I want to get out of here,
Lieutenant. Now."

Surprisingly, he didn't protest. Perhaps he was afraid she
might faint, bang her head on the tile floor and then sue the
city for harassment. God knows, and she knew, having
glimpsed herself in the bathroom mirror, she looked rotten enough to give anybody cause for alarm. She'd lost
weight steadily since Brian died, and she'd begun to ap-

pear skeletal even with makeup on and her clothes in order. Tonight, with every trace of color drained from her face, she looked like a death's-head.

Liz pushed her way out of the bathroom, ignoring a final question from the lieutenant. She grabbed her purse from the table as she passed by. "I'll be in the airport Hilton," she said tersely, knowing Rodriguez had no grounds to detain her. Not yet. Not until he contacted his counterparts in Seattle. Then Lieutenant Rodriguez was going to start asking himself how many coincidences he wanted to believe. How many dead roommates could a law-abiding citizen explain away?

"Do you need a ride, Miss Meacham?"

"No thanks. My car's right in the parking lot. I took the bus this morning because the roads were so icy, but it's not freezing anymore."

"Still, you want to drive carefully, Miss Meacham. We don't need any more accidents tonight."

Liz smiled bitterly. "I don't seem accident-prone, Lieutenant. At least not personally."

"You're lucky," Rodriguez said, but she felt his gaze follow her as she left the room.

Chapter Two

The traffic light flicked from amber to red and Liz drew her Honda to an obedient halt. When the light turned green thirty seconds later, she gazed at it blankly until the irate honking of several horns reminded her that green meant Go.

But go where? She drove across the intersection and stared into the darkness, trying to discover where she was. Alameda Avenue, according to the signpost. Alameda, heading west toward the mountains.

How did I end up here? she wondered. Her mind felt thick and slow-moving, and her hands sat clumsily on the steering wheel, alien attachments at the end of her arms. The simple act of guiding the car through traffic demanded intense concentration. She'd intended to drive straight to the airport Hilton. Instead, here she was on the fringe of some of Denver's most prestigious real estate. The Denver Country Club was only a few blocks away. The Polo Club was even closer.

So was Dexter Rand's Denver home.

The thought came and went without making any particular impact. Liz waited at another traffic light, then turned left. Dexter's house loomed ahead of her at the end of the cul-de-sac. With a shiver of anticipation, she recognized that she'd intended to drive here all along.

She parked the car against the only free stretch of side-walk and stared at the high brick wall surrounding Dexter's home. As if offering her a welcome, the lights from the upper windows gleamed through the dark evergreens that lined the driveway. Liz grimaced. A false impression, if ever she'd seen one.

The house was a handsome brick-and-timber affair, vaguely Tudor in style, with a spectacular yard designed for summer entertaining. Liz knew all this because she'd tempted fate once before, dropping Karen off for work one morning. But she wasn't sure why she had come here, to-night of all nights, or what she expected to accomplish. Dexter Rand was the last man in the world she wanted to ask for help or comfort.

I'll tell him about Karen before the police get to him. Maybe I owe him that much.

That simple decision exhausted Liz's mental capabilities. She got out of the car, locked it and pocketed the keys, feeling vaguely pleased that she hadn't done something dumb like leaving them in the ignition.

She wrapped her woolly scarf around her chin to shut out the biting wind, and walked up the driveway. *I'll just tell him about Karen, nothing more,* she reassured herself, listening to her boots crunch on the icy path. *I won't mention Seattle, or murder, or anything like that.* She needed to formulate her thoughts into simple instructions, or she knew her control would vanish into a shapeless fog of fear.

She rang the bell. A maid opened the door, and a muted babble of voices and laughter greeted Liz as soon as she stepped inside. Her heart sank. Of course! Dexter was giving a party. That was the reason for the welcoming lights and for all the cars parked along Pinewood Road. She should have recognized the signs. Dexter Rand, national hero, U.S. senator, former Air Force test pilot, and all-around important person, never came home from Washington without entertaining. His house was probably

crammed with local VIPs, not to mention aspiring VIPs
and the inevitable hangers-on who came for the free cocktails. It had been crazy to drive over here. It had been even
crazier to imagine she'd actually get to talk privately with
Dexter.

"Good evening, ma'am. May I take your coat?"

Liz blinked and stared at the maid. Her coat. The maid
expected her to stay and socialize. It was really funny, if you
stopped to think about it.

"Er...no, thanks," Liz mumbled. "I don't think I'm
staying." She attempted a smile. "I'm sorry. Wrong party."

Her smile was not much of a success. The maid's welcoming glance faded into a look of downright suspicion,
and she glanced over her shoulder, obviously searching for
a security guard, or at least a hefty male waiter. Liz didn't
want to be thrown out. She turned to go, fumbling for the
handle of the front door.

A sudden tension at the base of her spine caused her to
look over her shoulder, so that she and the maid saw Dexter at almost the same moment. The maid greeted him with
evident relief. Liz stared at him in numb silence. All she
could think of was that he looked even better in real life
than he did on television. His six-feet-two-inch body was
still perfectly proportioned, and his dark, coarse hair remained indecently thick, with no more than the occasional
thread of gray to mark the passing of the last nine years. On
him, even the crow's-feet around his eyes looked good. She
wished he'd gone bald or developed a beer belly. Except, of
course, that Dexter Rand never drank anything as ple-
beian as beer.

"This young lady was just leaving," the maid said.

"But not before I've had a chance to say hello, I
hope...." Dexter's professionally warm voice trailed away
into stunned silence. "Liz?" he asked hoarsely. "Liz, what
in the world are you doing here?"

"Karen's dead."

She hadn't meant to drop the news with such a devastating lack of finesse. If she had been in full control of her actions, she would never have come near Dexter Rand. They had successfully avoided each other for nine years, and this was hardly the ideal time to choose for a reunion.

"Karen? You mean Karen Zeit, my secretary? What in the world happened?" For a moment, but only for a moment, Dexter looked blank. Then his usual capacity for quick thinking under pressure reasserted itself. It was a skill that had made him invaluable as a test pilot. Liz had seen him use it to even greater effect when facing inquisitive reporters on the Hill. Whatever he was feeling, Liz knew he would reveal none of it.

"This is terrible news," he said, his voice tinged with just the right amount of sorrow. "A terrible shock, too. Karen seemed so healthy when she left here this afternoon. Was it . . . ? It must have been a car accident?"

The old, destructive desire to prick Dexter's damnable self-control stirred among the debris of Liz's emotions. She spoke without giving herself time for second thoughts. "No, not a car accident. They found her dead on the sidewalk outside her apartment building. The police think she jumped."

"She killed herself? Oh, my God!" For an instant Liz saw stark horror in Dexter's eyes, then he reached out and drew her further into the foyer, away from the front door. Control once again masked his expression.

"Poor Karen," Dexter said. "I'm sorry, so very sorry. I knew something was on her mind, and now I'm kicking myself for missing the signs that things were getting desperate." His gaze flicked over the name printed on the maid's fancy apron. "Gwen, could you help us out by finding Evan Howard, and asking him to come to my study as soon as possible?"

"I would, sir, but I don't know what Mr. Howard looks like."

"Blond, short, thirtyish. Slender build. Anybody on my staff can point him out to you."

"Certainly, sir. I'll find him right away. You want him in your study, you said?"

Dexter nodded, and Gwen, seeming reassured by Dexter's calm, take-charge tone of voice, walked off briskly in the direction of the main reception rooms. Liz wanted to mock the maid for being so gullible, so susceptible to Dexter's aura of control, but she couldn't. Why had she herself come here, if not to let Dexter take charge? In the last resort, wasn't that what she'd always wanted Dexter to do? Hadn't she always expected him to walk behind her, picking up the disorganized pieces of her life and rearranging them into some neat new pattern?

The thought was shocking in its novel perception of their relationship, and she shoved it angrily aside. Good grief, she must be closer to the edge than she'd realized if she was actually finding excuses for Dexter. Dexter, the inhuman superachiever. The man had exploited her from the day they first met.

"Let go of my arm," she said through her teeth. The anger felt good. Much better than the numb fear that had preceded it. "I'm leaving, Dexter."

"No, you're not. We need to talk." He gave a passing guest one of his patented thousand-watt smiles, slipped his arm around Liz's waist, and propelled her with iron force through the foyer, skillfully eluding the half-dozen people who tried to engage him in conversation. He finally stopped at a heavy oaken door and punched an electronic key code into the pad above the lock. He opened the door and stood back to let Liz pass. His manners always had been impeccable, she thought with a twist of irony. That was only one of the reasons she had found their constant fights so unendurable. She had screamed and yelled like a demented banshee, while Dexter politely—condescendingly—explained the error of her ways.

Even the distant memory of those painful times was enough to make Liz boil inside, a vulnerable nineteen-year-old again instead of a mature woman approaching thirty. She glanced around the room in an effort to calm her unruly emotions.

For anybody who knew Dexter well, the study contained few surprises. The room looked almost the same as the study Dexter had furnished in their Frankfurt apartment: comfortable and efficient, without any particular hint of luxury. The money in Dexter's family had been rattling around so long, he never felt any need to remind people that he had it. Nothing of the nouveau riche about good old Dex. Liz watched, fighting an unwelcome sensation of being transported back in time, as he opened a concealed cupboard in the paneling and revealed a small bar. He poured two brandies.

"Here," he said, offering one to Liz. "I need this, even if you don't."

"I don't drink in a crisis," she said, finally managing to look straight at him. "I learned not to."

He grinned, damn him, his gray eyes cruelly mocking. "Good lesson," he said, downing his own brandy in a single swallow. "You must've had a smart teacher."

"Experience. The best one of all."

For a split second, she felt the tension arc between them, and she knew her words had gotten to him. But when he turned around from the bar he displayed no emotion other than polite concern. He wasn't about to rehash old arguments, a fact for which she ought to be grateful.

"Let's sit down," he said, gesturing toward the sofa. "Damn it, I still can't believe she's dead! We spent two hours together this afternoon going over a speech, and she didn't give a hint of being desperate enough to walk out of here and kill herself. What happened?"

"The police think she threw herself out of the living-room window. I guess she must have...done it...right after she got home from work."

Dexter's eyes were shadowed with pain and a hint of some other emotion Liz couldn't identify. "That's terrible, almost unbelievable." He frowned. "Maybe I just don't want to believe it because I feel so guilty. How could she sit and chat about her plans for the weekend, when she intended to do this to herself a couple of hours later? How could I have missed all her signals of despair? Hell, she must have given me a dozen of them, if I'd been looking."

"Maybe not. Maybe something happened after she got home. A devastating phone call or something."

"I sure would like to think so." Dexter looked up, a new question obviously occurring to him. "How do you know all this, Liz? Come to think of that, how did you know Karen? She never mentioned your name to me."

Liz avoided his eyes. "She was—my roommate."

"You were sharing an apartment with my personal secretary?"

"Yes. Is that illegal or something?"

The pause before he replied was almost undetectable. "Not illegal. Surprising. Did she know about—us?"

"No."

"Odd that she never spoke about you."

"We'd been sharing the apartment less than two months. She probably had no reason to mention me. Why would she?"

He shrugged. "Things like that usually come up in conversation, although Karen never did talk much about her friends."

"I wasn't a friend, only a roommate. We didn't know each other at all well."

She spoke with more vehemence than the subject demanded, and Dexter scrutinized her intently for a moment before taking another sip of brandy. From his perspective, it must be hard to believe that Liz hadn't anticipated a meeting between the two of them from the moment she moved in with Karen. With an unwelcome flash of self-knowledge, Liz realized he was right to be suspicious. At some deeply buried level of her subconscious she had known that living with Karen would eventually bring her smack into the middle of Dexter's orbit. Thankfully, he asked her another question before she had time to pursue this uncomfortable new insight.

"What are you doing here in Denver, Liz? When we parted company, I didn't think anything would tear you away from life in the Big Apple."

If only he knew, Liz thought ruefully. If only he knew how grateful she'd been five years ago to find an obscure job in an obscure corner of southern Ohio. Better that he should never know. Pride made a great substitute for other emotions. She smiled brightly.

"It was tough leaving New York, but you know what companies are like these days. If you want a promotion, you have to be prepared to relocate, and I was tired of the entertainment industry."

"Why didn't you go back to skating, not even to teach?"

She pushed her fingers through her hair, her smile brighter than ever. "I doubt if anyone on the Olympic team would have me, and I'm not interested in anything else. There's nothing more pathetic than a second-rate athlete trying to eke out a living on the fringes of the sports world."

"You aren't a second-rate athlete, Liz, and we both know it. You went to pieces during that last championship, although God knows why. No skater spends years in training and then walks out onto the ice for an Olympic contest with her mind obviously elsewhere. I've always suspected your sister had something to do with it."

"Alison?" He was so far off the mark that it was almost funny. "Poor Alison. You never did like her, did you?"

"The fact that she was your twin didn't make her your friend, Liz. You never would understand that simple fact."

Liz laughed harshly. "Funny thing," she said. "Nine years and nothing changes. Isn't this about where our last conversation ended?"

Dexter stared into his empty glass. "You're right, and this isn't the moment for hashing over the past. We should be thinking about Karen. Did you discover...? Are you the one who discovered her?"

"No." Liz drew in a deep breath. "When I came home tonight, she was already dead. They'd already moved her. All I saw was the outline of her body on the pavement...."

Dexter put a hand over hers. "I'm sorry, Liz. Really sorry. That must have been a hellish sight to come home to."

She stared at his hand, fighting a ridiculous urge to give way to tears. The strength of his fingers had always fascinated her, especially the way he used that strength so considerately when he made love. In bed, Dexter had not been the cool, self-possessed man of his public facade. In bed, she had always been able to make him lose control. When they made love, she had glimpsed facets of another, more vulnerable man. In bed, she had sometimes thought that Dexter loved her.

He continued to cradle her hand in his clasp. "Why don't you think Karen committed suicide?" he asked softly. "Why do you think the police have got it all wrong?"

Liz jerked up her head and tugged her hand away, anger and a strange relief combining in an explosive mixture. "Damn you, Dexter! Why don't you ever ask the same questions anybody else would ask?"

"Because you don't want me to ask the standard questions. You came here for a reason, Liz, and that must be connected with Karen's death. If you believed she'd committed suicide, you wouldn't have come. Only something really important would reconcile you to seeing me again. We didn't exactly part friends, and I imagine my marriage to Susan only made things worse."

She sprang up from the sofa, turning her back on him. "I'm sorry about your wife," she said abruptly. "Nowadays you don't expect a woman as young as Susan to die of heart disease."

"Statistically it happens, but I guess we never anticipate people we love becoming part of the statistics." There was a tiny pause, and Dexter's voice roughened. "Amanda has found it really difficult to accept her mother's death."

Liz swallowed hard. "How old is Amanda now?"

"She's almost eight, and in my totally unprejudiced opinion, she's gorgeous." Liz could almost hear Dexter smiling. "She was born exactly a year after Susan and I got married. A great anniversary gift for both of us."

Nothing he said was news to Liz, but she'd felt obligated to get the topic of his wife and daughter out of the way. She heard the warmth, the gentle caring that crept into his voice when he spoke their names. Now she knew exactly how he sounded when he loved someone without reservation—and she wished she didn't.

"But you aren't here to discuss Amanda," Dexter said. "Why did you come, Liz? What's bothering you so much about Karen Zeit's death that you were prepared to talk to me face-to-face?"

As soon as he asked the question, Liz realized that she planned to tell him the whole truth, at least insofar as she could call her pathetic smattering of suspicions *truth*. She wasn't entirely comfortable with her decision, and walked over to the windows, keeping her back toward him when she finally spoke.

"I think Karen was murdered."

Silence. She was grateful that he didn't protest, or tell her in polite euphemisms that she was crazy. After a second or two, he simply walked over to where she was standing, turned her around and looked at her assessingly with those cool gray eyes of his. He asked only one question. "Why?"

"Karen isn't my first roommate to die. I was working in Seattle until I moved to Denver at the beginning of March. I shared apartments with two other people there, and both of them died almost the same way as Karen. Either a few weeks of living with me is enough to drive sane people crazy, or somebody is systematically killing off my roommates." She tried a smile, without much success. "Nice alternatives, huh? Liz the Witch, or Liz the Intended Victim."

"Not nice alternatives at all, and both of them hard to believe. First question, if you're the intended victim of a plot, why is somebody killing off your roommates? Why not murder you directly?"

"Maybe the killer makes mistakes?"

"You mean he's murdering by remote control, and the wrong person keeps ending up dead?"

"Something like that."

"Three times? Come on, Liz, even a psychopath would do a better job of fine-tuning his methods than that."

"Then how can it be murder, Dex?" The old nickname slipped out almost unnoticed. "Three unconnected suicides may be hard to believe, but three unconnected murders belong to the land of paranoid fantasy."

He put an arm around her and drew her back to the sofa. "We reach an obvious conclusion: the deaths aren't unconnected."

She held her body very straight against the cushions. "You mean I'm the connecting link?"

"You have to be. That's the only logical explanation."

"But Dex, I'd never even met Karen Zeit until two days before I moved in with her! And she had no links to either Brian or Jill. She came from a different part of the country, her work was different. All their work was different—"

"What did your other roommates do?"

"Brian was a university professor, and Jill was a social worker. Jill was in her twenties, Brian was forty-five and Karen was thirty-something. Dex, they have nothing in common."

"But they do. We just established that. They all shared an apartment with you."

"Which brings us right back to where we started. It makes no sense, Dex. Nobody has a reason to kill off my roommates."

"On the contrary," he said neutrally. "If you're the person doing the killing, everything makes perfectly good sense."

Liz felt herself turn cold with horror. "You think...you believe I murdered my roommates?"

"It seems—unlikely."

"Thanks for the ringing vote of confidence." Liz dug her fingers into the cushion. "Dex, for God's sake, I didn't murder those people. Don't you know me well enough to realize I could never kill anybody? Particularly not by pushing them out of a window."

"I don't think we know each other at all," Dexter said. "Not nine years ago and certainly not now. But that's beside the point, I guess. I was simply suggesting that there must be logical explanations for three roommates of yours getting themselves murdered. I pointed out the most obvious one."

The chilling fear that had been clawing at Liz for hours began to take on a sharper reality. "The police are going to arrest me," she said, her voice shaking. "Somebody's going to contact the police in Seattle and then it will all be over. I'm going to be arrested, Dex."

His grasp on her hands tightened reassuringly. "Not if I can avoid it."

"How can you keep me out of jail when you don't even believe I'm innocent?"

"I didn't say that, Liz. I simply suggested that we don't know each other very well." His gaze became unexpectedly sympathetic. "You're freezing, Liz. Let me pour you another brandy, strictly for medicinal purposes."

He was right about one thing: she was freezing, inside and out. And if she was headed for a jail cell, she might as well make the most of her remaining few hours of freedom. "All right, thanks. I think I could use some of your vintage cognac."

Dexter walked to the bar and reached for clean glasses. "Aside from the fact that you can't believe the coincidence of three roommates committing suicide within three months, do you have any other reason for thinking Karen and the others might have been murdered?"

She shook her head. "Not a thing, unless you count my feeling that they weren't suicidal sorts of people."

"Did you know them well enough to judge?"

"Not Karen, maybe. But the other two. Jill and I had been acquainted with each other for a couple of years. We belonged to the same health club. And Brian...I guess you could say we knew each other pretty well."

Carefully, Dexter returned the stopper to the brandy bottle. "Were you and Brian lovers?" he asked.

"We'd talked about getting engaged. We were living together."

"That doesn't answer my question, Liz."

"I think it does. If it's any of your business."

Before Dexter could say anything more, a perfunctory knock at the door was followed by the sound of the lock clicking open. A slender man with pale blond hair and a perspiring forehead erupted into the room, trailing an aura of generalized disaster.

"Dexter! Thank God you're here!"

"Hello, Evan. I'm glad Gwen managed to find you."

"Gwen? Who's she?" Without waiting for an answer, Evan rushed on. "Dexter, what in blazes are you doing hiding away in here? Holy hell's breaking loose out there, and nobody can find you. I just had a call from the police. Karen's been found dead outside her apartment, and the reporters are already swarming—'' Evan broke off abruptly, as he suddenly realized Dexter wasn't alone. He drew himself up, mopping his forehead with a silk handkerchief pulled from his breast pocket. In the blink of an eye he transformed himself into a dapper, deferential assistant.

"Oh, I'm sorry, Senator. I didn't know you were entertaining. When you've given your guest her drink, perhaps you could spare me a moment? In private? There are a couple of administrative matters that need your attention. When you've finished with your guest, of course."

"Let me introduce you two to each other," Dexter said, a definite note of wry humor in his voice. "Liz, this is my public-relations aide, Evan Howard. Evan, this is my former wife—Liz Meacham."

"Your ex-wife?" Evan looked as if he might faint. "How do you do, Ms. Meacham. I thought you lived in New York."

"Somebody hasn't been keeping your files up-to-date, Mr. Howard. I haven't lived in New York for more than five years."

"Liz lives in Denver," Dexter supplied. "She shared an apartment with Karen Zeit."

Evan dropped his handkerchief. "Holy hell," he said.

Dexter smiled. "Now that you've mentioned it, Evan, I guess that's pretty much what I was thinking."

Evan bent to pick up his handkerchief, and Dexter turned to hand Liz her brandy. For a split second their gazes locked in rueful, shared amusement. The unexpected moment of intimacy made Liz profoundly uncomfortable. She and Dexter Rand did not operate on the same mental wavelength. She didn't want to operate on the same mental wavelength as Dexter Rand. That was one of the illusions that had led her into trouble before.

Taking things calmly was obviously not one of the skills Evan had been hired for. "The media are gonna crucify you, Dex. Holy moly, what have I ever done to deserve this?"

"Signed on to my staff?" Dexter suggested mildly.

Evan ignored this remark. His eyes narrowed in acute concentration. "There's no way we can keep her name out of the paper," he muttered, staring at Liz without really seeing her. "They're bound to find out she was married to you—she's listed on all your official bios. World Champion Figure Skater, Liz Meacham." He nibbled his lower lip. "There must be some angle we could come up with. How about you approached Liz to teach the orphans in that school you sponsor? We'll tie it into the Olympic program somehow. Make it sound patriotic. Overcoming personal differences for the good of your country."

"Why in the world would I approach Liz? There are a dozen world-class skaters active in Colorado, and everybody in the skating business knows Liz hasn't been near an ice rink since she left Germany."

"You're right. Skating stinks." A gleam lighted Evan's eyes. "How about a reconciliation? Now there's an idea. You and Liz are getting together again. Remarriage in the air, and all that good stuff."

"No," Liz said flatly. "No. We'd never be able to pull it off. And how would a story like that help? It would just fan the gossip flames."

"How about telling the truth?" Dexter suggested. "There's a radical new approach for you to consider, Evan. You could tell the reporters that I had no idea Liz was living in the same apartment as my personal secretary, and that until tonight we hadn't spoken to each other in nine years."

Evan's expression turned sour. "Damn it, Dexter, nobody's gonna believe a dumb story like that! Your ex-wife lives with your personal secretary, who commits suicide for no apparent reason. Even you must see the scandal sheets will have the three of you locked up in some sort of bizarre triangular love nest before the first edition hits the streets."

Liz stood up. "I'm sorry, Dexter. I've really done you a bad turn by coming here. I've only been in Denver a few weeks, and half that time I've been out of the country on business trips. If I'd stayed away, we could have played down our past connection. After all, we both know it has absolutely nothing to do with this case. Isn't there some back way I could get out of here and avoid all the reporters who are probably lying in wait out front?"

Evan beamed his approval. "An excellent suggestion, Ms. Meacham. I'll let you out through the kitchen and arrange for one of the catering people to drive you home."

"But my own car's parked out front on Pinewood Road. How will I get it back?"

"Don't give your car another moment's thought, Ms. Meacham. If you'll let me have the keys, I'll see that somebody gets it home to you tomorrow, inconspicuously. What sort of car do you drive?"

"A Hond—"

"It doesn't matter what she drives," Dexter said. "You surely don't think we're going to smuggle her out of this house without causing comment, after at least twenty guests saw me walk down the hallway with her? I'll bet there are already at least a half-dozen rumors making the rounds about the 'mystery woman' I escorted into my study."

"Then what do you suggest? That we take her out front and introduce her as your ex-wife? Just when the story about Karen is breaking? Damn it, Dexter, you can't afford a breath of scandal with the crucial hearings before the Armed Services Committee about to resume. And this sure ain't a breath, it's a gale!"

"I suggest that we don't have much choice except to ride it out. My feeling is that Liz should spend the night here, so that we can work on our stories while you hold the reporters at bay. Then Liz and I'll meet the press together, tomorrow morning. Is that okay with you, Liz?"

It seemed slightly less okay than spending the night in a cage with a hungry tiger. The only thing that might possibly be worse was the prospect of driving to a hotel room and spending the night alone with her imagination and her suddenly overactive memories. She looked at Evan Howard. "Dexter's right," she said quietly. "I think maybe it would be best if I stayed here."

Evan's horrified gasp gave Liz a perverse twinge of satisfaction. She had met dozens of men like Evan during her skating career, and despised most of them. There was some consolation in the knowledge that if Evan Howard didn't like the idea of her spending the night in Dexter's house, then her decision to stay couldn't be all bad.

She thought she detected the merest flicker of surprise in Dexter's expression when he heard her response, but all he said was, "Handle the press for me, will you, Evan? Liz and I are going to put our heads together and see if we can come up with a few reasons why Karen Zeit might have been murdered."

"Murdered!" Evan's already pale complexion turned faintly green. Then he swung quickly on his heel. "Don't tell me," he said, "I don't want to know what you're talking about a minute before I have to. I'll do the best job I can with those reporters, but I'm warning both of you. You'd better come up with a damn good story."

"Don't worry." For the first time, Liz could hear a note of bitterness in Dexter's voice. "We're experts. We've done all this before."

Chapter Three

For once, Amanda's antics were not absorbing all of Dexter's attentions. He held her hand, relishing the contact of baby-soft skin against his palm, but answered her nonstop barrage of questions with only half his attention.

He had suspected a leakage of classified information from his Washington office for at least six months. An undercover FBI operative had been working secretly on Dexter's staff for the last two. So far, the investigation had been spectacular for its lack of success. As far as Dexter was concerned, Karen's death threw a whole new light on the situation. Was it possible that the leaks had originated in Denver, rather than Washington? Was that why none of the carefully planted red herrings were turning up anywhere?

Guiltily, Dexter acknowledged he was worried less about Karen's death than the part his ex-wife might have played in it. If Karen had been something more than the dedicated office worker she seemed, could Liz possibly be as bewildered and innocent as she had sounded the previous night? He didn't think so. There were limits as to how far he was prepared to stretch the long arm of coincidence.

One fact was irritatingly clear. Liz's unexpected arrival on his doorstep had thrown him for a loop, not least because of the impact her physical presence had upon him. Until last night, Dexter had assumed that his old, tumultuous feelings about Liz had all been resolved. It was a shock, and not a pleasant one, to discover she still exerted the same sexual fascination that had almost destroyed him the first time around.

The sun cast brilliant light but little heat and Dexter scowled, feeling the chill of the morning air now that he had finished his daily three-mile run. "What's the matter, Dad?" Amanda demanded, seeing his frown.

He heard the anxiety in her voice and quickly smoothed his expression. "Nothing's wrong," he said, squeezing her hand. "How could anything be wrong when you're out here playing with me?"

"We're not playing, just walking. I wish the snow hadn't gone away. We could've built a fort."

"We did that already this year. May is too late for snow. In a couple of weeks you'll be asking to go swimming."

"I like swimming. So does Spot." Amanda patted the Labrador who trotted patiently at her side.

"I know Spot likes swimming—he likes it too well! This year we're going to train him not to jump into the pool when we have guests."

She giggled. "Maybe. Spot likes swimming with lots of people, though."

"Unfortunately, most of my guests don't return the compliment." Dexter glanced at his watch. "We have five more minutes, honey, and then we have to go inside. What game do you want to play?"

"Catch."

"Okay." Dexter took a chewed-up tennis ball from his daughter and threw it toward a far corner of the backyard. Amanda and the dog bounded after it in hot competition. Spot—his daughter had insisted on the name, despite the fact that the Labrador's sleek black body bore not a single mark—was the inevitable winner. He obligingly fell over his front paws and allowed the ball to trickle out of his mouth into Amanda's waiting hands.

"I got it, Dad! I won!" She buried her nose between the Labrador's ears, hugging him tight before throwing the ball back toward her father. This time Spot wasn't prepared to be generous. Outstripping his mistress, he snatched the ball with all the skill of his retriever heritage and bounded off toward his favorite hidey-hole in the bushes. Panting, Amanda ran up and skidded to a halt alongside her father.

"He won't come back for ages. Play baseball with me?" She reached into the pocket of her oversize sweater. "I've got another ball."

"I wish we could, sweetheart," Dexter said regretfully. "But I have a meeting early this morning, and I need to change my clothes. There's no time for baseball."

"You always have meetings."

"I guess it seems that way sometimes." He rumpled her hair, loving the feel of curls tickling his fingers. "But the work I do is important, honey. Unfortunately, there just aren't enough people in Congress who really understand military technology, and I do. There are some decisions our government has to take where my opinion can really make a difference."

"'Cos you were a pilot?"

"Mmm, sort of. And because I'm an engineer."

"If it's so important, why can't I come to your meeting? Maybe I oughta learn about airplanes and things instead of dumb old math at school."

Dexter grinned. "Good try, honey, but you know the answer. The meeting's important for me, school's important for you. And if we don't hurry and get back inside, you won't have time to wash the dirt off your hands before your ride gets here. Then I'll be in trouble with Mrs. Morton again."

She gave one of the gurgles of laughter that always made his heart ache. "Don't be silly, Dad. Mrs. Morton can't be mad at you. You're a grown-up and she works for you."

"And you think that makes me safe from Mrs. Morton's wrath? Young lady, you have a lot to learn!"

Amanda chuckled again, understanding the teasing tone of his voice, if nothing else. "Do you have to go back to Washington next week, Dad? I wish you didn't."

"I'm afraid I do, honey." They had reached the kitchen door and he gave her a quick hug, trying not to let her wistful look get to him. Most of his colleagues in the senate couldn't understand why he spent every spare minute that wasn't devoted to the defense budget campaigning for adequate, federally funded day-care centers. But then, most of his colleagues weren't single parents and didn't understand the burden of guilt mothers and fathers felt when forced to spend long hours away from their children. He gave Amanda another kiss. "Have a good day in school and I'll see you tonight. That's a promise."

Dexter left his daughter washing her hands under Mrs. Morton's eagle-eyed inspection. He crossed the hallway at a brisk pace, wondering just how rational his plans for the upcoming press conference actually were. In the cool light of morning, he was beginning to see a dozen problems that hadn't been apparent the night before.

Face it, he told himself wryly. You were functioning strictly on the no-brain, multihormone level last night. You were so busy feeling furious about the past and horny about the present that you'd have agreed the moon was made of green cheese, if she'd suggested it.

The realization that Liz still retained the power to make him act like an idiot wasn't calculated to sweeten Dexter's mood. Once this press conference was over, he'd make damn sure he didn't see her again. If she needed help, he'd pass her over to Evan. Evan would have no trouble finding her a good private investigator or a first-class lawyer, and that was about all the personal attention he owed her.

Dexter took the stairs two at a time, stopping with great reluctance when he heard Evan's voice. "Senator, I'm so glad you're back from your morning walk with your daughter. You have somebody waiting to see you, Senator."

Not only did Evan sound twice as pompous as usual, he also wore one of his gloomiest and most official faces. Dexter's spirits sank a notch. "If it's a reporter, Evan, you know I don't have time for any personal interviews this morning."

"It's not a reporter, it's the police. A Detective Rodriguez. He wants to see you right now, Senator. He says it's urgent."

Dexter glanced down at his watch. When Evan called him "Senator" three times in as many sentences, it meant big trouble. "I have twenty minutes to shower, shave and change for the press conference we called. That means I can give your detective five minutes—unless he cares to wait until after the press conference."

A tall, slightly overweight figure in a raincoat appeared in the foyer behind Evan. "Five minutes would make a good start, Senator. There are a couple of facts in connection with Karen Zeit's death that I need to go over with you. I'm Lieutenant Rodriguez, by the way, with the Denver Police Department."

Dexter concealed his racing thoughts beneath a polite smile. "Good to meet you, Lieutenant, although the circumstances certainly aren't very pleasant. Why don't we go into my study? That seems as good a place as any for us to talk."

"I'll see that we have coffee and rolls set out for the press conference," Evan said. "Unless you need me to stay with you, Senator?"

"At this hour of the morning, if we want the reporters to act like human beings, coffee should definitely be your first priority." Dexter kept his response light, although he had already picked up the tension—hostility?—emanating from the lieutenant. "And check that Amanda gets off to school okay, will you, Evan?"

"Certainly, Senator. I'll be expecting you in five minutes. I'm sure Lieutenant Rodriguez understands how busy your schedule is this morning and will limit himself accordingly."

What the devil had the detective been saying to Evan? Dexter wondered. His aide rarely kept up the "deferential servant" act for more than a few minutes at a time, but this morning he was behaving like a bad imitation of Jeeves.

"You have news about Karen's death?" he said to the lieutenant, shutting the study door. "Have you discovered something that sheds light on why she committed suicide?"

The detective didn't answer directly. "That's a fancy lock you have there, Senator."

"I frequently have confidential papers in here," Dexter replied shortly. "We had a burglary some six months ago, and the security company suggested electronic locks. What was it you wanted to tell me about Karen?"

"Well, Senator, we've discovered several rather interesting things. First of all, I think you should know that we don't believe Karen Zeit committed suicide."

"You mean her death was accidental?" Dexter asked, knowing damn well that the lieutenant meant nothing of the sort.

Rodriguez looked at him without expression. "Karen Zeit contacted an agent with the Colorado Bureau of Investigations last week. She insisted that her life was in danger. She said somebody was planning to murder her."

"What?" Dexter made no effort to conceal his shock. He ran his hands through his sweat-stiffened hair, his mind racing. What in God's name had his seemingly quiet and unassuming secretary been involved with after hours? "I guess it's absurd to say that the idea of anybody wanting to kill Karen strikes me as ridiculous."

"Hardly ridiculous, considering that she *is* dead. I'm sure you realize, Senator, that the Bureau gets crazies coming in every day, telling us their life is in danger. Half of them think they're in communication with aliens from another planet, and most of the rest are borderline psychotics. Karen Zeit didn't quite fit the pattern, although she was too frightened to tell the agent exactly why her life was at risk. She wanted police protection, but wasn't prepared to say more than that somebody in a position of power was out to kill her."

"So did you give her protection?"

There was a tiny pause. "No, we didn't," Rodriguez admitted. "CBI funding doesn't stretch to looking after citizens who won't say who's threatening them, or why their lives might be in danger. It's all they can do to take care of the people who are obviously at risk."

"I think at the minimum I should have been notified of her concerns."

"Yes, that was an oversight."

"I have a suspicion, Lieutenant, that the people at the Bureau are taking Karen's worries much more seriously this week than they were last."

"Death does have an amazing tendency to concentrate the mind," the lieutenant agreed mildly. "Particularly when the death is murder."

"And you're sure Karen was murdered?"

"Our preliminary investigations have disclosed some interesting facts about Ms. Zeit's death. The pathologist has found evidence of bruising around her mouth and wrists. This bruising occurred some time before death, and not when she fell out of her apartment window. The pathologist suggests that the marks are consistent with the deceased being forcibly restrained and compelled to swallow something—sleeping pills and whiskey, perhaps? With the combination of drugs and alcohol found in her system, she would have been unconscious within ten minutes. Think how easy it would have been for a murderer to push her from the window of her apartment and quietly disappear into the shadows."

"But God in heaven, man, what reason would anybody have for killing Karen? She was a pleasant, efficient secretary, but she always struck me as completely—ordinary."

"In some lines of work, Senator, the ordinary sort of person is the most dangerous."

"If that's what you're thinking, Lieutenant, I recommend that you speak with Agent Waterman at the FBI. He's been rerunning some of the background checks on members of my staff."

"Has he indeed?" Lieutenant Rodriguez scribbled furiously in his notebook. "There is one other point, Senator. Did the deceased have any men friends that you're aware of?"

"She had one or two friends who were male. No steady boyfriend, as far as I know."

"No boyfriend, eh? Interesting you should say that, Senator, because Karen Zeit was nine weeks pregnant when she died."

Dexter felt a fresh surge of astonishment. "But how in the world could she have gotten herself pregnant?"

Rodriguez actually smiled. "The same way as any other woman, Senator. She was sexually intimate with a man."

"I understand the biology," Dexter responded impatiently. "But Karen was thirty-three years old and reasonably sophisticated. Why would she make a mistake like that? We're not talking about some high-school kid who's never heard of birth control."

"Why do you assume Ms. Zeit made a mistake? Perhaps she was in love with the father. Maybe she wanted to get pregnant, to force his hand in some way."

"But who was the father, for heaven's sake? Who could he have been? One way and another, Karen spent nearly sixty hours a week with me. That doesn't leave much time for an outside social life, especially one she's keeping secret."

The lieutenant's voice was very dry. "An excellent point, Senator."

Dexter's head shot up. "Oh no, Rodriguez. You're barking up the wrong tree. Karen Zeit was my secretary, and that's all she was. Quite apart from the fact that I would never have an affair with a member of my staff, Karen just wasn't my type."

"Strange you should say that, Senator. The first thing that struck me was how much she looked like your wife."

"Like Liz?" Dexter shoved his hands into the pockets of his sweats. "Oh, I see. You mean like Susan."

"You seem confused, Senator. What's so confusing about Karen Zeit's appearance? Either she looked like your wife or she didn't."

"I've been married twice," Dexter said curtly. "I suppose Karen looked a bit like my second wife, although their personalities were very different."

"I didn't know you'd been divorced, Senator."

"Then you must be one of the few people in the United States who doesn't know all the gory details, Lieutenant. My first wife and I practically got divorced on television."

"And your first wife's name was?"

"Elizabeth Meacham."

"Elizabeth Meacham!"

Dexter felt obscurely satisfied in having finally shaken Rodriguez's cast-iron calm. "Before you say anything more, Lieutenant, I know that my former wife was sharing an apartment with Karen Zeit. I also know that I have to be at a press conference in precisely eight minutes. Regretfully, our time together has just run out." Dexter walked over to the desk and pressed a button on the intercom system. Evan responded instantly.

"Yes, Senator?"

"I have to shower and dress. Maybe you could answer any other questions Lieutenant Rodriguez might have."

"I'll be right there, Senator."

Dexter turned to the detective. "If there's anything else you feel we ought to discuss, perhaps you could phone me some time this afternoon."

"A phone call won't be necessary, Senator. You've given me several useful leads to work on, and I'm sure if I have any more questions, we'll be able to fit a face-to-face meeting somewhere into your busy schedule."

The look Dexter gave the detective was hard with challenge. "I'm not planning to leave town, Lieutenant, at least for the next couple of days."

"That's very cooperative of you, Senator."

"No. I merely have several important meetings scheduled in Colorado. Good morning to you, Lieutenant."

Evan appeared in the doorway and Dexter turned abruptly on his heel, leaving the study without saying another word.

LIZ GLANCED AT HER WATCH. The press conference was scheduled to begin in five minutes, and Dexter hadn't been anywhere near her since he said a courteous good-night at ten o'clock the previous evening.

She certainly couldn't complain that her comfort had been ignored. Her bathroom was stocked with every toiletry she might need, including a new toothbrush. Her clothes had been whisked away last night and returned early this morning, cleaned and pressed by an expert hand. Promptly at eight, a delicious breakfast had been brought to her bedroom, and Evan Howard had stopped by no less than three times, ostensibly to ensure that she was keeping to schedule, but in reality to make sure she had the details of the agreed story fixed firmly in her mind. Evan didn't like wild cards in his neatly ordered system, and had made it abundantly clear that he considered Liz the wildest of the wildest. Considering her decorous life-style over the past few years, she found his opinion of her almost funny. Almost, but not quite. Today nothing seemed really funny.

Liz coiled her hair into a smooth knot and pinned it swiftly in place. She peered at her reflection in the brightly lighted bathroom mirror, grimacing at what she saw. Years of appearing before the public had left her an expert with makeup, and she had managed to transform her unkempt appearance of the night before into a neat, expressionless mask. Understated pink lips, understated pink cheeks, discreetly darkened lashes. Evan and Dexter would both be thrilled, she thought cynically. The doll-like woman in the mirror looked like the perfect appendage for a politician.

Only her eyes betrayed her. Blue and turbulent, they revealed far too much of what she was feeling. They stared back at her from the mirror, disturbing reminders of a passionate child-woman who no longer existed, except in dreams. Liz closed her eyes. When she opened them again, the blue-gray depths were wiped satisfyingly clean of expression. Now her lifeless eyes matched the porcelain texture of the rest of her face.

When Dexter came to the door two minutes later, she was able to greet him with a polite detachment that would have been impossible during their marriage. She inquired if he'd slept well, if Amanda had gotten off to school on time, if all the arrangements for the press conference had gone smoothly. Meaningless conversation that covered over the horrors of silence. Some things, she discovered, did get better with the passage of time.

Dexter waited for her to finish spouting conversational gambits, then assessed her appearance with the faintest of smiles. "You look well armored against the fiends of the press."

"I figured I might need to be."

"With luck, you'll be able to get away with saying no more than how sorry you are that Karen's dead."

"That's the plan," she agreed.

"Liz, there's no time to talk now, and we need to. Can you spare fifteen minutes after the conference?"

"If you think it's necessary. My office isn't expecting me until lunchtime." She looked at the stairs, which provided a convenient excuse for not looking at him. "Dexter, I owe you an apology. I shouldn't have come here last night. The last thing I want is for you to feel obliged to help me. In fact, there's nothing for you to help me with. Three of my roommates have committed suicide. It's a terrible coincidence, but one I'll have to learn to live with."

"There've been some developments you should know about—oh hell, there's Evan, and he's got the *Boulder Post* editor with him. Smile, Liz. We're on."

She had to admire the way Dexter handled the editor, with just the right mix of friendliness and reserve. He introduced Liz by name, without mentioning their previous relationship. The editor showed not a flicker of recognition.

All four of them walked into the main reception room together, and the buzz of voices from the assembled journalists faded into immediate silence.

Evan had been much too smart to set up anything as formal as a podium and microphone. Dexter walked to the center of the small space that had been left at one end of the room and faced the dozen or so reporters and three TV camera crews. Liz was surprised that so many media people had turned out on what surely must be a fairly routine sort of story. Unfortunately, this was a situation in which Dexter's unusually high profile didn't work well for him.

"I'm sorry that the occasion for our get-together this morning is such a sad one," Dexter said without preamble. "Karen Zeit had been my personal secretary for the past year. She worked long hours with tireless efficiency, and kept my personal and business schedules untangled with almost magical skill. She will be sorely missed in my office, and by her colleagues. I like to think that we had become friends, as well as employer and employee, so that her loss is a double blow for me. I think most of your questions can be answered far better by the police department than they can by me, but I'll do my best to respond to anything relevant."

Six reporters were on their feet. Dexter nodded to one of them. "Joan."

"You say Karen was your personal secretary, Senator. What exactly were her duties, and did you often work out of your home?"

Dexter accepted the question with a bland smile, far too old a hand to allow the sleazy subtext of her question to bother him. Liz almost felt sorry for the reporter when Dexter launched into a long, dry explanation of how his office was organized. Karen's duties, it seemed, had consisted chiefly of coordinating his schedule, serving as liaison with his office in Washington, and helping him with fund-raisers and charitable events. "She was kept very busy, but she had nothing to do with any of my Senate committee work," Dexter concluded. "We try to channel most of that through my Washington office. Since I'm on the Armed Services Committee, a lot of my work is classified and therefore off limits for Karen. She'd never received official security clearance, which all of my staff in DC has."

That's one in the eye for you, Joan. Liz watched the disgruntled reporter sit down, and allowed herself to relax very marginally. With luck and a bit more of Dexter's skill, they were going to get through this conference with flying colors. Perhaps she wouldn't even have to speak.

She had allowed herself to relax too soon. A reporter from one of the TV stations spoke up next. "I was talking to the superintendent at Karen Zeit's apartment building this morning, and it turns out that she was sharing her apartment with a young woman called Elizabeth Meacham. It's not such a unique name, of course, but you were once married to a member of our U.S. Olympic figure skating team, and her name was also Elizabeth Meacham. Is this just a strange coincidence, Senator, or is it possible that your secretary was sharing an apartment with your ex-wife?"

Dexter's grin was a masterpiece of rueful, good-natured resignation. "It's no coincidence, Harry, as I'm sure you realized." Dexter turned and smiled toward Liz. "We anticipated that this item of news would set all your journalistic noses twitching, so my former wife very kindly volunteered to join us here this morning. Liz."

Dexter held out his hand in a casual, welcoming gesture. Liz rose to her feet, stretched her neat pink-glossed lips into a smile and walked across the room to Dexter's side. The ten feet of padded carpet seemed to take so long to cross that they might as well have been ten miles of icy tundra. It had been a while since she last faced a roomful of journalists, but not long enough to forget how easily they could savage you.

"Karen and I met at a party a couple of months ago," she said. Her voice sounded husky and she cleared her throat, angry at the appearance of nervousness. Behind her, the silent strength of Dexter's presence gave her a burst of confidence. "We talked about sharing an apartment. When I found out who Karen worked for, I explained that Dexter and I had once been married. Neither Karen nor I thought that had any bearing on our decision to share an apartment, so I moved in."

The faces of the journalists blurred into a single, avid mob, all shouting questions at her. Deafened by the bombardment, she forced herself to maintain her inner calm. A question from one of the TV journalists caught her attention.

"Hard feelings toward the senator?" she said with a casual smile. "Oh, no. Dexter and I reconciled our differences a long time ago. We're both ten years older now, and events have taken on a whole different perspective." If she'd been a kid, she'd have had her hands behind her back crossing her fingers when she uttered that whopper.

The editor from the *Boulder Post* was on his feet. "Senator, I understand from sources inside the police department that the CBI is working on this case. I also understand that the autopsy results suggest that Karen Zeit didn't commit suicide. As of now, the police are treating this as a case of homicide. Do you have any comment on that?"

Liz plastered the noncommittal look onto her face so firmly that she was afraid it might never come off. Dear heaven, how long had the police suspected Karen had been murdered? She looked up at Dexter, marveling that he could appear so calm. At nineteen, she had never bothered to look below that surface calm. Now—instinctively—she recognized how much effort it was costing him to appear unconcerned.

"If the police autopsy suggests that Karen Zeit was murdered, then I certainly would have no grounds or expertise for disputing their verdict," Dexter said. "If it does turn out that she was murdered, I hope very much that her killer is found quickly and brought to justice."

Some sixth sense retained from her years under a constant publicity spotlight alerted Liz to the fact that the *Post* editor was disappointed with Dexter's reply. Her intuition warned her that the man had come here meaning to make a killing. In the split second pause as the reporter formulated his next question, she saw him coil for attack. "So you have no fears, Senator, that this investigation is going to touch close to home?"

"Karen was my personal secretary. Obviously I'm extremely interested in finding out how she died."

"And how about the note she left, Senator?"

"What note?"

"The one claiming you're the father of her baby and that you refused to marry her."

Chapter Four

Dexter never lost his cool amid the hubbub of the aggressive questions that followed. But despite his most skillful efforts, it took him almost half an hour to get rid of the clamoring journalists. Only the promise that he would issue another statement within forty-eight hours finally persuaded the reporters to sheath their pencils, pack up their equipment and leave.

From the evidence of their avid expressions as they rushed herdlike for the doors, Liz had no problem inferring that the phone wire would soon be vibrating with not-quite-libelous accounts of the thrilling story. She could already visualize the headlines. "Senator's Triangular Love Nest Explodes" would be one of the milder versions.

Evan turned out to be almost more difficult to pacify than the journalists. He paced up and down the study, his self-control obviously shot, trying—with a singular lack of success—to invent some way to put an acceptable public relations gloss on the sordid facts.

Liz watched Dexter soothe his aide, and reflected how much her ex-husband must have changed to employ someone like Evan. In the old days, Dexter's indifference to the press had been monumental, and he'd often been impatient with Liz's efforts to placate the powerful TV sportscasters. She was surprised to discover that she hoped he hadn't changed too much. Oddly enough, Dexter the Arrogant was far more acceptable to her than Dexter the Media Manipulator.

He finally handed the sweating and swearing Evan a glass of club soda. "Look Evan," he said, putting his arm around the distraught publicist's shoulder. "We have to face reality, tell the truth, and move on from there."

"Truth and reality never won any election I heard about."

"I'm still fighting you on that," Dexter said wryly. "In the meantime, you have to accept there's no way to turn Karen's death into a public relations coup for me. All we can do is control the worst of the damage by saying as little as possible and making damn sure that everything we say is true. Stop trying to achieve anything more, or you'll give yourself an ulcer."

"I already have an ulcer. I shouldn't be drinking this carbonated junk. Gas bubbles are murder on my stomach."

"Then let's work on saving you from ulcer number two." Dexter's jaw tensed slightly. It was the only sign of impatience he allowed himself. "We're all agreed that being suspected of murder makes lousy publicity for a U.S. senator, so stop sweating it."

"Why did she have to leave a note, for God's sake?"

"You heard what Rodriguez said. He thinks the note was part of an unmailed letter to me."

"Why did she need to write, for heaven's sake? She saw you every day!"

Dexter's smile was hard. "You didn't ask the more important question, Evan. Why did she write something that wasn't true?"

Evan remained silent, and Liz thought she detected a brief flash of hurt in Dexter's gaze. When he spoke, however, his voice was crisp and businesslike. "For what it's worth," he said, "I would like you to know there isn't a word of truth in Karen's note. If it isn't a forgery, she was fantasizing."

Evan's head shot up, and Liz thought she saw genuine astonishment in his eyes. "You're sure of that? You didn't get her pregnant? You're saying you two weren't—you know—intimate?"

There was a hint of weariness in Dexter's reply. "No, we weren't intimate. You're taking Lieutenant Rodriguez too seriously, Evan."

"No." Evan's voice was quiet now. "The truth is, Dexter, Karen told me in confidence that the two of you were lovers. You know, after that weekend you went up to Aspen together. She was...um...hoping to marry you. I told her not to count on it." He cast a worried glance in Liz's direction, then plunged ahead. "I warned her that you hadn't been taking your women...um...seriously since Susan...."

When had Dexter ever taken his women seriously? Liz thought cynically. Certainly not during his marriage to her.

"You repeated all this to Lieutenant Rodriguez?" Dexter asked.

Evan hung his head. "I had to. He kept on asking all these questions about Karen and you. I had to tell the truth, Dexter, you can see that."

Liz could barely refrain from asking why truth suddenly ranked so high on Evan's list of priorities. Dexter merely shrugged. "Whatever Karen may have said to you, I wasn't her lover and I didn't get her pregnant. Damn it, I never even kissed the woman, much less had sex with her! We had rooms on separate floors of the hotel, and worked on the final draft of a speech to the League of Women Voters that weekend in Aspen."

"Sure, Dexter, if you say so, but remember the police'll probably be able to run paternity tests on the fetus—"

Dexter cast a single, hard glance at his publicist. "That's good news."

Evan reddened. "Yeah, I guess it is. I'm sure their tests will prove the baby couldn't have been yours, of course."

"Of course." Dexter didn't bother to disguise the heavy irony in his reply. "If the lieutenant asks, tell him I'd be delighted to give a blood sample for comparative testing. Think positively, Evan. Count your blessings that it's two years until I'm up for reelection."

Evan visibly brightened. It was becoming clear to Liz that facts as concrete entities scarcely existed for him—how things would appear in the media made up his personal version of reality. "That's true. Two and a half years, actually. Hell, we have plenty of time to come up with a convincing explanation for everything."

Liz spoke for the first time. For some reason, she found Evan's lack of faith in his employer distinctly annoying. "There's even the faint hope that the police might have discovered what truly happened by then. In which case, you might not need to invent any stories about anything."

"I guess." Evan clearly placed about as much hope in the possibility of the police solving the mystery as he had faith in his employer's innocence. "What do you want me to do, Dexter? Should I work on a statement for you to make to the press tomorrow?"

"Right now we don't seem to have any clear ideas about what I should say, so that seems like an exercise in futility. Why don't you make an appointment to consult with Needinger?"

"Your lawyer? That's a great idea." Evan cheered up again. "Needinger has lots of clout at the police department. He can talk to Lieutenant Rodriguez and make sure we get all the up-to-date information. We don't want reporters springing any more surprises on us. That clunker from the *Boulder Post* this morning was enough for a lifetime. What are you going to do for the rest of the day, Senator? Do you plan to stick to your original timetable?

You have a dinner scheduled with the governor, remember?''

"You might cancel that, with my profound apologies. I'm sure he'll be relieved not to have to make polite conversation while we both sit and wonder how likely I am to be arrested before dessert is served.''

Evan winced. "Bite your tongue, Senator. How about the rest of your schedule?''

Dexter glanced at the calendar spread open on his desk. "I'm planning to spend the next hour or so talking to Liz. Seems to me we have some useful information to share, she and I.''

Evan viewed Liz with distinct lack of favor. "If you really think that's wise, Senator—''

"I think it's very wise,'' Dexter said firmly. "I'll keep the afternoon appointments. And could you call the agency for a temporary secretary? Bonnie's never going to cope on her own.''

"Very well, Senator.'' From the number of times he'd said "Senator'' in the past two minutes, Liz decided Evan once again felt in control of the situation. He gave a smooth smile. "I'll see you after lunch, when I've had a chance to check things out with Needinger.''

"If he needs to see you, you know my schedule.''

"Yes, Senator.'' Evan nodded his head toward Liz. "Goodbye Ms. Meacham. It's been a . . . um . . . pleasure meeting you.''

She actually felt her mouth twist into a small smile. "I hope your pleasures aren't always so traumatic, Mr. Howard.''

Her reply seemed to disconcert him. He smiled nervously, then hurried from the room with a final word of acknowledgment to his employer. Liz waited until the door closed. "For your sake, I hope he's better at his job than he seems,'' she said dryly. She flushed. "I'm sorry. That remark was uncalled-for.''

Dexter seemed amused rather than offended. "He's actually damn good at his job. He has a knack for turning
complex policy positions into easy-to-grasp, easy-to-read
statements, and he can charm a mob of hungry journalists
better than anybody I know."

Liz thought back and realized Dexter was right. Evan
Howard had shown no sign of being traumatized until
they'd been alone in the study. "Nursing him through a
nervous breakdown every time there's a crisis seems like a
stiff price to pay."

"He's not usually this upset. He's always a worrier, but
I must say Karen's death seems to have thrown him for a
total loop. He normally panics for ten minutes, then has the
whole situation under control ten minutes later."

"Maybe he's thrown because he thinks you killed her."

Her words fell into a little pool of silence. Dexter stopped
riffling through the pages of his calendar and looked up at
her. "What about you, Liz? Do you think I killed Karen?"

She gave an odd little laugh. "I wish I could say yes. After the debacle of our marriage, I rather like the idea of you
groveling in the courts over a messy crime of passion. It
would make you seem semihuman."

"Translated, does that mean you don't believe I murdered my secretary?"

She smiled wryly. "Crazy, isn't it? The evidence all points
to you, but somehow I don't believe you did it."

"Why not?"

"Maybe because I can't imagine you ever feeling passionate enough about a woman to kill her."

He looked away. "You're wrong," he said quietly. "I've
felt that passionate—and that desperate. But not over
Karen."

Susan, Liz thought, and was aware of a sharp little twist
of pain in her stomach. Why had he felt so desperate about
Susan? Was he implying that his second wife had been unfaithful to him? Surely not, although Liz considered it a

splendid irony of fate if she had. The adulterer finally stung by his wife's adultery.

"You're very quiet," he said. "Does that mean you're wondering if I'm guilty, after all?"

"No, I guess I'm quite sure you didn't kill her."

"Should I be flattered?"

"Maybe. Or perhaps I can't believe you're guilty because the evidence is too convincing."

"When there's a bullet-ridden body on the floor and the only other person in the room holds a smoking gun, it's reasonable to conclude that the person holding the gun had something to do with the bullet-ridden body."

"Are you trying to convince me you killed her, Dexter?"

"I'm trying to discover why on earth you believe I didn't. Knowing your opinion of my character, I can't believe it's a burning faith in my integrity."

"Let's just say I have a perverse intuition that this time the guy with the smoking gun didn't pull the trigger."

"You know who the police are going to suspect if they ever give up on me, don't you?"

"Yes. I know I ought to run to Rodriguez screaming that you did it. Because if you didn't kill Karen, that surely puts me right at the top of the police list of likely murderers. Except I know I didn't kill her, or my other two roommates. So maybe you didn't kill her either, despite all the evidence."

"Or get her pregnant?"

She glanced down at her hands. "I—don't know about that."

His voice sounded harsh. "I suppose I should be grateful for small mercies. I guess it's better to have your ex-wife consider you a lecher who's fooling around with the office staff than to have her think you might be a murderer."

Liz dug her nails into her palms. "You ... were unfaithful while we were married. How do I know what your sexual morals might be nowadays?"

"I was never unfaithful to you," Dexter said, sounding suddenly tired. "But let's not open that old can of worms. I don't think we can have a single thing left to say on the subject of our marriage. God knows, we said it all nine years ago, and most of it in front of a TV camera."

"I still have nightmares about that night." Liz had no idea why she suddenly made the admission that pride had kept inside for so many years.

"Which part of the night?" Dexter asked quietly. "The medal you'd just lost, or the public disintegration of our marriage?"

She hesitated before admitting the truth. "Both."

Dexter was silent even longer than she had been. "With the proper training, you could have come back in time for the world championship," he said finally. "You were a brilliant skater."

"The psychological moment had passed, I guess." Liz shrugged off the lingering regret that could still grab her by the throat when she gave it the chance. "At least the tabloids aren't interested in me anymore. That must be one of the few compensations for getting old and out of shape!"

Dexter's gaze flicked over her. "You don't look out of shape to me," he commented. "Your body's as spectacular as ever." He continued without giving her a chance to respond. "Look, Liz, why don't we make a deal? I'll agree that you're an innocent victim in the deaths of all three of your roommates, if you'll agree to give me the benefit of the doubt about Karen and her pregnancy."

"Does it matter if we believe each other?"

"I think maybe it does. The police aren't going to look very far for their murderer when they have you and me as such convenient suspects, and I'd like to find out what I'm being set up for. Because I sure as hell don't think it's coincidence that my secretary got herself murdered while she just happened to be living with my ex-wife.''

''You think I'm setting you up?''

''No, but it's a possibility. A remote one, but I've learned not to discount possibilities. Shall we talk about it?''

''For heaven's sake, why in the world would I bother to set you up?''

''Revenge?''

''Good grief, Dexter! Quite apart from the fact that killing three people seems a somewhat excessive revenge, I'm not neurotic enough or obsessed enough to have spent nine years waiting to get back at you because you're a terminal louse and we had a rotten divorce.''

''I see.'' He grinned faintly. ''You mean, a plot to castrate me would meet with your approval, but setting me up for murder goes too far?''

To her surprise, she found herself answering his grin. ''Something like that,'' she agreed. ''Although now that you mention it, I can't think why I didn't come up with the castration idea years ago.''

''No creative imagination,'' he said promptly. ''Your creativity all goes into your skating.''

She smiled, then sighed, feeling a sudden sadness. ''Nine years later, and we still come around to the same old topics, don't we? Dexter, I haven't skated in nine years. Wherever my creativity is going these days, it's not into the ice.''

He closed the desk calendar with a snap. ''You're right. We should stick to Karen's murder and not waste time rehashing the past. Would you be willing to help me come up with some ideas as to who might have killed her?''

''Surely that's something we should leave to the police.''

''Unfortunately, I think the police will soon decide that they have all the ideas they need.''

''You think they'll arrest you? Or me?''

''How about both of us?''

It was at moments such as these that Liz understood why people smoked. Her hands desperately needed something to do before the rest of her exploded. Dexter seemed to sense her panic. He emerged from behind the desk and crossed the room to sit beside her on the sofa.

"Liz, if we put our heads together, I think we can come up with several insights the police won't have. You see, we know quite a lot that they don't. For example, I know that Karen wasn't pregnant with my baby and that we didn't have an affair. You know that you didn't kill her or your other two roommates."

"Okay, but where do we go from there?"

"At a minimum, it gives us a couple of avenues to explore. Who was the father of Karen's baby, and why were your roommates killed? Those aren't going to be burning questions on the police investigation."

"But Dexter, that brings us back to where we started out last night. I haven't the faintest, remotest idea why my roommates were killed. I've spent the past day and a half trying to imagine any possible connecting link between the three of them. Believe me, there isn't one."

"Were they friends? Acquaintances?"

"Of course they weren't!"

"How do you know?"

"Because they never mentioned each other! Because they moved in completely different circles! Because there's no *reason* for them to have been friends!"

"We don't know of any reason for them to have been murdered, but they were. Okay, maybe they weren't bosom buddies, but are you sure that they'd never met?"

She stared at him, eyes wide with the shock of realization. "No, I don't know that they'd never met," she murmured. "Not for sure. But when I moved in with Karen I told her that I'd been living with a woman called Jill Skinner, who'd died. If Karen knew Jill, why wouldn't she have said so?"

"Liz, stop reacting and start thinking. If Karen and Brian and Jill shared some secret that got all three of them murdered, do you think any of them were going to worry about a little secret like not telling you that they knew one another?"

"Are you saying that they conspired to trick me into moving in with them for some deep, dark purpose we know nothing about?" Even to her own ears, her voice sounded distinctly breathless.

"I'm saying you should consider the possibility. And they didn't have to share a deep, dark purpose. People conceal information for all sorts of reasons. After all, you never told Karen that you'd been married to me."

"That was different. There was no reason to mention a relationship that didn't—doesn't—exist anymore."

"How do you know your roommates didn't have a similar sort of reason? Maybe Brian had been married to Jill. Or Karen."

"No! He'd been single for years. He told me his marriage ended right after grad school...." Her passionate denial trailed away into unconvincing silence.

"You see?" Dexter said softly. "You never checked up on Brian's story, did you?"

"People usually tell each other the truth—"

"But not always." Dexter got up and walked over to his desk. Depressing a button, he spoke into the intercom. "Mrs. Morton, could you please make us a pot of coffee and a couple of sandwiches? Thanks." Turning back to Liz, he looked at her thoughtfully. "Who first suggested that you should move into Karen's apartment?"

Liz cast her mind back, trying to visualize the crowded room at the party where she had first met Karen. "I did," she said. "I'm almost sure of it. Karen asked me all the usual questions, like how long I had been in Denver, where I was working, that sort of thing. I told her I'd just started a new job at Peperito's, and that I was looking for a roommate. She told me that by coincidence her roommate had just moved out—"

"As far as I know, Karen never had a roommate. The subject came up once, and she specifically told me she lived alone." Dexter must have caught some fleeting change in Liz's expression because his eyes flashed dark with irritation. "We were talking about a spate of burglaries in her neighborhood, Liz, not a prospective seduction."

"Maybe it was the burglaries that changed her mind."

"Could be. Who was giving this party? Whoever it was, must be a friend of Karen's."

"Pieter Ullmann."

"The skater?"

"Yes, he won the gold at the last Olympics."

"I detect a tinge of acid in your voice. Didn't he deserve his gold?"

"Sure he did. He's probably the best male skater since Scott Hamilton. I'm just tired of athletes who think an Olympic gold is the master key to unlock every woman's bedroom door. Pieter skates like an angel and has a mind like a sewer. Unfortunately, when I'm around him, I keep forgetting the angelic part and smelling the sewer."

Dexter laughed. "So why did you go to his party?"

"Mikhail invited me to go with him. Pieter was—is—his star pupil at the moment."

"Of course, I should've remembered. There was enough press coverage of them both during the winter games." Dexter's voice was carefully neutral. "How is Mikhail these days? I haven't seen him since he first arrived in the States after his defection, but I heard lots of good things about his teaching program, even before Pieter carried off the gold."

"Mikhail's the best figure-skating coach in the United States," Liz said, smiling affectionately as she thought of her brother-in-law. Now that Alison was dead, and their mother barely aware of her surroundings, Mikhail was Liz's closest substitute for a family.

"He's never tried to persuade you back onto the ice?"

"We don't have any sort of professional relationship. Mikhail always admired Alison's skating style much more than mine. That's what first attracted him to her."

"Technical perfection over fire and heart?"

"Alison was a magnificent skater!"

"You always said so," Dexter agreed. An odd note of hesitancy crept into his voice. "Are you thinking of marrying him, Liz?"

She could justifiably have told Dexter it was none of his business, that he'd lost the right to pry into her affairs years ago, but somehow she found herself confiding the truth. "No, never," she said. "He was Alison's husband. Alison was my twin, and the two of us had always been so close, at least until you and I got married. I could never think of Mikhail as anything except a brother."

A light tap at the door heralded the arrival of Mrs. Morton with a carafe of steaming coffee and a plate of smoked-salmon-and-cucumber sandwiches. As soon as the housekeeper left the room, Liz took a generous bite of sandwich and grinned across at Dexter.

"There are a few advantages to being filthy rich," she said, leaning back against the sofa pillows. "In my next life I'm going to reincarnate as somebody who presses buttons and makes sandwiches appear."

"Take care that the masters of the universe aren't listening, or you may come back as a music-hall conjurer."

She laughed, then sobered abruptly, the sandwich losing its appeal. "Smoked salmon was Karen's favorite, too. Oh God, Dexter, she didn't deserve to end up splattered on a parking-lot pavement."

"No, she didn't. Nobody deserves to die that way. But at this point, we can't do anything to help her except try to find her killer. Which I guess brings us right back to your decision to move in with Karen. With all the advantage of hindsight, would you say that it's possible you were maneuvered into sharing an apartment with her?''

"Of course it's possible—''

"But not probable, you think?''

"I don't know!'' Liz's voice faded into silence while she tried to remember the exact chain of events. "I don't know about Karen,'' she said finally. "But if it'll make you feel better, I can be more positive about my decision to move in with Jill Skinner. That wasn't my decision, it was Jill's. I was numb after Brian died, and she virtually made the move for me. At that point, I was so shattered I'd have moved in with Dracula if he'd been prepared to pack my suitcases and hire the U-Haul. So if you want to suspect some vast conspiracy with me as the helpless pawn, the person to start with is Jill Skinner.''

"Tell me about her,'' Dexter suggested. "And about Brian.''

It was easier to discuss Jill, so she did that first. "Like I told you last night, Jill and I knew each other for at least two years, but we weren't close friends. We went to the same health club and sweated through the advanced aerobics class, then commiserated about our aching muscles over fruit juice in the locker room. We saw each other three times a week, but until we shared an apartment, I don't think I knew anything more about her than that she had a terrific body, she was around my age, and had a job as a social worker.''

"And once you moved in with her?''

"I found out that she was neat, a vegetarian, a sympathetic listener, and that she took care never to intrude into my space. She had a lot of friends, but she socialized with them in restaurants, not in the apartment. Dex, what can I say? She was a great roommate, but we weren't bosom buddies.''

"What about her friends?''

"As I said, she had lots of them. Male and female. She was out most nights."

"Did you like her friends?"

Once again, Liz fell silent. "I don't think I ever met any of them," she admitted finally. "Except maybe to say hi at the door."

"In fact, if you added up everything you know about Jill, you just might be able to fill two sides of a small piece of paper."

Liz felt a chill ripple down her spine. "That's an underestimation, but not by much."

"What about Brian? Did you know him any better?"

"Of course I did! I was living with him, for heaven's sake!"

"You were living with Jill and Karen, too."

"No, I was sharing an apartment. It's different."

"Is it? Aside from what he was like in bed, do you know any more about Brian than you do about Jill and Karen?"

"Yes," she said, through gritted teeth. "Unlike some people, I don't hop into bed with anybody who looks good in a pair of pants."

"Well, bully for you." Dexter's smile was lethal. "So what intimate details do you know about our friend Brian?"

"He was a professor at the university," she replied. "He had a doctoral degree in electrical engineering. He was forty-five, and a wonderfully calm, considerate human being. He'd been married once when he was a student, but the marriage only lasted a few months before his wife left him for another man." She smiled grimly. "As you can see, we had a lot in common."

"Failed marriages, or chips on your shoulders?" Dexter inquired with excessive politeness.

She wished she could think of some brilliant, scathing retort that would reduce him to dust. Of course, she couldn't. "Brian had a very well-balanced personality," was the best she could come up with.

"I'm so sorry," Dexter pretended sympathy. "Was he boring in bed, too?"

He had been incredibly boring in bed, but Liz had no intention of stepping into that particular nest of vipers. Not with Dexter, of all people. She got to her feet, carrying her plate and cup over to the heavy silver tray Mrs. Morton had left on a side table. She smiled with freezing politeness.

"I've just noticed it's noon already. I have to get to work. My boss isn't too understanding when it comes to taking time off to cope with personal crises. Murder or no murder, he's going to want my latest market-research figures charted and on his desk."

Dexter reached out and captured her hand. He exerted almost no pressure, but somehow she felt incapable of walking away. "Liz, I'm sorry. I owe you an apology. We left a lot of things unresolved between us when we split up, and I think we've both been carrying around some excess emotional baggage, but that's no excuse for what I just said."

"It's been a tough morning," she said, not looking at him.

"Things are likely to get tougher, not easier. This isn't the moment for me to start hurling insults."

"No, I guess it's not. Maybe we should both try to count to ten before we speak to each other."

He broke a moment of silence. "Where are you going to stay tonight?"

She blinked, dismayed by the question. Where was she going to stay? Dear God, she hadn't given that problem a moment's thought. One thing was for sure: she couldn't go back to her apartment, wherever else she went. At the moment, she felt she would never be able to live in an apartment—any apartment—again.

"I hadn't thought about it," she admitted. "But it should be easy enough to find a room near the office. There are dozens of motels around the airport."

"You could stay here," he said. "We have plenty of room."

"Thank you very much for the offer, but I don't think—"

"Liz, we could help each other, if you'd only spend some time with me. We haven't even started to work out a list of Karen's friends—"

"Dexter, we already agreed that I know almost nothing about Karen, and even less about her friends."

He put a finger against her lips, gently silencing her. "I'll bet you don't know half of what you know," he said lightly. "Liz, please consider it. For both our sakes."

She closed her eyes, cursing silently. She never had been able to resist Dexter when he gave her one of his tender, sincere looks. She'd grown up a lot in the last nine years, but the extra maturity didn't seem to have done a darn thing for her susceptibility to Dexter. She had more self-control these days than she'd had when she was nineteen, but his offer was still incredibly tempting—partly because she didn't want to spend the next few nights pacing up and down a lonely motel room with the specters of Karen and Lieutenant Rodriguez looming over her shoulder.

"All right," she said, drawing in a deep breath. "If you really think it would be helpful, I'll pack a suitcase after work and join you later on this evening."

"Wonderful." Dexter's smile was warm, happy, intimate—and made her want to scream in protest at its devastating effect on her hormones. Why couldn't he have developed sagging jowls and a belly to match? She held her body stiff as he gave her a quick, friendly hug.

"See you tonight, Liz. I'll be waiting for you."

Chapter Five

Liz barely survived her afternoon at the office. The combination of an overloaded desk and colleagues consumed by curiosity proved as exhausting as the morning's press conference. Since she'd only recently started work at Peperito's, her colleagues had not yet become friends, and their fascination with her sudden notoriety inevitably came across as prying. Even her boss, a middle-aged workaholic, took ten minutes off from studying his sales charts to bludgeon her with questions. He seemed to have a tough time deciding which part of the breaking news story was most deplorable: Liz's past career as a—failed—skater; her short-lived marriage to the famous Senator Rand; or her involvement in a juicy murder that was clearly destined to remain on the front pages of Colorado's newspapers for several weeks.

Liz was literally shaking with fatigue by the time she turned the key in the lock of her apartment door and pushed it open. The sight of Pieter Ullmann lounging in Karen's favorite armchair proved the final straw to her self-control.

"What the blazes are you doing here?" she demanded. "Who let you in?"

"And I'm thrilled to see you, too, darling." Pieter switched off the television set, jumped gracefully to his feet and bounded across the room to drop a kiss on her cheek. She turned her head just in time, and his kiss landed on her ear.

"Knock it off," she said wearily. "Who let you in, Pieter?"

"Your superintendent's wife," he said cheerily. "I gave her my autograph, and she was thrilled. Her granddaughter sleeps with my picture under her pillow."

"How touching. However, I don't sleep with your picture under my pillow and I already have your autograph, so I'd be grateful if you'd leave. I have a bunch of things to do tonight."

"I came to offer you my sympathy," he said, sounding mortally wounded by her curt rejection. "And my help."

"Thanks. The sympathy's accepted, the help isn't needed. Goodbye."

He winced. "Liz, darling, try to show a few social graces."

She threw her coat onto the nearest available chair. "I'm too tired to be socially gracious. Go home, Pieter."

"Being the generous person that I am, I'll ignore your hostility and invite you to come back to my apartment. What do you say, Liz? I'll call the caterers and we can have a quiet dinner, just the two of us. Champagne. Lobster. Whatever you want."

"And then a quiet little night in bed? Just the two of us?"

Pieter smiled. "Darling, my bedmates are much too ecstatic to be quiet. If you'd only allow yourself to let go now and again, you'd know that my performance in the bedroom is even more spectacular than on the ice. So you know how wonderful that must be."

Liz freed herself from his arms and made her way to the kitchen. "The trouble is, Pieter, I'm old-fashioned enough to think the bedroom is a place to make love, not take part in a performance."

"Darling Liz, you can't be that old!"

Against her will she laughed, and the laughter turned into a yawn. "Believe me, I'm that old. And tired, as well." She opened the fridge, realizing as she peered inside that she was almost grateful to Pieter. Finding him in the apartment had taken some of the sting out of her return.

"If you don't want to go and pursue more promising quarry, you could stay and have a drink. It looks like you can have white wine, soda or orange juice."

He sighed. "I'd better say orange juice, since Mikhail is your brother-in-law and you'll probably report back to him. You two are like Siamese twins."

"Good grief, Pieter, I'm not that much of a witch! Besides, despite all your weary man-of-the-world act, I know damn well that you keep to your training program, whether Mikhail's on your back or not. You can't fool me. I know what it takes to reach Olympic standard as a figure skater."

He took a swallow of orange juice and grimaced. "Liz, darling, I can see that this is one of your nights for being a bore."

"I agree, so why are you staying? Pieter, I mean it when I say I'm not coming back to your apartment."

"Dearest Liz, if you don't want to have the best night of your life, that's your business. My sole purpose at this moment is to make you happy. If you want me to hang around drinking orange juice, that's what I'll do. It's creepy to think of you being here alone. Karen was really inconsiderate to get herself murdered in your apartment."

"Gee, you're right!" Liz loaded her words with sarcasm. "If she'd had a smidgen of good taste, she'd surely have asked her murderer to search around and find some other window to push her out of. Murderers are always so cooperative about that sort of thing."

Pieter stirred an ice cube into his juice with a finger. "You're not going to spend the night here alone, are you, Liz?"

"No," she said, a little surprised by his sudden seriousness. "I'm not staying here. I'm going to a friend's house."

"Whose?"

"Nobody you know. We ... um ... work together." She silently apologized for the lie, but had no intention of telling gossipy Pieter where she was really going. "I just stopped by to pack a suitcase. In fact, I have to get started on my packing right now." She picked up her diet soda and walked toward the narrow hallway of the apartment.

Pieter followed her into her bedroom without bothering to ask permission. Bedrooms and the ice rink were his natural habitat, and he obviously felt equally at home in both. He kicked off his shoes and stretched out comfortably on her bed.

"Am I in the way, Liz darling?"

"No more than usual." She opened a drawer and dumped a pile of sweaters onto his stomach. "Here, choose me a couple, would you?"

Pieter obligingly began sorting through sweaters. "Liz," he said with determined casualness. "Did you see much of Karen over the past few weeks?"

"Not much. I was in Mexico City meeting with Peperito's suppliers until Friday."

"Oh. Did she say anything to you about—um—anything?"

Liz belatedly remembered it was at one of Pieter's parties that she had first met Karen. She straightened from her search through the bottom of the closet for a missing sneaker, and turned around to face Pieter.

"How well did you know Karen Zeit?" she asked quietly.

He stared at one of her turquoise sweaters as if he'd never seen such a mesmerizing garment. "Not well. I scarcely knew her at all, in fact."

"Well enough to take her to bed?"

A flash of Pieter's usual brittle manner reappeared momentarily. "Dearest Liz, even you should realize it's the people you don't know that you go to bed with. With someone you know, you might have to talk afterward."

Liz's gaze remained cool. "I take it that means you and Karen were bedmates?"

"Then you take it wrong." Pieter got off the bed and handed Liz two pink sweaters. "Here, pack these. You look like death warmed over. You could use some color in your clothes, because you sure as hell don't have any in your cheeks."

"Thank you." Liz took the sweaters, her voice softening. "Pieter, are you sure you're not the father of Karen's baby?"

"Yes, damn it, I'm sure! The baby wasn't mine! It couldn't have been, because we never slept together."

"Then why are you yelling?"

"Because she came on to me like gangbusters, and a whole bunch of my friends know that."

"I didn't know you ever turned down a willing female, Pieter."

"You don't know a hell of a lot," Pieter said tightly. "About me, or about your roommate. From the way Karen approached me, I'd guess half the men in Denver could have been the father of her baby. But whoever the father was, it wasn't me." Pieter swallowed the last of his orange juice, muttered an obscene epithet and pushed himself off the bed. "Damn Mikhail and his training schedule. I'm planning to go out and party."

"Pieter, don't go for a minute! Have you told the police what you know about Karen?"

"I don't know anything about Karen."

"You know she came on to you."

He laughed harshly. "Are you crazy? In the first place, I don't know a thing about her general behavior. All I know is how she behaved with me. And in the second place, don't you think I have enough problems with the media without asking for trouble? I've already got two teenagers suing me in paternity suits, and I swear to God I've never set eyes on either of them."

"The police think Dex—Senator Rand is the father of Karen's child."

"That's their problem. Or his. Anyway, it sure isn't mine." Pieter zipped up his jacket and strode out of the bedroom. Liz hurried after him.

"Pieter!"

He stopped but didn't turn. "Yeah?"

She swallowed, surprised at the words that came out. "Take a cab home from the party if you drink too much."

"I could do that." He swung around and looked at her, his eyes shadowed. "Have you thought about taking a vacation, Liz? Somewhere a long way away from Denver?"

"I only just moved here, for heaven's sake!"

"Looks like now would be a real good time to move on."

"Pieter, what are you trying to tell me?"

He shrugged, reaching for the door. Liz had the feeling he was regretting having come, regretting even more having spoken so freely. "Nothing, babe. I guess I'm just running off at the mouth. See you around, huh?" He left the apartment, slamming the door loudly behind him.

LIZ'S PACKING still didn't go as quickly as she'd hoped, even after Pieter left. She was interrupted by two phone calls. One came from the nursing home in Durango where her mother was being cared for. The ostensible purpose of the call was for the head nurse to reassure Liz that Mrs. Meacham remained unaware of her surroundings and was therefore not at all worried by the news stories that had been blasting forth all day on the lounge TV. But Liz couldn't help suspecting that the real purpose of the call was to find out if she'd been arrested.

The second call came from a journalist offering Liz five thousand dollars for "the inside story on your affair with Senator Rand."

It had been so long since she'd needed to field this sort of call that Liz let the journalist rattle on while she stared at the receiver, literally bereft of words. Finally she gathered her wits together sufficiently to respond.

"The senator and I are not currently having an affair. We did not have an affair in the past, nor do we plan to have an affair in the future. That's my exclusive inside story and you're welcome to it. For free." She banged down the receiver. "I hope that broke your eardrum," she muttered.

Her suitcase finally packed, she was almost at the front door of the apartment when the phone rang again. She hesitated, not wanting to confront another journalist—or Lieutenant Rodriguez, for that matter. When the phone continued to ring, the conviction grew that it was Dexter, calling to say he'd changed his mind about having her stay with him. Reluctantly she snatched the receiver from the cradle and barked, "Hello!"

"You sound horribly fierce, Lizushka. What is all this that I hear is going on up there in Denver?"

"Mikhail!" With a sigh of relief, she sank into the chair alongside the phone. Mikhail had married Alison just as Liz's own marriage to Dexter was going down in flames. He had defected from the Soviet Union during the world figure-skating championships five years ago, shortly after Alison had died in an Aeroflot plane crash. Drawn together by shared grief, he had been Liz's closest friend and confidant ever since his arrival in America. The warm sound of his accented voice made her smile, and she felt herself relax for the first time in hours.

"I'm sorry I sounded so aggressive. I expected you to be a reporter."

"Ah! That explains everything," he said with a laugh. "You and the reporters are never friends, yes?"

"No, we sure aren't. This morning's session with the wolf pack reminded me how much I love obscurity."

"I was at the rink all day and I didn't hear the news until I came home and turned on the TV while I cooked supper. Lizushka, this is terrible. Another of your roommates is dead, and you have been seeing Dexter Rand? What in the world have you gotten yourself into?"

"I don't know, Mikhail. I just absolutely and completely have no idea."

"But how did you get mixed up again with that monster Dexter? I know how bitter you felt after your divorce, and rightly so."

"Karen Zeit worked for him."

"And you never knew this? In all the weeks you shared an apartment with her, you never discussed her job?"

Liz felt herself blush. "I knew Karen worked for Dexter," she admitted.

Mikhail said nothing, but she could feel the silence gradually fill with his concern. "I thought we were friends," he said at last. "Good friends. Why didn't you tell me about Karen's job?"

"It . . . there was nothing to tell."

"Are you sure, *dorogoya*?" He spoke the Russian endearment softly. "I don't want you to get hurt again. Are you quite certain that the smiles you exchanged with the senator on the TV were just for the reporters?"

"I'm a hundred percent positive! That news conference didn't mean a thing in terms of our personal relationship. We just decided that it would look better for both of us if we joined forces to meet the press, that's all."

"With you and Dexter, things are not likely to be so simple, Lizzie. I hoped you'd finally gotten over your hang-ups for this ex-husband of yours."

"I have!" she declared vehemently. "Don't you see, Mikhail, it's because he means nothing to me that I was determined not to move out of Karen's apartment. I never planned to see Dexter, or speak to him, so what difference did it make who she worked for?"

A rueful note crept into Mikhail's voice. "As it turned out, *dorogoya*, rather a lot."

"But I had no way of knowing Karen would be killed. No way of knowing that I'd be thrust into Dexter's orbit again. Besides, this will all blow over. Believe me, I have no intention of staying within his striking range."

There was another worried silence before Mikhail spoke again. "Liz, do you not think it is time to tell the police about what has happened to your last two roommates? They already believe Karen was murdered. How is it going to look when they find out you were living with two other people who both died by falling out of windows?"

"Brian shot himself first," she said, as if that made the situation somehow less suspicious.

"Shot himself—or was shot? Do you not realize that the police will soon ask you this very question?"

"But I haven't done anything," she protested. "Eventually they'll find the people who are responsible, and in the meantime, I refuse to worry. In this country people are innocent until they're proven guilty."

"The United States is a wonderful place, Lizushka, the best in the world. But in this country the police want to write SOLVED across their file covers, just like in Russia." His voice was husky, his accent strong enough to add a beguiling touch of emphasis to his vowels. Liz felt a familiar rush of affection.

"Mikhail, you worry far too much about me. I'm not nearly as vulnerable as you think."

"I do not think you are vulnerable. But you are my sister, the twin of my Alison. Of course I must worry. How can I remain calm while the police bumble around, searching for a solution? How do we know that the murderer will not turn his attention to you while the police plod through their 'routine investigations'?"

She shivered, then said staunchly, "If somebody wanted to kill me, Mikhail, they would surely have done it by now."

"Who knows what this crazy murderer's motivations might be?"

Her control wavered, perilously close to breaking. "Oh God, Mikhail, don't you realize it's the pointlessness of all this that's driving me crazy?"

Mikhail backtracked immediately, obviously upset that his concern for Liz's welfare had made him add to her worries. "I am a fool," he said softly. "You are right not to concern yourself about a problem that cannot have anything to do with you. There is no reason for anybody to wish to kill you."

She made an effort to laugh. "It's not as if I'm going to leave somebody a trillion dollars when I die."

"And you live like a nun, so it cannot be a crime of passion. *Dorogoya*, let us stop talking about this horrible situation and turn to more pleasant subjects. I did not call to alarm you, but to issue an invitation. You will not want to be alone tonight, so I will drive up to Denver and bring you home to my house. You can spend the night with me in Colorado Springs and take my car into work tomorrow. The drive will be a little long for you, but we shall have dinner together tonight and enjoy each other's company over a glass of wine, so that you will say the long commute was worth it. You know you can stay with me for as many days as you wish. Forever, if you would only agree to it."

His generous offer produced an immediate wave of guilt in Liz. During the past twenty-four hours she had scarcely given Mikhail a thought, so exclusively had her attention been focused on Karen's death and her own meeting with Dexter. The obsession with Karen's death might be understandable, but the obsession with her ex-husband was not. Why in the world hadn't she remembered Mikhail when she'd been trying to come up with an alternative to checking into an hotel? Why had she so meekly agreed to spend another night with Dexter?

"Mikhail, I would love to come to Colorado Springs," she apologized. "But I've already agreed to go to..." She let her words trail off, as reluctant as she had been with Pieter to admit where she was going. Mikhail wouldn't gossip, but he would call her a fool—which she probably was—and right now she didn't feel strong enough to face another brotherly lecture.

"I've already promised to spend the night somewhere else," she amended. "With a friend from work." She blushed at the lie.

"Well, I'm glad you've found a place to stay. Is this new friend male or female?"

She could hear the hurt behind the cheerful words and felt like a worm. It seemed more important than ever not to let Mikhail find out where she was going. He simply wouldn't understand that her decision to spend the night at Dexter's house was entirely practical, based on her need to find an answer to the mystery of Karen's death. Mikhail had known her well at the time of her marriage breakup, and would never accept that she was cured of her infatuation. Knowing that she was spending a second night in her ex-husband's house, he would read all sorts of false significance into the arrangement.

"A married man with a child," she said finally, sticking as closely to the truth as she could. "Pieter Ullmann was pestering me to spend the night at his apartment, and since I didn't feel in the mood to become his bedtime bunny of the week, I accepted an invitation from a...from a colleague."

"Has Pieter been bothering you?" Mikhail's voice was sharp. "That boy is a great skater, but he's about as mature emotionally as a two-year-old."

"The poor guy's only twenty, isn't he?"

"Twenty-one, going on fifteen."

Liz laughed, chiefly from relief that her brother-in-law wasn't pursuing the question of precisely where she planned to spend the night. "I learned to handle the Pieters of this world a long time ago," she said. "You forget how many young men I met who were dazzled by their own Olympic medals and thought I ought to be dazzled, too."

He joined in her laughter. "You're right. You have worked so hard at becoming the efficient woman executive that I forget you were once poetry on ice, and everybody's heartthrob. Well, *dorogoya*, since you are determined to desert me, I shall eat my Stroganoff alone. Think of all that sour cream and fresh paprika and weep."

"I will for sure! It'll probably be hamburgers and French fries for me, if I'm lucky."

"Serves you right for abandoning me. Will you come down to the Springs on Saturday? We will share our favorite meal."

"It's a date," she said, relief flooding her because she had brushed through this difficult conversation without mortally wounding Mikhail's sensitive Russian soul.

"Goodbye, Lizushka."

She was halfway to Dexter's house before it dawned on her that her arrangement to spend the night with her ex-husband had been a somewhat casual thing—scarcely a commitment graven in stone. To avoid hurting Mikhail's feelings, all she had needed to do was call Dexter and explain politely that she no longer wished to accept his invitation.

Liz wondered why this obvious solution had not occurred to her earlier.

It required very few minutes' reflection to decide it would
be wiser not to inquire too deeply into the workings of her
psyche.

THE MEETING with Igor, his contact from the embassy in
Washington, D.C., didn't go as well as he had hoped. He'd
noticed that their meetings in Denver nearly always ended
on a sour note, and he wondered if Denver's high altitude
gave Igor a headache. Certainly, tonight had been one of
their less pleasant sessions, despite the fact that Karen had
been so successfully taken care of.

Everything had started off well enough, although he'd
been too smart to relax and rest on his laurels. Igor was
notorious for his habit of lulling his minions into a false
sense of security before letting fly with brutal criticisms.

He had set the right tone for the meeting by providing
Igor's favorite food. The KGB man had beamed at the
generous supply of greasy packages set out on the table,
and had selected a jumbo-size box of French fries and a
double hamburger.

He himself didn't eat such poisonous foods, of course.
He merely watched as Igor squirted ketchup onto the fries,
making swirls of bright red sauce. He reflected cynically
that Igor couldn't have been allowed to do enough finger
painting when he was young. Soviet nursery schools had
always been big on patriotic songs and notoriously indifferent to child psychology.

After several minutes of munching, Igor looked up from
his earnest consumption of French fries. "So, Karen Zeit
is dead. It was time. Past time. She was becoming nervous, I think." Igor had an annoying habit of stating the
obvious.

"Yes, Comrade Secretary. As I told you, she feared the
FBI investigation authorized by Senator Rand would blow

her cover. There is an FBI agent working in the senator's Washington office, and unfortunately, our operatives haven't yet identified him. Karen was very worried. As you know, her past wouldn't stand up to detailed scrutiny."

"I am all too aware of the limitations of the identity we provided. With this murder investigation going ahead full steam, we work under time pressure." Igor munched through a mouthful of burger. "At least the main part of our mission proceeds according to plan. The trap has been satisfactorily set. The senator is already receiving some very unfavorable press."

"Yes, Comrade. And the press conference with his ex-wife can only work to our advantage."

"Ah yes! The former wife of the senator. I am glad that you yourself bring up the subject of Ms. Meacham." Igor licked up a drop of ketchup with a long, pink tongue, closing his eyes in appreciation of the exquisite flavor. "If Congress would only stop trying to sell democracy to the third world and concentrate on hamburgers, the Americans would be invincible."

He smiled, as he was supposed to. Igor liked to be thought of as a humorist. "I expect Congress wishes to export both hamburgers and democracy, Comrade Secretary."

Igor wiped his fingers delicately on a paper napkin. "Hamburgers transplant better than democracy. But, to return to the subject of Ms. Meacham. I hope you have that situation firmly in hand? She is the high-risk element of our operation. She must be seen in public with the senator, but she cannot become too close to him."

"I understand, Comrade Secretary. Ms. Meacham is completely under control."

"Hmm." Igor managed to express a great deal of doubt in a small grunt. "It is one thing for Ms. Meacham to appear at a press conference with her former husband. It would be an entirely different matter if the two of them should start to become—intimate. You have assured me that the hatred between Elizabeth Meacham and Dexter Rand makes any exchange of information extremely unlikely. I trust you have not miscalculated."

He was beginning to sweat, and surreptitiously wiped his palms on the edge of the tablecloth. "Believe me, Comrade Secretary, there is no chance of that. Elizabeth Meacham despises the senator after the way he treated her at the time of their divorce. I have heard this same story repeated on all sides."

"And your own observation?"

"Agrees completely with what I've heard."

"I expected her to be with you tonight. Where is she?"

"I invited her to have dinner with me, but she refused. However, there is no cause for alarm. She's spending the night with one of her colleagues."

"If she is not precisely where we want her to be, then there is cause for alarm. Your much-vaunted success with other women is of no value to us if you cannot attract Ms. Meacham sufficiently to control her movements."

He couldn't stop his gaze sliding disparagingly over Igor's bulging waistline and clumsy, peasantlike hands, then immediately realized it was a mistake to have allowed his disdain to show.

"Comrade Champion," Igor said softly. "My duty to the motherland does not require that I should have a desirable body. My duty requires only that my wits remain sharp and that I possess a profound understanding of the American political system. It is clear that I am fulfilling my duties. Are you fulfilling yours?"

"Yes, yes, of course, Comrade Secretary. Is Karen Zeit not dead? Is Senator Rand not in trouble?" He decided it might be smart to make no further mention of Liz Meacham.

"Who was the father of Karen Zeit's baby?" The question was slashed across the table with the sting of a whip.

He made the fatal mistake of lying. "Senator Rand—"

"Would never take his secretary to bed. He is the model of bourgeois propriety. You are the father of her baby, Comrade. Is that not so?"

Regretfully, he realized he had little choice but to tell the truth. "It isn't certain, Comrade Secretary, but the child could be mine. Karen fell hopelessly in love with me, and her infatuation jeopardized the safety of our operation. I had sex with her only to keep her content. Naturally, I had no idea that she would be so careless as to allow herself to become pregnant."

Igor banged his fist on the table, and the little packets of ketchup jumped with the force of the blow. "You play me for a fool, Comrade Champion. Do you expect me to believe that Karen never told you she carried your child? What reason could she have had to become pregnant, if she did not want you to marry her?"

Thank God, he had murdered Karen. Now she would never be able to contradict his story. He lifted wide, innocent eyes to meet Igor's accusing gaze. It was a blessing that he had always had such marvelously honest eyes. "Comrade Secretary, I swear to you that Karen never once mentioned to me the fact that she was pregnant. Perhaps she knew the child wasn't mine."

Igor grunted. He was a past master of the expressive grunt. This one conveyed scorn, disbelief and indifference in almost equal measure. "We have more important problems to worry about at this moment, I suppose. Our government is running out of time. Our secret lobbying against the new F-19B fighter jet has not been as successful as we hoped. This is an effective weapon, Comrade, and by some miracle, many U.S. senators on the Defense Appropriations Committee understand that fact."

"The new president isn't much in favor of expensive weapons development."

"But on this occasion, there is rare bipartisan support for the project. Except for one or two die-hard pacifists, the F-19B has met with nothing but approval. It is undetectable by radar. It is faster than any other plane now flying. It can carry conventional arms as well as nuclear warheads, and it can come in low to pinpoint a target. Possession of such a plane would give the United States an enormous strategic advantage. Therefore we cannot allow it to go into production. And unless we can convince Dexter Rand to campaign actively against it, the Senate Appropriations Committee is likely to vote funds for production of the plane within a few weeks."

"I understand, Comrade Secretary. I realize that Dexter Rand must be made to declare publicly against the plane. We need to control his vote. His chairmanship of this senate committee has already proven disastrous to the interests of the Soviet Union."

Igor gave another of his grunts. "From our point of view, he does far too good a job of separating useful military technology from projects that are never going to work. Who would have thought the senators would be smart enough to select a military expert to chair their armaments committee?"

He didn't bother to answer what was clearly a rhetorical question. Senator Rand's appointment to the Appropriations Committee had been causing gray hairs in Moscow ever since it was first announced. He spoke reassuringly. "The details of our plan to control the senator have been meticulously worked out, Comrade. With luck, Dexter Rand will soon be a useful tool in our hands instead of a thorn in our sides."

"Luck doesn't factor in our government's planning, Comrade. I trust that you have left no part of this operation to luck."

Inwardly he cursed the aggravating old buzzard. Outwardly he smiled. "The plans have been perfected to the last tiny detail, Comrade Secretary. We will deal with the senator and with Elizabeth Meacham before the end of the week." He paused for a moment, then pressed ahead with the question that was at the forefront of his mind. "Have the necessary personnel arrived from Moscow?"

Igor's response was curt. "She is already in the embassy."

"There is—a message for me?"

"She looks forward to seeing you soon."

He would have liked to ask more questions, but knew that Igor would delight in withholding information. "Do you want me to review the details of our plan for the abduction, and for Elizabeth Meacham's murder?"

"No." Igor rose to his feet. "I am well aware of your plans. Have you forgotten that I approved them in the first place? I am spending the next few days collating the evidence that will prove that Senator Rand murdered Ms. Meacham. Just be sure that your own part of the operation is carried out with similar efficiency."

"It is all taken care of, Comrade Secretary. We shall need the photographs when the senator goes to Washington."

The damned old buzzard grunted again. "A word of warning, Comrade Champion. Neither the senator nor Elizabeth Meacham is a fool. Each of them knows that they did not commit murder. Take care that their efforts to save themselves do not unravel our plans."

"Their efforts to extricate themselves from the trap cannot succeed," he said, with a touch more confidence than he actually felt. "There are no trails for them to follow. We've made sure that whatever line of investigation anybody pursues, they will find only dead ends."

"Very dead, I trust." Igor put on his jacket. "Dead is highly desirable."

He wasn't sure he'd understood. "I'm sorry, Comrade Secretary? If you would be so good as to clarify..."

"One of your collaborators is no longer useful to us, and unfortunately he knows too much. Take care of him, Comrade. Take care of him soon, before his nerves get us all into trouble."

He rose to his feet, relieved that the interview had ended on a relatively positive note. Killing was easy. "I understand, Comrade Secretary. The matter will be taken care of expertly. I will kill him myself."

"No more windows, Comrade. I'm getting tired of windows."

"Certainly, Comrade. There are many other ways. I think perhaps a knife."

Igor grunted.

Chapter Six

Dinner was long over by the time Liz finally returned to Dexter's house. The housekeeper answered the door and directed her to a family room overlooking the backyard, where Dexter and his daughter were engaged in a game of dominoes. From the fierce frown of concentration wrinkling Amanda's forehead, Liz concluded that the game was being taken very seriously by at least one of the participants.

"Your visitor, Senator Rand. Miss Meacham's here."

"Thanks, Mrs. Morton." Dexter stood up and came across the room to greet Liz, and the housekeeper left, insisting on carrying Liz's case up to the guest room.

"Glad you made it back. Amanda and I were beginning to wonder what had happened to you."

"I'm sorry. I was delayed at the office and then I couldn't decide what I needed to pack. But I should have phoned."

"Don't worry about it. You had other things on your mind. Do you need dinner?"

"No, thanks. I stopped at Burger King on the way over."

He grinned. "Shush, don't let Amanda hear those magic words. She had to suffer through chicken breasts, mushrooms and fresh fruit salad. She tells me I'm the meanest dad in the world to keep ordering such yucky meals."

Liz's smile was only a touch strained. "Sounds like you're bringing up a deprived child, Dex. Don't you know that too much nutritious food damages the psyche?"

His eyes softened as he glanced over at the table, where his daughter was occupied in building a long, low wall of dominoes. "She's gorgeous," he said simply. "Not a hint of damage so far. Come and meet her."

Liz gripped her purse a little tighter. "Does she . . . um . . . does she know we were married?" she asked, trying to think up some reasonable excuse for hanging back. She couldn't very well say *I hated her mother so much, I don't want to meet her.*

"I told her, but she doesn't seem to find the information relevant. As soon as she realized you weren't about to become her stepmother, she lost interest in our relationship."

Liz followed Dexter across the room, curiosity to meet Susan's child still mixed with a confused grab bag of other emotions. Her stomach knotted painfully when Dexter rumpled Amanda's hair in a casual gesture that spoke volumes about his love.

"Hey, honey, I'm sorry about our game. This is Elizabeth Meacham. She's the friend of mine I told you about, and she'll be staying with us for a few days."

Somebody had obviously taught Amanda very good manners. Or maybe, Liz thought with a touch of bitterness, courtesy to inferiors was bred into the genes of people like Dexter and Susan—part of their birthright, along with their infuriating self-possession. Amanda hopped off her chair, dark curls bouncing. *Susan's curls. Susan's green eyes. But Dexter's arrogant, stubborn chin.* Amanda held out her hand. "Hello, Mrs. Meacham. It's nice to have you here."

Liz took the tiny hand into her own. It felt warm, a little bit sticky and oddly trusting. She swallowed hard, resisting the craziest impulse to reach down and sweep the child into her arms. Surely she was imagining the vulnerability she saw in those stunning green eyes? "Hello, Amanda." She sought for something to say that was both suitable and honest. Her gaze fell on the dominoes. "Who's winning?"

"It's kind of a draw at the moment." Amanda squinted up at her father. "Will you have time to finish the game, Dad?"

He glanced down at his watch. "It's past your bedtime already, young lady."

"But it's Friday. So there's no school tomorrow."

Dexter sat down at the table with a mock sigh. "I guess we'll have to finish, then, or you'll claim you won."

She giggled. "No, I wouldn't. I have to let you win at dominoes, 'cos I always beat you so bad at Nintendo."

Dexter shot a rueful glance in Liz's direction. "Don't let this child get you in front of a TV set with a joystick. Believe me, it's a totally humiliating experience."

The jealousy Liz felt as she watched Dexter joke with his daughter was intense and shocking. She realized that she resented Susan's success in carrying Dexter's child to term more than anything else. Nowadays she almost never thought about the possibility of becoming a mother herself, and yet for a moment, she felt a pang of loss so sharp that her miscarriage might have occurred nine days instead of nine years ago.

Dexter glanced up, his eyes darkening with sudden concern. "Liz, are you sure you're okay? You look awfully pale."

"I'll be fine." She flashed a determined smile, something she seemed to be doing a lot lately. "But I might go and beg a cup of tea from Mrs. Morton, if she's still in the kitchen."

"She's probably gone to her room. If so, help yourself to whatever you want."

"Thanks." Liz's main purpose wasn't to drink or to eat; it was to escape from the unbearably cozy scene of domestic intimacy. "Good night, Amanda, I'm glad to have met you. See you tomorrow, Dexter."

"Night, Mrs. Meacham."

"I'll join you in the kitchen as soon as we've finished our game."

"There's no need—"

"We have things to talk about," Dexter said quietly. "For one thing, we need to decide what we should do tomorrow. Also, Lieutenant Rodriguez came to see me again this afternoon."

She swung around, looking at him inquiringly. "He's been checking our alibis," he said. Glancing at his daughter, he added, "I'll talk to you later."

"You need a six, Dad," Amanda interjected.

Dexter laid down a domino with a triumphant flourish. "Ha-ha! Now you need a six, too, and I don't think you have one."

Liz left the room. She doubted if either Dexter or his daughter noticed her departure.

THE DOMINO GAME lasted less time than she would have expected. Dexter came into the kitchen just as she finished pouring out her cup of orange-and-cinnamon tea.

"Would you like some?" She gestured to the pot.

"Thanks, but you sit down. I'll get it." He searched in a couple of cupboards until he found a cup and saucer—he evidently didn't spend much time in the kitchen—then sat next to her at the polished wooden table. "Rough day?" he asked softly. "You look beat."

She stirred her tea with great concentration, although she never took sugar. "No worse than yours, I expect."

He smiled grimly. "That leaves plenty of scope for rough. How were things at the office?"

"Busy. Awful."

His smile relaxed slightly. "Rarely have two small words conveyed such a wealth of information. That sums up my day perfectly." He took a sip of tea. "As far as I can tell, the police have moved us up from being run-of-the-mill suspicious characters into being prime suspects. The preliminary pathology results show that Karen died around four-thirty. The highly efficient Lieutenant Rodriguez has checked our schedules and determined that neither of us have alibis. He clearly suspects us of working in collusion to do away with poor Karen."

"He thinks we were working together?"

"He's convinced of it. We were planning to marry again, you see, only Karen inconveniently became pregnant and wouldn't have an abortion. Since U.S. senators from Colorado can't hope to get elected with sex scandals featuring prominently in their résumés, you and I hatched this plan to toss Karen from a window and make it look like suicide."

The scenario was so preposterous that she would have laughed if she hadn't been so scared. "That's pretty far-fetched as a motive for you to commit murder. It's flat out ridiculous for me. What in the world am I supposed to get out of all this?"

"Me. And my money." He caught her look and his mouth twisted into a wry grimace. "My dear Liz, the lieutenant can't be expected to understand that you wouldn't take me if I came gift-wrapped in million-dollar bills."

She had the oddest impression that she could hear pain beneath his flippant words. "For a double layer of packaging I might consider it," she said.

He looked at her long and hard. "That's a considerable improvement over the situation nine years ago. My lawyer said the sound of my name was enough to make you turn green by the time our divorce case hit the courts."

She looked away. "I was very young then."

"Yes." He hesitated. "So was I, you know. Not in years, perhaps, but in experience."

Liz turned around and stared at him in astonishment. "How can you say that? You were the most sophisticated man I'd ever met! You'd already traveled half across the world. You were the Air Force's ace test pilot. You were a millionaire—"

"And I knew no more about falling in love and being married than you did," he interjected quietly. "Aside from acute hormonal spasms when I was in my teens, I'd never been in love until I met you. A lot of the time we were together, my emotions were..."

He didn't finish his sentence and she prompted him. "Yes?"

"Out of control is the best way to describe it, I guess."

She twirled her teacup on its saucer. It was Dresden porcelain, she noticed, antique and beautiful. Probably imported into the States by Dexter's grandfather, who had once been American's ambassador to Germany. It was Germany where Liz had competed in her last, disastrous skating championship. She cradled the delicate china in her hands, as if by doing so she could contain her memories of that awful time.

"What are you thinking about?"

"The Olympics," she replied honestly.

He didn't have to ask which Olympics. They both knew. "That was a bad night for you," he said. "For both of us."

"I was six weeks pregnant," she said suddenly. "I'd torn a ligament in my ankle and I felt so sick I thought I was going to throw up every time I turned my head."

His body stiffened with shock. "Pregnant! Liz, my God! Why didn't you tell me?"

She traced the thin gold rim of the cup with her thumb. "I was...afraid you'd be mad at me. Because you said you didn't want children and you thought I was taking birth-control pills."

"And you weren't taking pills?"

She shook her head, then laughed, mocking her younger self. "I wanted to trap you into staying married," she admitted. "So I used the oldest trick in the world. And then, when I found out I really was expecting a baby, I was too scared to tell you. Not to mention telling my coach, who'd have thrown a fit at the prospect of his star athlete going on maternity leave." Her mouth twisted into a painful smile. "I'd worked out the perfect trap, except I was afraid to spring it."

"What happened to the baby, Liz?"

"I miscarried a couple of months later."

"And you still didn't tell me? Good God, was I really such a monster?"

She finally looked up at him. "I don't know. By that time, I couldn't see you clearly anymore. Susan was always in the way, blocking my view."

He stretched out a hand, then allowed it to fall back into his lap without touching her. She realized now—as she never would have nine years earlier—that he was afraid of offending her, afraid of her rejection. His voice when he spoke was tight, not with impatience as she would once have thought, but with regret. "I never was unfaithful to you during our marriage, Liz. Whatever Ali... Whatever anyone may have told you, Susan and I never made love until after you'd divorced me."

"Alison never suggested you and Susan were lovers," she said. "Susan told me herself."

Silence descended, thick, heavy and fraught with tension. "If Susan told you we were lovers during the time you and I were married, then she lied," Dexter said at last. "I'm sorry, Liz. I must have been doing a lousy job of handling my relationships for them to have gotten so screwed up."

"It was a long time ago," she said, and suddenly the trite words were true. She pushed the cup of tea away, leaning back in the chair to ease cramped muscles. "A long time ago, in a faraway place, with people who've changed so much they're hardly the same.''

"You've changed," he agreed. "You're softer. More beautiful."

"Thank you." She was shocked by the intensity of pleasure his comment provoked. She got up from the table, carrying the teapot over to the sink so that she could hide the sudden color staining her cheeks. "We'd better get this conversation back to the present, Dexter, or the lieutenant will be pounding on the door to arrest us and we'll have done nothing except trade compliments about how mature we've gotten since we savaged each other in the divorce courts."

"I wish that sounded funny. The bit about the lieutenant coming to arrest us, I mean. But the fact is, I have no alibi. I left a meeting with the manager of Stapleton Airport at three forty-five. I should have arrived here about twenty minutes later. I actually arrived home at five o'clock."

"What happened?" she asked, returning to her chair.

"I went to the library," he said wryly. "The main one, downtown. The meeting with the airport manager had finished a half hour earlier than we expected, and I've been wanting to double-check some facts in a book on Denver's old, ethnic neighborhoods. Nobody was waiting for me, so I grabbed the chance."

"Did you check the book out? There might be a time on the computer."

"No, the book's for reference only. And before you ask, no, I didn't speak to any of the librarians. I knew where the book was shelved and I went straight there."

"It's a lousy alibi, Dex. Don't you have a research staff to double-check facts for you? Important senators don't visit the library unless it's an official visit."

"Liz, honey, you're singing the lieutenant's song. But you're no better off than I am. Rodriguez claims you left

your office at the crucial time without telling anybody
where you were going."

"Of course I didn't say where I was going!" Liz protested. "That was the whole point of the exercise. The darn
phone hadn't stopped ringing all day, so I hid in one of the
typists' offices, trying to catch up on my paperwork."

"Where was the typist?"

"Out sick with the flu."

"Well, good luck telling that one to the lieutenant."

Liz laughed, then sobered abruptly. "When I'm with
you, I forget to take the situation seriously. Then, as soon
as I'm alone, all the reasons why I should be panic-stricken
come rushing back. I mean, we could end up in the electric
chair, Dex."

"In Colorado they use the gas chamber."

"Gosh and golly, now I feel much better!"

He smiled, reaching out to clasp her hand. Her stomach
danced a little jig. "We're going to find out what's behind
this, long before things reach that stage, Liz."

Several seconds passed before she gathered her wits sufficiently to move her hand. "Pieter Ullmann was at my
apartment tonight," she said, breaking the momentary silence. "From the remarks he dropped about Karen, I guess
several people could have been the father of her baby."

"He'd had an affair with her?"

"He said not. But he also claimed she came on to him in
a big way."

Dexter frowned. "Odd, isn't it, how we get to know
people in such a one-dimensional fashion? I can't even
picture Karen as a sexually active woman, let alone a sexually aggressive one. Now that it's too late, I'm feeling
guilty because I spent so little time thinking about her as a
person. Maybe if I'd been more attentive to her needs, none
of this would have happened."

"You're being too hard on yourself. She was an employee, Dexter, not a close friend."

"She was a damn good administrative assistant, that's for sure. We always seemed to exchange the usual chitchat about our personal lives, and yet once the lieutenant started questioning me, I realized I knew almost nothing about her. Not even trivial things like whether she preferred Beethoven or Bruce Springsteen."

"Rodriguez thinks you're concealing information."

"Of course he does. Unfortunately I'm not. In fact, I wish I knew something—anything—that would give us a starting point to unravel what was going on in Karen's life. I suppose you haven't come up with any wonderful new insights since this morning?"

"Nothing wonderful. But I've been thinking a lot about what you said last night. About how my roommates must have had something in common, something that linked them."

"And you thought of a link?"

"I'm not sure. It's so tenuous, you may think it's silly to mention it."

"At this point, nothing's too silly to mention."

"Well, like I told you, Brian was an engineer and Jill was a social worker, and Karen's basic training was secretarial. But in a weird sort of way, all three of them worked for the government, although their jobs were so different it almost doesn't coun—"

"Explain their connection to the government," Dexter interrupted, his body radiating a sudden tension.

She was startled by his intensity. "Karen's link is obvious. She was your personal assistant, and you're a U.S. senator."

"Go on. What about Jill?"

"She worked as a civilian employee for the navy. The naval shipyards in Bremerton are so huge, they basically employ the whole town, so I never gave her employer a second thought when you asked me last night. She worked in the personnel-management division."

"And Brian?"

"He was a professor of electrical engineering at the university, but he didn't do much teaching, and I think his recent research was in the field of electronics. Almost all his income came from projects funded by the government, and a lot of his work was secret, I do know that."

"Have you any idea what he was working on when he died?"

"Not specifically. Even if it hadn't been secret, I wouldn't have understood what he was doing. Electronic microcircuitry isn't exactly my area of expertise. He mentioned once that he was part of the design team for a new fighter jet that was on order for the Air Force. He was brilliant at his work, everybody agreed on that."

"A new fighter jet," Dexter muttered. He stared abstractedly into the middle distance, then finally rose to his feet. "I need to make a phone call to Washington," he said. "Come into the study, will you? Liz, I think—just possibly—you may be onto something."

"Mind telling me what? You think it's significant that all my roommates worked for the government?"

"Yes, I do, although at the moment I don't see precisely how. What we need is information, and I should get that from my phone call."

Dexter opened the door to his study, shut it behind them, then pressed a section of wall paneling next to the bar. A small, concealed door sprang open to reveal a scarlet telephone. Dexter punched in a long series of numbers, gestured to indicate that Liz should take a seat on the sofa, and waited in patient silence for about thirty seconds.

"This is Senator Rand," he said finally. "I want to speak with Agent Harry Cooper. Patch me through, please."

Liz glanced at her watch. It was ten o'clock in Denver, midnight already in Washington, DC. Agent Cooper either kept late office hours or slept with his scarlet phone next to the pillow She leaned back against the cushions of the sofa, listening to Dexter identify himself again, first by name and then by a series of numbers.

She wondered why she felt so little surprise at Dexter's active response to her suggestion of a job link among her dead roommates. Perhaps the unreality of her situation was beginning to affect her. From the day Brian died, she had felt distanced from her everyday life, as if she could only react to events, not take charge of them. Three days earlier, for example, she would have said that being alone with Dexter was as unlikely as the possibility that Karen Zeit would be murdered. Now Karen was incontrovertibly dead, and she was spending the second night in a row with her ex-husband. Her world had lost it familiar boundaries.

"Professor Brian Jensen," she heard Dexter say. "An electrical engineer. Full professor. Possibly working on the F-19B fighter jet project. The control panel for all the F-19s came out of Seattle. I want you to find out anything and everything you can about him. He supposedly committed suicide four months ago."

There was a short silence, followed by Dexter's reply. "In Seattle. He shot himself, then fell out of his apartment window. There must have been a police investigation."

Another pause, much longer this time, then Dexter's reply. "I need this information, Cooper. I need it soon. I'm asking as a personal favor. I'll beg, if you want me to."

Silence. "Thanks, Cooper. I owe you one. By the way, I'm beginning to wonder if the leak is from Denver, and not from DC. You might want to talk to your chief about that. Maybe we have the undercover operative in the wrong place, which would explain our lack of progress. If we do, Karen's death gives us the perfect excuse to introduce somebody at this end. I'm going to need a new assistant."

Another pause. "Fine. But please, just make sure she can type and knows something about party politics." A final brief moment of silence, and then Dexter said good-night, hanging up the phone and closing the wall cabinet.

"Is that a secret phone?" Liz asked, not sure whether to be impressed or amused.

"Not very secret. Everybody who has access to this room knows about it. But it's supposedly 'safe.' The signal's scrambled, so it's protected against wiretaps."

"Do all senators get a safe red phone?"

"Not all of them. A lot depends on their committee assignments. I chair the Senate Committee on Defense Appropriations, so a great deal of top-secret material comes into my hands. Not only secret because of policy decisions, but because the technology is new."

"And that's why you got the phone?"

"Part of the reason." Dexter came and sat beside her on the sofa. Their knees touched, and she carefully moved away.

"I feel like I'm dragging out your teeth without benefit of anesthesia," she said. "Can you tell me what that phone call was all about?"

"There have been leaks of classified information from my Washington office," Dexter said slowly. "Nothing too important until a couple of months ago, when the specifications for a section of the new F-19B fighter jet turned up for sale on the international black market."

"But how do you know all this? Presumably black-market arms dealers don't go around shouting to the world about their sale item of the week."

"I can't answer your question, Liz. I've already revealed far more than I officially should. Let's just say certain government agencies manage to keep effective tabs on who's selling what to whom."

"Are you allowed to tell me why those government agencies decided the black-market specifications came from your office?"

"Top-secret documents have an extremely limited distribution, and each copy is marked with identifying data. The specifications that turned up on the black market were obviously photocopies of material that had come from my office."

"If you haven't found out who was responsible for the original leak, how do you stop future ones?"

"Liz, I know I sound like a bad actor in a thirties movie, but the answer is: *We have our ways.*"

"Do your ways work?"

"Hopefully. So far they seem to be working."

"It's certainly a strange coincidence that Brian should have been working on the F-19 plane when he died."

"Very strange. Which is why I've asked my contact at the FBI to run a comprehensive check on Brian Jensen's background."

"Couldn't you ask the FBI to run checks on Karen Zeit, as well?"

"You heard my conversation with Harry Cooper. The FBI is short of money and staff, and they're already expending too much of both on my office. I had to beg to get anything done on Brian Jensen. Unless the Colorado law-enforcement authorities ask for FBI assistance, we haven't a hope of persuading the Bureau to run two background checks simultaneously. Besides, Karen lived with you and worked with me. Between the two of us, surely we ought to be able to come up with some information about her, once we start digging."

"I brought her address book with me." Liz searched in her purse, then produced the slender maroon notebook with a flourish. "There aren't too many names in it, which should make it easier to track people down."

Dexter took the book and quickly thumbed through the pages. "The lieutenant slipped up, didn't he? Why didn't he take this away with him?"

"Karen kept it with her recipe books in the kitchen. I guess the police passed right over it."

"Hmm. Your name's here with a work phone number, so is mine with a DC address and number. Here's Evan

Howard's home address and phone number." Dexter flicked over the pages. "Home addresses and numbers for all the people in my Colorado office. Phone numbers for the hairdresser, the doctor and the dentist. An address for Pieter Ullmann. No phone number. And there are a dozen names I don't recognize. How about you?"

Liz leaned over so that she could see the pages as Dexter turned them. Her body was pressed against his from shoulder to thigh, and suddenly, over the chasm of nine years' separation, she felt the achingly familiar rush of sexual awareness. She couldn't move away without drawing attention to her reaction—which Dexter had given no sign of sharing—so she drew in a deep breath and reminded herself that she was a mature woman of twenty-eight, not a hormone-flooded teenager of nineteen.

"Rachel Landers is a woman Karen took gourmet cooking lessons with each Saturday. They went somewhere in Colorado Springs." Liz was delighted to hear that her voice sounded cool, crisp and businesslike. Unfortunately, the rest of her wasn't doing so well. She drew in another deep breath. "Bev Dixon and Rita Kominsky are tennis partners. I don't know any of the others. They all seem to be men."

"Did you notice something odd, though?" Dexter's voice was a little husky and he coughed to clear it.

"They're all Denver or Colorado Springs addresses," Liz said, wondering why he didn't move away, now that they'd finished looking at the address book. "Is that what you mean?"

"Yes." Dexter's voice was still husky. "Karen only came to Colorado from Kansas City two years ago. You'd think she'd have one or two friends from Kansas that she kept in touch with."

"Maybe she filed those addresses somewhere else."

"Maybe." Dexter closed the notebook with a snap and got purposefully to his feet. Liz tried hard not to feel bereft.

"Anyway," he said, "it seems to me our Saturday morning is mapped out for us. We have to try to talk to everybody on this list, starting with the people whose names neither of us recognize."

"Sounds good. What about Amanda, though? Won't she resent it if we leave her alone all day?"

"Mrs. Morton takes her to karate class in the morning—"

"Karate! I thought little girls were supposed to dream about ballet and pink tutus."

He grinned. "Amanda seems to prefer white trousers and stinging chops to the head. Anyway, she always brings a couple of friends over for lunch afterward, so she won't miss me. But I have promised to spend the evening with her."

"That works out well, because I've agreed to have dinner with Mikhail."

"Are you planning to spend the night with him?" Dexter's question was a miracle of neutrality. "Just so as I know whether to lock up the house or not," he added.

Liz looked at him steadily. "No," she said. "I'm not planning to spend the night with Mikhail tomorrow, although I often do."

Dexter turned away, his movement abrupt. "Would you like a nightcap? A brandy? A diet soda?"

"No thanks. But you're right, we should get to bed."

Her words fell like stones into the sudden silence, weighted with a meaning she had never intended to give them. Dexter shoved his hands into the pockets of his pants, as if he didn't know what else to do with them.

"It's still there, isn't it?" he said quietly. "For both of us."

"I don't know what you me..." The lie died away, unfinished. "Yes," she admitted, meeting Dexter's gaze. "It's still there. But I realize now that people don't have to...to get involved just because they're attracted to each other."

Dexter came and stood in front of her. His dark brows lifted, giving him a sardonic, almost derisive air. "You think now we've talked about it, we'll be able to ignore the tension between us and get on with more important things?"

"We should be able to. We're mature adults."

"How adult?" he murmured, pulling her into his arms and holding her lightly against his lean, hard strength. Liz tried to ignore the shiver of delight that coursed through her, but she didn't move away.

His head bent slowly toward her, his breath warm against her skin. Against her will, her eyes drifted closed, so she didn't see the moment when his mouth covered hers, but she felt his touch with every fiber of her being.

With a quiver almost of despair, Liz melted into his arms. Why did Dexter's kiss turn her to fire, where other men's attempts at lovemaking left her cool and faintly bored? The years of separation hadn't dulled her memory of what it was like to share Dexter's bed, and when he trailed tiny, seeking kisses around the edge of her mouth, she had a brief moment of madness when she wondered what depth of pleasure would be in store, if she allowed herself to follow him up the stairs into the welcome darkness of his room.

His hands left her shoulders and slid into the tight knot of her hair, pulling out the pins so that he could run his hands through the silken strands. For a single insane minute she allowed herself to be drawn unreservedly into the kiss, until the heat flooding her body triggered some primitive warning that soon she would leave herself with no choice but to surrender.

Panting, shaking, she drew herself away. "No!" she whispered. "Please, Dex, don't make me feel this way...."

As soon as she had spoken, she realized just how much those few words revealed. Dexter, thank God, didn't challenge her. Instead, he lightly touched a forefinger to her lips.

"You taste even better now you've grown up," he said.

Chapter Seven

The first part of Saturday morning taught Liz how frustrating—not to mention exhausting—a supposedly simple investigation could be. She and Dexter called first on Karen's tennis partners, who agreed that Karen played tennis regularly and well. None of them had any idea who her other friends might be, or what she did when she wasn't playing tennis.

Dexter suggested that their next move should be to check out the men on the list. Six of the dozen men listed in Karen's notebook weren't home. Another had moved out of state, leaving no forwarding address. Four were at home and willing to answer questions, but had nothing more to say than that they'd met Karen only recently and didn't know her very well.

The last person on their Most Wanted list turned out to be an airline steward, who'd just flown back to Denver from Hong Kong. The news of Karen's death clearly came as an unpleasant shock to him, since he hadn't read any American newspapers for a couple of days. His surprise might have contributed to his willingness to talk but he— like all the others—denied being a close friend of the dead woman.

"Karen was just somebody I met at a party, if you know what I mean."

"Yes, I know what you mean," Dexter responded neutrally. "Did she spend more than one night with you?"

"How d'you know she spent the night?" The steward's voice contained a heavy touch of belligerence. "I never said anything about taking her home, and I sure didn't get her pregnant."

"Karen mentioned something once...." Liz carefully didn't specify what her roommate had mentioned, and the steward jumped in.

"Hey, whatever she said, it wasn't any great love affair between us, you know. She was feeling lonely and upset about some guy or other who'd dumped on her, and I offered her a few hours of fun. To take her mind off things, you know? We only met a couple of times after that first night."

Dexter spoke quickly. "Did she tell you anything about the man who'd been treating her so badly? His name, perhaps, or where he lived?"

The steward gave a reminiscent smile and winked. "Hey, she might have done, if you know what I mean. I guess I never paid too much attention to what Karen said. That little lady was some bundle of fire, a regular crackerjack in bed. We were really something together." He caught Liz's eye and saw that his kiss-and-tell boasting wasn't going over too well.

"Maybe I do remember one thing," he amended. "This guy who'd dumped on her—she mentioned once that she worked for him. Like he was her boss, if you know what I mean, and he was taking advantage."

Dexter's face revealed nothing of what he was thinking. "Yes," he said. "We know exactly what you mean."

Liz quickly asked another question, but the rest of their conversation revealed little more than that the steward remained very impressed with his own skill in the bedroom.

"He and Pieter Ullmann sound like soul mates," Liz commented as they returned to the car. "We should introduce them to each other."

"He certainly seems like a bad choice of companion, if Karen was feeling unsure of herself," Dexter agreed. He clicked the seat belt closed, not looking at Liz when he spoke again. "Feel free to report what we just learned to Lieutenant Rodriguez. In fact, it's probably your civic duty to report everything the man said."

Liz stared out of the window, although she didn't really see either the budding trees or the sunny stretch of suburban road. Despite the steward's damning words, she had the strongest conviction that Dexter wasn't the father of Karen's baby. She wondered if she was a complete fool to continue believing in his innocence. Nine years ago, she had allowed sexual attraction to overcome her common sense and even her own self-interest. Was she doing the same thing again?

Dexter's voice broke into her reverie. "For what it's worth, Liz, I'll repeat that Karen and I were never lovers, so I can't be the father of the child she was carrying. Although, God knows, after what that steward said, there's no reason for you to believe me."

"Actually there is." Liz's thoughts became clearer in her own mind as she spoke. "In the first place, I don't think you'd ever get involved with somebody working in your office. Why would you bother when you have so many other choices? Washington is full of eligible women who'd love to be the mistress of a young, powerful senator, and you like being a senator too much to risk your job over a love affair with one of your staff."

He smiled ruefully. "I'm not sure if that's a flattering assessment of my character or not. Anyway, it's something of a moot point, because I don't think most people would buy your reasoning. Elected officials have affairs all the time with partners who are flagrantly unsuitable. Despite all the aggressive journalists dogging their footsteps, they always assume they'll be able to keep the details of their personal lives hidden.''

"You may be right. But there's a more important reason why I don't believe you killed Karen. I've seen you with Amanda and I'm sure you'd never murder a woman who was carrying your baby. If Karen had been pregnant with your child, you'd have married her—even if only to have a fighting chance of claiming custody.''

"Rodriguez would say Karen might not have told me she was pregnant.''

"He can't have it both ways. If you didn't know she was pregnant, you had no reason to kill her.''

Dexter sent her one of the smiles that always made her heart turn over. Damn him. "Thanks, Liz,'' he said simply. "I appreciate the vote of confidence.'' He turned on the ignition. "Well, if you're not bound and determined to head for the nearest police station, we have an interesting question to resolve. If Karen didn't mean me when she referred to her boss, who did she mean?''

"An old boss from Kansas City?''

"Could be.''

"Why did she leave her last job?''

He frowned in concentration. "She'd worked on somebody's political campaign, and they'd lost, if I'm remembering correctly.''

"Who checked her references?''

"Evan Howard does all the screening of candidates for my Colorado offices. I'll ask him to check the personnel files and get back to me with some names and addresses.'' He gestured to the notebook lying on Liz's lap. "Do we have any other hot leads in Denver?''

"Except for the people who are out of town, there are no more men left on our list.''

"Then let's go visit one of the women. Unless you're hungry?''

She shook her head. "Not at all."

"Then how about visiting some of the people from my office? Maybe she indulged in heart-to-hearts over the watercooler."

"We could try them. But Rachel Landers's home is much closer than anybody who works for you. She has an apartment on Havana, and that's only ten minutes from here."

"Okay." Dexter headed the car west. "Rachel Landers? Wasn't she the woman Karen took cooking classes with?"

"Yes. They went to some retired master chef in Colorado Springs. If Karen ever mentioned the chef's name, I've forgotten it, but he's obviously darn good. Karen always came back to Denver with the most delicious food. I never accepted invitations to eat out on Saturday nights."

"She never invited you to go with her to cooking class?"

"She was too smart for that. You know me and kitchens?"

"Still?"

"Still." She smiled. "Not many people have my astonishing level of skill, you know. There can't be many adult females in the world routinely able to scorch water."

Dexter's grin changed to a frown. "You know, I could have sworn Karen didn't enjoy cooking, although I can't remember why I have that impression."

"You must be mistaken. Nobody could prepare food like we ate on Saturdays, unless they enjoyed cooking. Karen was a real expert, Dex." She peered out of the window. "Here's Rachel's building. Her apartment number's 304."

Rachel Landers, a plain woman of about thirty-five, eyes almost invisible behind pebble-lensed glasses, was at home and more than willing to cooperate. Delighted to be entertaining a United States senator and a former world figure-skating champion—even if the morning newspaper had implied they might well be guilty of murder—she insisted on serving them freshly brewed coffee and homemade pastries.

"I can see you put your gourmet cookery classes to wonderful use," Liz said, finishing a mouthful of flaky, raspberry-filled turnover.

Rachel blushed with pleasure. "When you punch numbers in a bank all day, it's nice to do something creative on the weekend. I made those pastries last night. They're quite simple, once you learn how to manipulate the Greek phyllo dough."

Liz suddenly realized how surprising it was that they had found Rachel at home. "Has your class been canceled for this morning?" she asked.

"Oh no, but it'll take me a while to find another ride." She pointed to her glasses. "I see quite well close up, but I'm not safe behind the wheel of a car. Chef Robert is the best teacher in the Rocky Mountain region, and Karen made his class possible for me. I was very grateful to her. I shall miss her a lot. For the ride and for the company."

Liz savored her last bite of pastry. "That was wonderful, Rachel. You're an even better cook than Karen was."

"Thank you." A hot red blush crept up Rachel's neck. Not a flush of pleasure, Liz realized, but of acute embarrassment.

"Did you and Karen meet at a cooking class?" she asked, wondering what could possibly have upset Rachel in such an innocuous compliment.

"No." The blush receded. "I do a little bit of catering on the side, and a customer recommended me to that nice young man who won the Olympic medal for figure skating. Oh, you probably know him, since you're in that line of work yourself. Pieter Ullmann. He was so young to be hosting a party, but he'd just won his gold medal and he was celebrating."

Liz felt a little leap of excitement. "You met Karen at Pieter's house? That must have been over a year ago."

"Yes, like I said, it was just after Pieter had come back from the Winter Olympics."

Liz wasn't sure whether to be excited or disappointed. On the one hand, it was interesting to learn that Karen's acquaintance with Pieter stretched much farther back than he'd been willing to admit. On the other hand, she'd been half hoping that Rachel would reveal some entirely new name and set of relationships. She smothered a small sigh of frustration, recognizing that she and Dexter were clutching at straws. There was no good reason for a casual acquaintance like Rachel to have any deep insight into Karen's personality and friends.

Dexter returned his coffee cup to the tray. "How many of Chef Robert's classes had Karen actually attended with you, Miss Landers?"

Again the ugly red flush stained Rachel's neck and pushed into her cheeks. She sat down hard on a nearby chair. "I don't know what to say, Senator," she mumbled, flashing a wary glance from Dexter to Liz. "You see, I read in the papers that she was pregnant."

"What has Karen's pregnancy got to do with her cooking lessons?" Dexter asked. "Was she having an affair with the chef?"

Rachel stared fixedly at her sensible, low-heeled shoes. The flush had now crept up to the tips of her ears. "The cookery classes were just a cover," she whispered. "Karen never attended them."

Liz stared in surprise. "Never attended? But who cooked all that wonderful food she brought home?"

Rachel hung her head even lower. "I did. Karen paid me for everything she took home. There's only me, you see, and I can't eat everything I prepare."

Dexter leaned forward, and although his voice remained calm and soothing, Liz could see tension in every line of his body. She reflected that nine years earlier she would have heard the calm and totally missed the inner tension. Odd how she had been married to Dexter and perceived him less clearly than she did now, when they were mere acquaintances.

"Why did Karen bother to set up such an elaborate pretense?" Dexter asked. "Do you know why she wanted everyone to think she was attending cookery school, when she wasn't?"

Rachel looked away, blinking rapidly behind her pebble glasses. "Yes, I know. She was—having an affair."

"With a married man, you mean?"

"That's what I assumed. Why else would she have to sneak around and hide what she was doing? I sometimes wondered if her lover was in an important public position, as well as being married, you know?" Rachel threw an embarrassed, inquiring look in Dexter's direction.

"I'm not married," he said quietly. "I admired Karen as an employee, but that was the extent of our relationship, and we never had an affair."

"Oh, of course not! I never meant...I don't want you to think, Senator...I'm sure you wouldn't dream..."

Liz took pity on Rachel's floundering efforts at a disclaimer. "Karen never mentioned the name of her lover to you, Miss Landers?"

"Oh no, she never said anything specific about him. Just how much she loved him and then, toward the end, how he wouldn't treat their relationship seriously. How he'd taken advantage of her loyalty." She looked up, her expression apologetic and more than a little guilty. "I know I shouldn't have covered up for Karen. Some poor wife probably spent her Saturday mornings wondering what her husband was up to. But Chef Robert is such a wonderful instructor, and he teaches the business side of catering as well as the food presentation. It's my dream to set up a full-time catering service...." Once again her voice trailed away.

"I doubt if Karen would have ended her affair, even if you'd refused to cover for her, Miss Landers. She'd have found another alibi. I don't think you need carry around too big a burden of guilty conscience.''

Dexter's words seemed to cheer Rachel, and she perked up enough to insist on pouring them another cup of coffee and boxing a chocolate torte for them to take home.

"I'll call on you when my daughter needs her next birthday cake," Dexter promised, and Rachel's answering smile was so gratified that her plain face became almost attractive.

"Do you want to chat with some of your employees now?" Liz asked when they had said their farewells and returned to the car.

"You don't sound thrilled at the prospect."

"I just think we're going to hear more of the same stuff we've been hearing all day. You might as well save yourself the hassle of driving all over Denver, and talk with them on Monday." Liz got into the car and waited while Dexter filtered into the stream of traffic. "Surely if one of your employees knew anything really startling about Karen, they'd have told you by now."

"I'm sure they would. It's getting late anyway, so we may as well head for home."

Liz muttered in exasperation. "Dex, have you noticed that Karen never said a word about her love life to you or to me, but she seemed willing to reveal her deepest emotional problems to virtually everyone else? People who were barely acquaintances."

"I did notice. I also noticed that she may have talked a lot, but she never seemed to give people any practical details about her lover. Was he old or young? Handsome or ugly? Rich or poor? Where did he work? Where did he live?"

"Presumably he lived in Colorado Springs. That's where she went every Saturday."

"Maybe. Or maybe not. It's only a forty-five-minute drive from the southern suburbs of Denver to the Springs, and there are a dozen motels along the highway."

"We know that he was married, and that Karen claimed he was her boss," Liz pointed out.

"Do we? I'd say those are conclusions people drew, which might tell us more about the people drawing the conclusions than they do about Karen. The fact is, we've spoken to eight people this morning, and not one of them really knew anything about her or her lover. In fact, nobody seems to know anything more about her than you and I."

"But why would she be so secretive?"

Dexter shrugged. "The obvious answer is that she had something to hide."

"You mean she was scared to reveal the name of her lover?"

"Something like that. It seems to me that either Karen or her lover stood to lose a lot if their affair became public knowledge."

"Nowadays, it's difficult to imagine how any affair could be that threatening."

"I may have become paranoid in the last two days," Dexter remarked, "but I keep thinking that if Karen had wanted to set me up as her murderer, she couldn't have done a better job. All this rushing around town, muttering dire things about her cruel boss and her broken heart. Naturally everyone concluded she was talking about me."

"I agree, but she couldn't have known she would be murdered, so she couldn't have been setting you up, even if she had some obscure motive for revenge."

"She couldn't have been setting me up for murder," Dexter agreed, "but how about for a paternity suit?"

"And the murderer just took advantage of the groundwork Karen had laid, so to speak?"

"It sounds possible, don't you think?"

"Except that Karen was an intelligent, educated woman. She must have known that blood tests today can determine paternity with ninety-nine percent accuracy. And if you weren't the father, how could she set you up?"

Dexter frowned as he turned the car off Alameda and headed toward his home. "Maybe she was just going to *threaten* me with a paternity suit, unless I paid her and her lover lots of money."

"That's it!" Liz squirmed around inside her seat belt so that she could look at Dexter. "Of course, that's it, Dex! She hoped you would pay up to avoid the bad publicity. She knew all the voters would say 'there's no smoke without a fire,' and that half of them would read about the lawsuit but never get around to reading the verdict, when you were proven not to be the father. Sometimes an accusation doesn't have to be true for it to cause a heck of a lot of damage."

"I guess that's possible," Dexter agreed slowly. "Except that sort of scheming doesn't fit the efficient, bland Karen I knew."

"But then it seems you didn't know her very well. Neither did I."

"True. She's the last woman I'd ever have suspected of being promiscuous. I feel like I'm watching a character in a play, who's repressed Miss Prim-and-Proper in Act One. Then in Act Two she fixes her hair, rips off her glasses and bingo!—she's a sultry bombshell."

"I guess this morning's investigations have taught us something," Liz said. "For whatever reason, Karen was playing a part with both of us. And she lied a lot."

He grimaced. "Great return for seven hours of running around town. Damn, but I wish we could come up with a few more names to check out. At least then I'd have the illusion we were achieving something."

"Remember five or six of the men listed in Karen's address book weren't home."

"I'll try to reach some of them by phone early this evening, or first thing tomorrow." He glanced at his watch. "Probably tomorrow. Today's pretty well shot. Normally I'd ask Evan, but he's worked two eighteen-hour stints back-to-back. He deserves the rest of the weekend to himself."

Liz glanced at her own watch. "I hadn't realized how late it is. I'll have to hurry if I'm going to be in Colorado Springs by six-thirty."

Dexter made a smooth turn into the long driveway leading to his house. "I have a dinner meeting tonight with a dozen or so suburban mayors, and it would be wonderful if you could join me."

"I'm sorry," she said. "I've already accepted another invitation. Didn't I mention that I was having dinner with Mikhail?"

"Possibly. I don't remember." Dexter's voice was cool. "Are you sure I can't persuade you to change your plans? Take pity on the poor journalists. Think how exciting they could make their Sunday editions, if we turned up together at the same function."

Liz felt a wave of frustrated irritation, an unpleasant reminder of feelings that had been all too common in the days of her marriage. "No, you can't persuade me to change my mind," she said, her voice as cool as his. "Offering myself up as journalistic fodder isn't my idea of Saturday-night fun. Besides, I've not seen Mikhail since Karen died, and I'm looking forward to relaxing with him for a couple of hours."

"He's done some outstanding work for the Special Olympics Committee," Dexter said. The praise seemed torn from him, as if it hurt to admit any good points about Liz's brother-in-law. For some reason, Mikhail—along with Alison—had always been high on Dexter's list of nonapproved persons. For the first time, Liz thought to question why.

"What in the world has Mikhail done to make you despise him, Dexter?"

"Nothing," he said curtly. He punched the button on the remote-controlled garage-door opener, then broke a momentary silence by turning to her and giving a rueful smile.

"Sorry," he said. "I'm being a pain in the neck. The fact is that I don't like Mikhail, and I've no reason to dislike him. It makes me feel guilty, which is why I snap every time someone mentions his name."

Liz didn't reply for several seconds, then she turned and met Dexter's gaze with a dawning sense of wonderment. "Do you know, Dex, that's the first time in our entire relationship that you've ever admitted to possessing a single irrational feeling?"

"You sound as if you think that's good."

"It's more than good. It's marvelous! I feel like breaking into a rousing rendition of the 'Hallelujah' chorus."

His eyes gleamed. "Feel free," he said, drawing the car to a halt inside the garage. "As I remember, you have a lovely voice. Although I never recall hearing you sing *The Messiah*."

Against her will, Liz felt her cheeks flame with heat. She had a tuneful but oddly throaty voice, which imparted a sensual promise to even the most innocuous of tunes. Dexter had once told her that she could make "Yankee Doodle Dandy" sound like a love song. Liz had only ever sung for him in the privacy of their bedroom, and her songs had almost never reached the end. They would both be lying on the bed, tugging at each other's zippers and buttons, long before the final verse.

"Dexter, we don't have time for chitchat," she said, avoiding his gaze. "It's over an hour's drive from here to Mikhail's house, and I still have to shower and change."

Dexter wasn't to be deterred from his line of questioning, although he led the way out of the garage into the rear hallway. "Do you still play the guitar?" he asked.

"Not in the past few months," she said. "I haven't felt much like playing since Brian died."

Dexter halted his swift progress along the corridor and turned to face her. His hands lightly touched her shoulders. "I'm sorry, Liz," he said softly. "I have this urge to catch up on what's been happening in your life, and I keep forgetting this is the third time within a few months that you've lost a friend."

The warmth of his hands felt almost like a caress. The sensation was strangely comforting. "The odd thing is," she admitted, "now that I know there's a chance my roommates were all murdered, I actually feel better. I've felt so unbearably guilty from the moment Brian died. You know, going over and over in my mind if there had been any clues that should have warned me he was in trouble."

"And were there?" Somehow she found herself held in a loose embrace, while one of Dexter's hands stroked gently up and down her back.

"He'd been irritable on occasion and he apologized by saying his research wasn't going well. But if he didn't commit suicide, then his mood can't be important, can it?"

Dexter's arms tightened around her. "Probably not, but—"

"Senator!" Evan Howard appeared at the end of the corridor, noticed that his boss was not alone, and gave Liz a halfhearted nod. Without haste, Dexter released Liz from his grasp and returned Evan's frazzled greeting with a friendly smile.

"You look as if this hasn't been a good day, Evan."

"It's been an awful day. Karen's file is missing from our personnel records, and some squirt of a police sergeant virtually accused me of destroying it to protect you. Then Lieutenant Rodriguez came around and when he found out you weren't home, he acted like you'd caught the first available flight to South America."

"He must have been reassured when you told him we'd only gone to Aurora."

"Hell, Dexter, how can you joke at a time like this? Do you know what the lieutenant has discovered? There are no records for Karen prior to the time she arrived in Denver. Her name and social-security number were fakes. Or at least they were stolen. They belonged to some baby who died in a car accident."

"Fakes!" Liz exclaimed. "So we don't even know Karen's real name?"

"Nothing. We don't know anything about her."

Liz subsided into stunned silence, while Dexter stared abstractedly into the distance, his expression unreadable. Evan began to look calmer, now that his revelations had produced a suitably amazed response. He shepherded the unresisting Liz and Dexter into the living room.

"What about our reference checks?" Dexter queried. "We always run a routine credit check, and call at least two work references. How can we have done that for someone who has no past?"

"Of course she had a past when I checked on her!" Evan almost exploded. "Damn it, I spoke to Harry Spinkoff's campaign manager. A guy called John Booth. I even remember the name, because I thought how odd it was for parents to inflict the same name as Lincoln's assassin on their kids."

Dexter cut into what was obviously becoming an endless flow of aggrieved reminiscence. "And you gave all this information to the police?"

"I told them she passed our investigation with flying colors. Banks, doctors, credit bureau, security—the whole caboodle. Everything checked out. Except they don't seem to believe I did any of it, because I can't find the darn file. How could it possibly go missing right at this crucial point? We never lose paperwork."

"Of course it isn't missing," Dexter said with a touch of impatience. "It's been stolen." He got up and walked to the door, seeming to remember Liz's and Evan's presence only at the last minute.

"I have to make a couple of phone calls," he said, and left the room without any further attempt at an explanation.

Evan pulled out his handkerchief and patted his forehead. "Why doesn't he just admit the darn baby was his and have done with it?" he muttered.

Liz looked at him coldly. "Possibly because it wasn't."

"Then who took the file? He's the only person with access to those cabinets apart from me."

Her temper flared, chiefly because she was furious with herself for defending Dexter. Why was it that after only a couple of sweet smiles, she was ready to jump through the hoop for the darn man?

"He's the only person with legitimate access, Mr. Howard. Hasn't it occurred to you yet that somebody is trying very hard to set Dexter Rand up for murder?"

Chapter Eight

After coping with Evan Howard, not to mention all the other frustrations of the day, it was a relief to turn into Mikhail's neat, flower-bordered driveway. Over the past few years, since his escape from Soviet Russia, Mikhail had become more than a brother-in-law to Liz; he had become her closest friend. She had moved to Colorado at his urging, and even before her move, when she had been living in Ohio and then in Seattle, they had seen each other frequently. Their shared interest in skating and their mutual love of Alison gave strong roots to their friendship.

Mikhail already had the door open by the time she parked the car. "The caviar's on ice!" he called out. "So's the vodka."

She grinned, appreciating the familiar routine in a world suddenly adrift. "Those slimy fish eggs are all yours, Mikhail, and you know it. Where's my fried chicken?"

He made a comical face of disgust, tossing his brown, windblown hair out of his eyes. "Your grease-and-cholesterol snack is warming in the oven. You can smell it right out here."

"Mmm-mmm. Yummy. Thank heaven you're not my trainer, you old grouch." She brushed her cheek against his in greeting. "Pieter is welcome to you, slave driver, gold medal and all."

"Pieter never breaks his training," Mikhail responded tranquilly. "That's part of the reason he won at the Olympics. Your trainer wasn't strict enough with you."

"So you keep telling me." Liz walked into the family room that led off the kitchen and curled up in her favorite armchair. "Ease up, old codger! I'm not in training for anything anymore."

"Except a heart attack," he muttered in mock disapproval. "And old codger, what means this?"

"A term of affection," she said, her eyes bright as she glanced up at him. "Oh, Mikhail, I'm glad to be here. These past few days have been hell."

"Now you are here you can relax." He poured her a vodka and tonic, adding a slice of fresh lime before handing her the glass. He took his own vodka neat, Russian-style, without ice. That, apparently, didn't offend his health consciousness. He put a platter of dip and raw vegetables on a coffee table comfortably within reach of Liz's chair, then took his own seat nearby. "Do you want to talk about things, Lizushka?"

She was surprised to find that she did. She launched into a detailed account of finding Karen's body, trying her best to share with Mikhail the horror she had felt in experiencing the same terrible trauma three times within four months. She described as honestly as she could the strain of the press conference and the frustration of her unproductive investigations with Dexter. The only element missing from her story was the unexpected ambivalence of her personal feelings toward her ex-husband. Since she wasn't ready to admit those feelings even to herself, she saw no reason to expose her idiocy to Mikhail's brotherly scorn.

When she finally ran out of steam, he took her glass and insisted on refilling it. "Your first drink barely smelled the vodka bottle," he said, when she reminded him that she had to drive back to town. "Besides, what is this nonsense, *dorogoya*? You don't have to drive anywhere, you can stay here. You should stay here. Why must you rush back to Denver?''

She blushed, knowing that Mikhail didn't approve of Dexter any more than Dexter liked Mikhail. "I need to look in at the office tomorrow and clear up my mountain of paperwork." It wasn't precisely a lie. She had every intention of spending the morning in the office.

Mikhail frowned, and she tried to gloss over a tight little silence. "How a company as small as Peperito's can generate so many internal memos, I'll never know."

"Too many desktop computers," Mikhail said, banishing his scowl. "Once everybody finds out how to make columns on their screens, they feel compelled to invent figures to go inside their columns." He tossed off his glass of vodka in a single swallow. "You haven't told me the whole story, have you, Liz? You're not just going back to Denver. You're staying with that monster of an ex-husband, aren't you?"

She swished the lime around in her drink. "Yes. How did you know?"

His smile was rueful. "Lizushka, you are the world's worst liar. Your nose turns pink with embarrassment if you try to tell the smallest fib."

"Right at the moment, he isn't being much of a monster, Mikhail. He's too busy trying to find out what was going on in Karen's life."

"*Dorogoya*, you are not only the world's worst liar, you are also the world's most softhearted fool. Your miserable ex-husband knows exactly what was going on with Karen. He was having an affair with her and got her pregnant. Can you not read the newspapers, Liz? Have you not heard the police detective interviewed on TV? What is his name, this lieutenant?"

"Rodriguez," she said absently. "Mikhail, I know the evidence looks damning. But when the lieutenant finds out about my other two roommates, he's going to think I'm involved in something, too. And Lord knows, nobody could understand less about what's going on than me.''

"And because you are guilty of nothing, you assume Dexter is equally innocent? *Dorogoya*, you should move to the Soviet Union. My former government needs citizens like you.''

She laughed, more than a little embarrassed by her apparent gullibility. "Most people would say you're right, Mikhail, I'm sure. But in my heart of hearts, I know Dexter isn't any more guilty than I am. Dexter is too smart to plan a crime and leave himself such an obvious suspect. Someone is setting him up.''

The oven pinged and Mikhail rose to his feet. "And just who do you think is setting up the great Senator Rand? Who could possibly plan such a thing? They would need to know that Karen was pregnant, for one thing—''

"Half the town seems to have known that," Liz said. "In fact, I had moments today when I wondered if Dexter and I were the only people in Denver who didn't know Karen was having an affair with a married man.''

Mikhail smiled sympathetically, wrinkling his nose as he handed Liz her plate of reheated chicken and biscuits. "Well, perhaps you are right, and anyway, it is not of great importance to us whether or not your ex-husband seduced his secretary. While we eat, let us talk of more cheerful subjects. I have happy news to report to you, Lizushka.''

A tiny break in his voice caused Liz to look up. "Mikhail?'' she asked. "It isn't—is it your mother?''

He nodded, stretching his mouth into a huge grin as he reached behind the cushion to produce a letter written on heavy, embossed paper. "You have guessed it," he said. "Read what I have received from the embassy.''

Liz laughed, sharing his happiness. "Mikhail, I don't read Russian.''

"I forgot. Alison, you know, had begun to learn.'' For once, the mention of his dead wife brought no sadness to

Mikhail's eyes. "In brief, the letter says that my mother has completed all the necessary paperwork, and that regional approval has been given to her request for an exit visa."

"Thank God for *glasnost*," Liz breathed. "Oh, Mikhail, what wonderful news!"

"I do not become too excited," he cautioned. "But my mother requires only one more step, this one from the ministry in Moscow."

Liz had spent five years following Mikhail's tortured efforts to secure an exit visa for his elderly mother. Their hopes had been high on several occasions in the past, so she knew better than to assume "one more stamp" would be a trivial detail in the endless progression of setbacks and false hopes. "How long do you think the final approval might take?" she asked cautiously.

"One day is sufficient for my mother to travel to Moscow, if she receives permission to buy an airline ticket." He shrugged with Slavic resignation. "If the authorities decide to be difficult, then we may still be talking of years."

Liz sought for something comforting to say, and found little. Her faith in Soviet officialdom was no deeper than Mikhail's. "Surely the embassy wouldn't have written the letter unless things were looking good?"

Mikhail smiled sadly. "Lizushka, you know better than that. But I allow myself a little bit of hope and today—yes, today I am truly optimistic. I do not allow myself to think that tomorrow I may again be in the depths of despair. Now eat up. Your chicken gets cold, and I have more good news. I spoke yesterday on the phone with my mother."

"But that's great! The authorities allowed your call to go through without any hassle?"

"They did. And she sounds in excellent health, most cheerful. She has been receiving the money I send, and has bought a new cooking stove." Mikhail chuckled. "She is the envy of the neighborhood, and very pleased with herself."

Liz swallowed hard over the sudden lump in her throat. "Mikhail, you know I'm counting the days for you."

He gave her hand a grateful squeeze. "I know, *doro-goya*. And since we are talking of mothers, what is the latest news from Durango?"

"The head nurse called the other day, and I visited with Mom two weeks ago. Nothing much seemed to have changed."

"She doesn't recognize you at all?"

Liz shook her head. "Nothing. The doctor commented recently that her type of memory loss is very rare. She can remember the names of public figures, like the president, for example, but she has to keep being reminded of the names of her nurses."

"It's as if her personal life doesn't exist."

"Exactly, and of course that's the most painful thing of all. When I call her Mom, she looks right through me. At least she doesn't have to mourn Alison, although I often wonder if there's a psychological component to her memory loss."

"The doctors insist that her symptoms are entirely physical, don't they?"

"Of course. They can see the brain damage on their machines. Why would they bother considering that the machines don't tell the whole story?"

Mikhail patted her gently on the arm. "You hope for miracles, Lizushka. Could you not try to remember only the good times before your mother's stroke, and forget about yearning for the impossible?"

"Most of the time, that's what I do. The rational part of me has accepted that she's never going to be cured. The stroke after Alison's death destroyed the part of her brain that stores family memories."

"Certainly she is content with the life she leads, and her physical problems do not become worse. I was down south to judge a skating contest last month, you know, and I paid a quick visit to the nursing home. Really quick, though. It was little more than in the front door and out the back, with just time to say hello as I walked through her room."

"You're too good to us, Mikhail," Liz said impulsively. "Most sons-in-law have to be nagged into tolerating the occasional family get-together. You pay half my mother's nursing home expenses, and then visit her as well, even though she doesn't recognize you. You know how much I appreciate your caring, don't you?"

He grinned. "*Dorogoya*, you thank me a minimum of three times per visit. How could I not know? But your thanks are unnecessary. Your mother is also the mother of Alison, who was my wife, and in Russia we hold such relationships close to our hearts. The great American capitalist system has made me rich, simply because I can teach people how to skate and win competitions. How else should I spend my money, if not on the mother of my wife?"

Liz pushed away the remainder of her chicken, assailed by a sudden memory. "The anniversary of Alison's death was last week. With everything that happened, I'd forgotten. I'm sorry, Mikhail."

"After five years, I have discovered that the pain fades, and all that is left are happy memories. Now when I think of Alison, I recall her beauty on the ice and her warmth in my arms. Believe me, I do not dwell in my thoughts on the crash that took her from me."

"If the grief is finally fading, maybe it's time for you to think of marrying again."

He put his hand to his heart, rolling his eyes in pretended passion. "Liz, my love, you wound me with your careless words. I think of marriage all the time, but you will not have me, so what am I to do?"

She smiled. "I was serious, Mikhail. Don't you want to find yourself some nice American girl and produce dozens of little Olympic champions?"

"One day," he said, sobering. "But the right woman has not yet appeared. Alison is not an easy woman to replace, as you will realize. In the meantime, I hope it won't offend your sisterly ears if I confess that even though I have not yet found the mother of my children, I do not spend every night alone in an empty bed."

Liz just managed to conceal her start of surprise. Intellectually she had never expected Mikhail to remain celibate. In addition to being one of the best-looking men she knew, he had a tempting athletic body and an appealing gleam in his dark gray eyes. Moreover he worked in a glamorous job that kept him surrounded by beautiful, lissome females. Emotionally, however, she was shocked by his admission, mostly because Mikhail had always kept his sexual activities screened from her view.

"You are blushing again, Lizushka." Mikhail's voice was warm and faintly quizzical. "I did not think American women knew how."

She laughed. "I've been cursing my pale skin since high school. You know I turn scarlet for every reason under the sun—and sometimes for no reason at all."

"I know," he said softly. "And you know that my love for Alison will always be buried deep in my heart—"

"But you can't love only a memory," Liz interjected. "You can't and you shouldn't. There's no reason in the world to apologize because you enjoy feminine company, Mikhail."

The doorbell rang, breaking the slight tension between the two of them. "One of your luscious lovelies?" Liz queried lightly.

He pulled a face as he walked to the door. "More likely an angry mother whose child I refused to take on as a student. I think sometimes to buy a guard dog." He opened the door. "Pieter! I wasn't expecting you tonight. Nothing's wrong, I hope? No pulled muscles or sprained wrists?"

Pieter's voice came low and urgent. "Mikhail, I'm in big trouble. The police came to see me. They found a letter in Karen's papers—"

"You'd better come in and calm down, Pieter. Liz is here."

"Hell, Mikhail, you don't understand. The police have found this letter, and it looks like my writing. The police expert swears it is my writing. Hell, man, that letter is big trouble for both of us."

Mikhail's voice took on the cool authority of trainer to athlete. "Pieter, come inside and sit down. We'll talk about this when you stop pacing on my doorstep like a caged tiger. This is America, not Russia. The police do not jump to conclusions without proof."

"This letter is proof, man." But Pieter sounded calmer, and he greeted Liz with some of his usual cockiness. "Hello, beautiful."

"Hello, Pieter. Forgotten my name?" she queried dryly.

He looked at her blankly, and Mikhail thrust a small shot glass into his hand. "Here, drink this. Trainer's orders."

Pieter took a tiny sip of the vodka, then put the glass aside, glancing at Liz almost defiantly. "I'm okay now," he said to Mikhail, holding out his hands. "See, steady as a rock and I'm sitting down like a good boy."

He's embarrassed, Liz thought, finding this sudden reminder of Pieter's youth almost endearing. *He's still young enough to be embarrassed because he doesn't like hard liquor.*

"So tell us what caused this visit from the police," Mikhail said, settling into his own chair.

"They found a letter, shoved inside one of Karen's journals. Man, it's trouble. It reads like I'd been involved in blood doping before the last Olympics, and Karen was trying to blackmail me."

Liz gave an exclamation of concern. "But Pieter, didn't you explain to the police that blood doping's only useful to endurance athletes? There would be no point in you trying to boost your blood supply for a figure-skating competition."

"That is irrelevant," Mikhail said impatiently. "Pieter claims he didn't write the letter, so what we must do is contact our lawyer and insist on having a copy submitted to an independent graphologist." He banged his fist on the counter and muttered some obscure Russian curse. "This whole stupid mess over Karen is becoming ridiculous. She was a boring woman, who could not remain alone in her own bed for fear of what she would discover about herself. And now Liz and Pieter are drawn into her silly problems."

"You think the . . . um . . . what's-it—what you said . . ." Pieter's vocabulary ran to nine different translations of *Let's make love, beautiful woman,* but few English words longer than two syllables, Liz reflected.

"You mean the graphologist."

"Yeah. Will he be able to prove I didn't write the letter?" Pieter asked hopefully.

"I am sure. Come, we will phone the lawyer right away and you will find there is no problem."

Liz admired the ring of confidence Mikhail was able to inject into his voice. She didn't know all that much about graphology, but she had the impression it was an inexact science and that handwriting experts often showed an alarming tendency to disagree on whether or not documents had been forged. Mikhail, however, obviously knew his student well. Under his trainer's calming influence, Pieter looked a different man from the frightened young person who had appeared on the doorstep ten minutes earlier.

"I'll clear up in here while you phone," Liz offered, carrying the debris of her chicken into the kitchen.

"Thanks," Mikhail responded, his mind clearly with the lawyer.

Liz covered the remains of the caviar with plastic wrap, returning it and the vodka to the fridge. She had stacked the plates in the dishwasher, wiped down the counters and plumped up all the cushions before Mikhail and Pieter reappeared.

"The lawyer's coming right over," Mikhail said briefly.

"Great. In that case, I'm going to leave you guys to it," she said. "I've been a bit short on sleep these past few days, and an early night would be welcome."

Both Mikhail and Pieter protested that there was no reason for her to go, but she felt their secret relief when she insisted that she needed to get back to Denver. She knew Mikhail well enough to guess that he was a great deal more worried than he cared to admit. Quite apart from any problems Pieter might face, Mikhail could not possibly afford to have the rumor getting around that his athletes indulged in illicit practices in order to win.

She gave Mikhail a hug as he walked her to her car. "Don't worry," she said. "The letter's obviously ridiculous, and anybody who knows anything about figure skating will be able to tell the police that. It must be a forgery."

"You are so swift to rush to everyone's defense," Mikhail said, his smile wistful. "Even Pieter, whom you do not like. *Dorogoya*, did it never cross your mind even for an instant that Pieter is so nervous because the letter is his?"

"And true, you mean?" Liz couldn't disguise her bewilderment. "Are you saying that you suspect Pieter did infuse himself with extra blood?"

Mikhail hesitated. "I...shall be very careful not to ask," he replied slowly.

Liz drew in a deep breath. "I'm not naive," she insisted. "But why would he do such a dangerous thing for such a minuscule advantage?"

"You were once in the finals of the Olympics, Lizushka. If you had thought that an extra dose of your own blood might—just might—give you the chance to win, can you swear you would not have taken the chance?"

"Yes, I can swear," she said. "Oh, don't get me wrong. Not because I'm so superethical, although I like to think I am. But I'd have been in such dread of discovery by the Olympics Committee that any possible edge I might have gained by injecting the blood would have been wiped out by nerves."

"Pieter, I think, does not share your sensitivities. If he wished to deceive the Olympic Committee, he would believe he could do so, and get away unpunished. I do not say that he blood-doped. I say only that it is possible. And to anybody except you, of course, I will swear that the very idea is nonsense. We are so free with our discussions, Lizushka, that sometimes I forget that I should not burden you with the truth of my thoughts. I have, perhaps, given Pieter's career into your hands. I ask that you do not voice my doubts to the police, although I shall understand if you feel you must speak."

"The police already know about the letter," Liz said. "They have graphologists they can consult. My opinion as to whether or not Pieter might have blood-doped is irrelevant."

"Thank you," Mikhail said. "I had better not leave Pieter alone any longer, or his nerve may once again fail him. Drive safely, Liz."

"I'll call you tomorrow to find out what the lawyer said."

"Fine. And by next weekend, let us hope the police have made an arrest, so that we can put all this nonsense behind us."

LIZ WAS BONE-WEARY by the time she pulled the car into the garage at Dexter's house. The fatigue, she realized, was mental far more than physical, the result of too many questions chasing too few answers around and around her brain.

Dexter had given her a set of house keys, and she opened the door leading from the garage to the kitchen, stopping abruptly when she realized she wasn't alone. Dexter sat at the table, his face lined with a weariness that matched her own. The stubble of the day's beard made a dark shadow across his face. His tie hung loose, and his shirt buttons were unfastened. Perversely, he didn't look rumpled, merely devastatingly sexy and more than a touch vulnerable, she had to admit. Liz mentally armored herself. Dexter was at his most dangerous on those rare occasions when he allowed himself to appear vulnerable.

"You're home early," he said. "I'm surprised Mikhail didn't barricade you in his spare bedroom, rather than let you come back to my house."

"It's been a long day," she said, ignoring his taunt. "Several long days, in fact. I wanted an early night. How was your dinner?"

He rattled the ice cubes in his glass. "The dinner was murder, if you must know." He laughed harshly. "No pun intended."

"The suburban mayors insisted on talking about Karen?"

"No." He looked up, his eyes veiled and hard to read. "They wanted to talk about us. About you and me."

"There is no *us*, for heaven's sake!"

"Try telling that to the suburban mayors. I ought never to have suggested you should stay with me, Liz. Evan was right when he said the reporters would find out you were here and put their own construction on the facts."

"You're not responsible for my choices, Dex. You didn't bind and gag me."

"But I've exposed you to the worst sort of media gossip, and I know how much you hate that."

"I'm older now, and not at all famous. Journalists bother me less." She walked over to the fridge and poured herself a glass of chilled water. "What precisely were the suburban mayors accusing us of?"

"Precisely isn't quite the word. 'Vague but all-encompassing' would be more appropriate. They seemed to have two main schools of thought. Most of them believe that you and I are passionately in love and killed Karen because we found out she was pregnant with my child."

"Didn't it occur to them that it would have been simpler for us to pay Karen to keep quiet?"

"*Simple* isn't a favorite mayoral concept," he replied dryly. "If you'd ever read an official town-zoning plan, you'd know that mayors aren't noted for their common-sense approach to life's everyday problems."

"And most of the mayors believe you and I were dumb enough to commit a murder where we were the most likely suspects?"

"Seems so. Or else they believe—"

"Am I going to like this theory any better?"

"I doubt it."

She sighed. "I may as well hear the worst. Tell me anyway."

"You and I are passionately in love, and Karen committed suicide when she found out about our relationship."

She frowned in exasperation. "This is crazy, Dexter! Why would you have been impregnating Karen, if the two of us are passionately in love?"

"That interesting question doesn't seem to have occurred to the mayors. Or their spouses."

She sipped her water, avoiding his eyes. "Why are they so set on the passionately-in-love part of the story?"

He shrugged. "We were married once before. Now you've reappeared in my life, they refuse to believe we're just good friends."

"Would they believe wary acquaintances?"

"Is that what we are?" he asked quietly.

"I don't know." That was true. "I haven't thought about it." That was a lie.

It was his turn to stare with great concentration into his glass of melting ice cubes. "I had a phone call this evening from the chairman of the Reelect Dexter Rand Committee."

"Let me guess," Liz said flippantly, wanting to move the conversation from ground that seemed suddenly treacherous to her emotions. "He asked you please not to murder any more secretaries before next November. Right?"

"No. He asked me to get married. To you."

All at once, Liz's hands were ice-cold. "I see," she said carefully. "Did you tell him we already tried that once? With spectacularly disastrous results?"

"He knew already. He'd like us to try again."

"What did you say?"

"No comment."

"A political career sure does demand sacrifices," she said, determined to keep her tone light. "Are you thinking that you might be willing to get remarried to me, simply to keep your voters happy?"

"I would never marry anyone, least of all you, for such an inadequate reason."

She lifted her head and met his gaze head-on. "You still hate me that much, huh?"

"I don't hate you, Liz. I never did."

"Gee!" she said with heavy sarcasm. "At last I understand. You've been suffering from unrequited love. All those months when you damn near froze me to death with your icy looks and frosty behavior were because you needed to mask the real you, and your burning fire of uncontrollable passion."

"Yes," he said simply. "That's exactly what happened."

Inwardly she was shaking, but all she said was a flippant. "Give me a break, Dexter."

"I'm telling you the truth. Finally."

"Your love for me was so overwhelming it left you tongue-tied? Come on, Dexter. Are you forgetting about the pilots who elected you Stud Supreme of the Frankfurt military base?"

"For heaven's sake, Liz, there's a difference between acquiring an asinine reputation as a stud, and being a man who's mature enough to handle a complex relationship with a woman."

"And when you married Susan you were suddenly mature?"

He was silent for a long time. Eventually he pushed his chair away from the table and stood up, turning his back on her. "I never loved Susan," he said. "That made a big difference."

"It's easier to be married to someone you don't love?"

"Maybe." Slowly he turned around to face her again. "Susan was a wonderful mother and the perfect political hostess. We were good friends, who respected each other's life-styles. I would say our marriage was as happy as most others."

Dex was describing the sort of marriage she might have had with Brian, Liz realized. In retrospect, she could scarcely believe she had almost let herself be sucked into such a cold, bloodless relationship.

"Would you want another marriage like that?" she asked.

His eyes strayed to her mouth and remained there, causing her entire body to flood with heat. "Last week I would have said yes."

She could guess—perhaps—what had caused him to change his mind, but didn't ask for confirmation. She didn't want to hear again that he shared her own unwilling sexual awareness. Dexter was a perfectionist, and given the mess they had made of their marriage, she understood how he might feel the need to rewrite their joint past by entering into a new, more mature relationship in the present. Unfortunately, she also knew—God, how she knew!—that she couldn't afford to risk getting too close to Dexter. While he might end up feeling more comfortable, she would end up badly burned.

His gaze lingered on her mouth, causing her tongue to thicken and her planned answer to die unspoken somewhere deep in her throat. Her instinct for self-preservation seemed to have taken a holiday, because she didn't run screaming for safety when he closed the small gap between their bodies and wrapped her in his arms.

"God, I missed you, Liz," he murmured, and the hesitancy in his voice touched off a response that no amount of aggressive male confidence could have provoked. Her knees felt shaky, blood pumped thickly through her veins, and her body ached with a sweet, familiar pain. She closed her eyes, knowing what would inevitably follow, but wanting him too much to care.

Their kiss was like every other kiss they had ever shared, and yet it was utterly different. Her body still ignited with the same, immediate force. Her veins still ran hot with fire, and her stomach still knotted tight with desire. But something in his touch was different, just as her response was different from everything that had gone between them in the past. This time, his lips moved over hers with supplication as well as expertise, and her response lacked the old humiliating element of helplessness. Her body's reaction was primitive, fierce, elemental, but it was a reaction given of her own free will.

They couldn't continue a kiss of such intensity for long without progressing to a stage of lovemaking Liz wasn't ready to contemplate. Reluctantly she pulled her mouth away, turning her head to one side. His body pulsed against hers, and for a moment his lips hardened demandingly.

Then she felt him relax, and he rested his forehead against hers for a fleeting moment before stepping away.

"Maybe you should go upstairs first," he said. "And you might want to consider locking your door."

She tried to laugh, but it came out as a breathy, husky sound, not at all what she had intended. "Dex, you're long past the stage of finding yourself swept away by overmastering passion."

"Am I?" he asked. "Funny, I was just thinking that I hadn't felt such a strong urge to push a woman to the floor and fall on top of her since..."

"Since?" she prompted, knowing that if she'd been smart, she'd have remained silent.

"Since the only time I ever did it before," he said. "In Frankfurt. With you."

Liz wondered how many fingers she would need to burn before she finally realized she was too close to the fire. She drew in a deep breath and from some hidden corner of her soul extracted a remaining shred or two of willpower.

"Good night, Dexter," she said with convincing firmness, then spoiled the whole effect by turning tail and running from the kitchen as if her life depended on it.

Chapter Nine

The office was blissfully empty on Sunday morning. Liz
worked assiduously on her paper mountain and succeeded
in reducing it to a modest-sized hill. Wanting a break before tackling the fine print of the latest market-research report, she contemplated the rival merits of McDonald's and
the local health-food bar. She had just reluctantly decided
that the health-food bar was the winner, when the phone
rang.

"Elizabeth Meacham," she said absently, wondering if
there was any way to convince her taste buds that bean
sprouts were more enjoyable than French fries.

"Liz, this is Evan Howard."

The PR man's voice came low and urgent over the phone,
and Liz's attention snapped back with a jerk.

"Evan? Is something wrong? What's happened?"

"I need to see you urgently. At my house. We'll be safe
there. I have something important to tell you."

The muted roar on the line was pierced by the distinctive
beep of a car horn. "Are you calling from a phone booth?"
she asked. "I can scarcely hear you."

"Yes, but I'm going home right now. Liz, you have to
come and see me." His voice sounded frankly desperate,
although she knew enough to take his desperation with a

grain of salt. Evan was not a man notable for his calm disposition.

"I don't know where you live," she said. "And what about calling Dexter—?"

"No!" His command was sharp, instantaneous. "No! Don't say a word about this meeting to Dexter. It would be dangerous for both of us."

"Evan, you have to tell me what this melodrama is all about. If it's connected with Karen's death—"

"My address is 244 South Clark," he interrupted. "Clark intersects with University. Be there as soon as you can." The hum of an empty wire warned Liz that Evan had hung up.

She grabbed her purse and dashed for the parking lot. Despite Evan's penchant for self-dramatization, she had detected a note of true fear in his voice, and she had an uncomfortable conviction that what he was about to tell her was something important—and quite possibly something she didn't want to hear. About Dexter? As far as she knew, she and Evan had no other mutual friends.

She drove too far south, and it took her longer than it should have done to find Clark. The street, part of a pleasant residential neighborhood, was Sunday-morning quiet, but the sunshine and peace didn't reassure her. Oppressed by a sudden sense of urgency, Liz parked the car haphazardly against the sidewalk and dashed up the steps leading to number 244.

The house was a typical Denver bungalow, recently restored. The door had been carved into the sort of artsy-craftsy look Liz would have expected from Evan, and she had to search to find the doorbell, which was nestled against the stem of an opulent bunch of cast-iron grapes. An electric buzzer sounded loudly within the house when she pressed the bell, but elicited no response. For a man who had been so insistent in his request that Liz come calling, Evan didn't exactly seem to be panting by the front door for her arrival.

She pressed the button a second time, her sense of urgency dissipating into the more familiar irritation Evan usually provoked. The buzzer once again faded into silence. The street remained empty and somnolent. Infuriated by her wasted trip, she searched around for a note or some other sign that Evan had been expecting her. Again nothing.

"Next time I'll know better than to come tearing out to meet you," she muttered, straightening from her foray into the flowerpots. She blew a stray strand of hair off her forehead, gave the bell another halfhearted push and surveyed the door one final time.

She had no idea what impelled her to test the handle, except maybe a generalized feeling of frustration. To her astonishment, it gave under her fingers, and when she pushed, the door swung open.

Feeling a bit like Goldilocks, Liz stepped into the narrow hall. "Evan?" she called. "Are you home? Is everything okay?"

She took two or three cautious steps into the hallway, and then two or three more. Nothing greeted her save the echo of her own footsteps. Staring around, she saw a series of half-open doors leading into silent rooms.

Belatedly it dawned on Liz that she was not terribly smart to be walking into an unknown house in response to a phone call from a man she scarcely knew. In fact, in retrospect she realized she couldn't even be entirely sure that it was Evan who had called her. The connection crackled, the caller had spoken softly, and the noise of passing traffic had drowned many subtleties of inflection.

With the sudden conviction that at any moment Karen's murderer was going to burst out of the hall closet and bop her on the head, she swung around and ran back down the hallway.

She had almost covered the short distance to the front door, when a slight, almost inaudible sound caused her to glance to her left. Coming back along the hall, her angle of sight into each of the rooms was different. For the first time, she noticed a foot, encased in a black leather loafer, poking around the edge of the living-room door.

Liz stopped, her breathing shallow and her stomach churning with dread. Instinctively tiptoeing, she crept into the living room.

Evan lay on his back, his face drained of color, his eyes closed, one hand resting limply around the knife handle protruding from his rib cage.

"Oh God! Dear God, no!" Liz whispered in agonized supplication. She fell on her knees alongside Evan's body, ripping open the neckline of his shirt, desperately seeking the pulse she was certain she wouldn't feel.

When he groaned, she jumped with shock, her hand slipping into the patch of blood that was congealing around the knife. His eyes flickered briefly open, then closed.

"A doctor," she instructed herself, wiping her hand on her skirt. "I must call the doctor." She half rose to her feet, pausing when Evan opened his eyes again.

"Liz…" Her name was no more than a breath of sound, and she leaned over him in order to hear, bracing herself on the floor above his shoulder to prevent her weight from resting on his blood-seeping wound.

"It's all right," she murmured. "Everything's going to be okay, Evan, I'm here."

"Liz?"

"Yes, I'm Liz. I'm here, and I'm going to get a doctor."

His eyes blurred, and although he stared straight at her, she wasn't sure he knew to whom he spoke. "They will have to kill you…." he said. He made a horrible gurgling sound, which Liz realized was meant to be a laugh. "I didn't know…. I was a fool…. I loved her so much. I did it for her."

"Who did you love?" she asked urgently. "Was it Karen?"

He didn't answer. "Evan," she said. "Oh God, Evan, who did this to you?"

His thoughts seemed to follow their own track, or perhaps he hadn't even heard Liz's question. "He is...so beautiful...and so danger—" His eyes rolled upward and he fell silent.

"No!" she protested. "No, damn it, you're not going to die!" She cupped his lips under her mouth, trying to force air into his lungs. Only when she was panting and dizzy with exhaustion did she stop the hopeless task.

She leaned back, pushing her sweat-soaked hair away from her forehead, and in that moment became aware of the dried blood coating her hands. She stared hypnotized at the ugly red splotches, her body gripped by an uncontrollable shuddering. A groan of horror pushed its way out of her throat, but she didn't—couldn't—move. She was still kneeling beside Evan's body, bloody hands wavering in front of her eyes, when the door to the living room banged open.

DEXTER HAD A PREMONITION of disaster as soon as he arrived at Evan's house and found the front door unlocked, but no sign of a police squad car. *A setup, then? Maybe. But then again, maybe not.* He had the feeling that whatever was going on, his enemies very much wanted him to remain alive.

Careful not to make any sound that would betray his presence, he slipped into the narrow hallway. His body tensed reflexively, alert for any hint of danger as he looked around. There was no sign of Evan, and nothing seemed disturbed, but the house was much too quiet. The silence vibrated with a special kind of menace, and the hallway smelled of death.

No sound came from the living room, but he would stake his life on the suspicion that someone was in there. His life, perhaps, was what he would be staking. With infinite care, he edged toward the living-room door. He knew better than to attempt any form of unarmed combat when he was out of training, but his old skill at moving noiselessly hadn't been lost. So far he wasn't taking much of a risk.

He paused before making the final, dangerous move past the half-open door of the living room. If somebody was lying in wait behind that door, he would be virtually without defense. As he paused, he heard someone groan. A woman. He would swear it was a woman. He would swear it was Liz.

Dexter reached out and banged the door open, adrenaline surging as his body fell automatically into the attack mode. The door crashed against the wall, telling him nobody was concealed behind it. He took a single step into the room, then froze.

Liz, her face and hands smeared with blood, was three feet away from him, crouched over Evan's—obviously dead—body.

For a moment she didn't seem aware of his presence, then her head jerked up, and she stared at him from terrified blue-gray eyes. Eyes that had haunted his dreams for the past nine years. Even now, as his pulse calmed and reason took over, he recognized his instinctive, involuntary response to her beauty.

"What happened?" he asked. The question came out brusquely, not only because of Evan's death, but because he was tired of remembering, tired of yearning for the unattainable, tired of wanting a mental rapport with Liz that would match their physical awareness.

She didn't say anything, but her eyes widened in panic. Her mouth opened, then closed again, and he realized that she was literally incapable of speech.

He walked to her side, a brief glance at Evan confirming that there was no need to rush for a doctor. Dexter had seen violent death too often during his years as a fighter pilot, and he felt a wave of bitter anger against the person who had so brutally ended Evan's life. He controlled the anger and the accompanying grief. At this moment he needed facts, not emotion.

"What happened?" he asked Liz again, more gently this time. He knelt down to brush his thumbs swiftly across Evan's eyes, restoring a tiny measure of dignity to the sprawling body. Then he put his arm around Liz and helped her to her feet.

She flinched at his touch, as if she couldn't bear the warmth of human contact so close to violent death, but he was relieved to see some of the wildness leave her eyes. "I didn't do it," she said. "Dexter, I didn't kill him."

"I never thought you did." He spoke the truth. Despite the compromising situation in which he'd found her, he knew Liz hadn't killed Evan. Like many athletes, she was indifferent to her own physical pain, but she'd always been squeamish about other people's. There might be some facets of Liz's character that remained mysterious to him, but he knew she could never have thrust a knife into a man's chest and then knelt beside him to watch him die. He smoothed a hand along her spine, calming her as he would have Amanda. "How did you get in? Was the front door open?"

"Yes. I j-just w-walked in."

"Did you see anything suspicious?"

"No. The house was empty.... Evan was—like that—when I found him."

She had always been a hopeless liar, and he knew at once that she wasn't telling the truth. Evan might have been at the point of death when she entered the living room, but he hadn't been dead. That was why she was covered in blood. She'd tried to save him.

"What did Evan say to you before he died?" Dexter asked quietly.

She looked at him with renewed horror, as if she couldn't bear to hear the question, and he saw full-blown panic return to her face. "The police," she muttered. "Oh God, the police!"

She tore herself out of Dexter's arms and dashed blindly down the hall, bumping into an ornamental stand and sending a china vase crashing to the floor. He doubted if she even heard the vase fall.

He followed her into the kitchen, his most immediate concern to calm her down before he called the police. She rammed the faucet full on and splashed steaming water onto her face, scrubbing with a ferocity that suggested she wanted to wash away not only Evan's blood, but all memory of the scene in the living room.

"Did you call a doctor?" he asked. If she had, they needed to worry about the imminent arrival of somebody who was going to ask a series of very awkward questions.

"No, I didn't call anybody. I've got to get out of here! You should go, too." Liz was clearly hanging on to her self-control by the merest thread. "Did you touch anything?" she demanded. "We have to get rid of our fingerprints." She elbowed past him without waiting for a reply, a roll of paper towels clutched in her hand.

"Liz, stop! Talk to me for God's sake! You can't dash around wiping off fingerprints!"

"Watch me!"

He caught hold of her arm. "Sit down, calm down, and tell me what happened."

"Sit down! Calm down!" She laughed, and began rubbing feverishly at the front door handle. "I'm getting out of here, Dexter, just as soon as I've cleaned off my prints. If the police find me anywhere near Evan's body, they're going to have me handcuffed and in a squad car as soon as they can spit out a Miranda warning. I don't blame them, either. If I were in Lieutenant Rodriguez's shoes, I'd arrest the pair of us."

Despite her panic, Dexter knew she had a point. His lawyers weren't likely to leave him lingering in jail longer than a couple of hours, but did he really want to subject himself to all the publicity an arrest would cause? On the other hand, he and Liz had discovered a crime and had a duty to report it. Sometimes, he thought wryly, duty was a damn nuisance.

"Nothing's going to bring Evan back to life," Liz said, almost as if she had read his thoughts. "And since I can't help him, I don't see any point in getting myself arrested."

She was right, Dexter conceded. Moreover, he suspected he might be playing straight into the murderer's hands if he and Liz were found here, hovering over Evan's body. Like the audience that is distracted by the conjurer's dazzling display of silk scarves, so that the crucial card can be slipped up his sleeve, Dexter had the feeling that the police and the FBI were having their attention directed to the murders of Evan Howard and Karen Zeit, while some much more complex evil was being plotted elsewhere.

"Where do you plan to go?" he asked.

"To the airport. To some place faraway."

"Is Boston far enough?" he asked, coming to a decision. "I planned to take Amanda to stay with her grandparents, anyway. If we left this afternoon, I'd just be moving things up a couple of days."

"I couldn't possibly impose on your parents—"

"Please come," he said, not even sure himself why her company seemed so important. "We have a lot to discuss, a lot of information to share, and there's no time now."

She was suddenly very still, and he knew that he had touched a sensitive nerve. It occurred to him for the first time that she probably suspected him of being involved in Evan's death. Her question confirmed it.

"Why did you come here?" she asked. "I thought you planned to spend the morning with Amanda."

"I did. But somebody called, claiming to be a police officer, and said Evan had found Karen's missing personnel file. He asked me to come over here right away. Since there's no sign of a policeman or a file, I guess we can safely assume the call was a fake. What brought you?"

"A phone call. Evan insisted he had something very important to tell me." She looked away. "He also told me it would be dangerous to get in touch with you."

"Dangerous?" Dexter tried without success to fit this piece of information into the puzzle. "Who was it dangerous for? Did he say?"

She hesitated for a second or two. "For me. For Evan. Not for you. At least, I don't think for you."

"I see." In fact, he saw a lot more than he wanted to. Like the reason for her panic at the sight of him. "Liz, I didn't kill Evan."

The color had once again completely faded from her face. "That's what you said about Karen, too."

"You're right," he replied quietly. "It looks suspicious, doesn't it?"

"Yes." Her reply was no more than a whisper.

"You told me you didn't murder Karen, though she was your third roommate to die. And you told me you didn't kill Evan, though I found you hunched over his body, covered in blood."

"I was trying to give him mouth-to-mouth resuscitation."

"I believe you."

He let the words fall into the sudden silence of the hallway. He thought she was about to speak, when the blare of a police siren shattered the quiet. Liz tensed, her entire body going ramrod stiff.

"Do you think they're coming here?"

"Doesn't sound like it, the direction's wrong. But we'd better leave, just in case. There's a back entrance. Let's take it." He didn't point out that if they'd been set up, somebody would have notified the police, for sure. For once, he was grateful for the fact that response time to emergency calls was less than wonderful.

She hesitated, momentarily irresolute. "Afraid you're aiding and abetting a murderer, Liz?" he queried softly.

"Just—afraid."

He sensed her continuing resistance and her doubt, but there was no time for explanations, even if he could have provided them. He took her hand and pulled her along the hall toward the kitchen. "Liz, we don't have time for any more protestations of innocence. We've got to get out of here."

She obviously agreed with that, if not with his innocence. "My car's in front," she said, as they emerged into Evan's backyard.

He stopped and listened for a moment before taking her hand. "No police around that I can hear," he said, guiding her down the narrow path to the front of the house. "Drive your car to the airport and leave it in long-term parking. That's as good a place to get rid of it as any. Then book us three one-way tickets on the next flight to Boston. Do you have money?"

"A credit card."

"Good. I'll meet you at the departures gate."

"My clothes . . ." she said. "The blood—"

"Stop off at one of the big discount stores on the way to the airport. Change in their ladies' room and throw away the skirt you're wearing. And I'll pack a suitcase for you at the house."

The sound of another siren sliced through the air, and this time it didn't conveniently fade into the distance. Dexter sprinted toward his car. "I'll pick up Amanda," he said.

"Give me one hour. Get moving, Liz! You don't have time to stand around thinking!"

HE WAITED until he was safely home before placing the call to Igor. For some reason, he felt the need for familiar surroundings before he confessed what had happened. Anyway, his home phone was as safe as a phone booth, and a lot quieter. They sent in professionals to sweep the phone line regularly, and he himself was expert at checking for bugs. Not that anybody suspected him, so there was no reason in the world to anticipate a bug. Even Igor—who was paranoid about security—had agreed that he could make sensitive calls from his home in perfect safety.

It wasn't easy to dial the number. His fingers, poised over the buttons, shook. Igor did not tolerate mistakes on the part of his underlings, nor did he believe in effete capitalist notions like forgiveness. Igor eliminated his mistakes, thus preserving his reputation and saving the Soviet state a great deal of money in pension benefits.

He wondered if this was a mistake he could cover up. Damn Elizabeth Meacham to hell! She'd always seemed such an asexual creature, he'd been sure the senator wouldn't have a chance of getting close to her. Particularly since their divorce had been so bitter. But Evan had sworn he'd seen them kissing—in the kitchen, of all places, and it hadn't been a friendly peck on the cheek. Thank God, he'd been instructed to kill Evan Howard. It was one thing to admit that Elizabeth Meacham seemed closer to the senator than was desirable. It was another thing to admit they had been observed locked in a passionate kiss. That was a piece of information he'd make sure never filtered back up to Igor. It was grotesque to think of Liz responding to Dexter Rand, after the number of times she'd turned him down!

He put the receiver back into its cradle and drew in a series of short, deep breaths. An old trick learned in competition, but it calmed him, just as it had done before the Olympics.

No point in delaying this call any longer. He drew in one final, cleansing breath and punched out the numbers quickly, before he could lose his nerve. After all, he had a success to report along with the failure. Evan was dead. Quickly and cleanly dead, although there had been that split second when his hand had wavered. He wasn't quite sure why that had happened. He couldn't possibly be losing his nerve for simple things like killing. Not now. Not when their plans were so close to success. Not when the intolerable wait was almost over.

"Yes." Igor always answered the phone himself on the first ring. It was a small, chilling example of his efficiency.

"Evan Howard has been taken care of in accordance with your instructions," he said. His voice, he was pleased to note, sounded strong and confident. "You were correct, as always, Comrade Secretary. He was no longer reliable. He threatened to tell the police that Elizabeth Meacham was in danger."

"Did he know the Meacham woman is to be killed?"

"I'm sure Evan knew nothing." He hoped to God that was the truth. "Karen Zeit was immensely effective in bending her lovers to her will, Comrade Secretary, but I'm afraid that—toward the end—she was not always discreet." Because she had developed this insane obsession that they should marry. How many people had she blabbed to before he silenced her? "Evan should never have known my name," he added. "Karen was totally unprofessional in revealing it."

"You chose Zeit. You ran her. You should have controlled her. If you hadn't impregnated her, she might have been more reliable."

"Yes, indeed, Comrade. But no harm has been done. Neither Karen Zeit nor Evan Howard knew why Elizabeth Meacham must be killed. In fact, I doubt if Evan knew much more than the fact that Karen wished very much for a job on the senator's staff. It was the order to destroy Karen's personnel file that disturbed him. As you suspected, he was beginning to think far too much about what was going on.''

"Karen Zeit and Evan Howard are now part of the past. We are concerned with the present and the future. Our visitor from Moscow is now fully prepared for her task. The final stage of our plan may be set in motion. I assume Senator Rand is being followed?''

"Yes, Comrade.''

"Where is he? Is he implicated as ordered in Evan Howard's death?''

He drew in a deep breath. "The police, unfortunately, did not arrive in time to find him in Evan's house. I have been informed that he is now at home.''

Igor grunted. "This is your official order to set the next stage of operation in motion.''

"Yes, Comrade Secretary.'' Should he admit that Liz had been at Evan's house? Should he drop a hint that maybe—just maybe—Liz and the senator were becoming more intimate than was desirable? If he spoke up, the plan could be amended, if necessary. If he remained silent, life would be easier now, but might be impossible later. He wiped away the sweat that was beading on his forehead.

"There is one more thing, Comrade.''

"Yes?''

"Elizabeth Meacham and the senator...''

"Yes?''

"They have spent a great deal of time together over the past few days. It seems that our assumption that they would be mutually hostile and avoid each other was not entirely correct.''

"Our assumption?'' Igor asked softly. "My plan was based on your assessment of Elizabeth Meacham's likely behavior, Comrade Champion. Are you telling me that I must revise my plan?"

"I suggest only that you keep in mind that the senator has seen the Meacham woman quite frequently over the past few days."

Igor grunted. "I will ensure that my plans cover all eventualities. Your task is so simple, Comrade Champion, that I hope sincerely you will not screw up."

The American slang was so unexpected that for a moment he couldn't reply. He swallowed and said finally, "The kidnapping will proceed on schedule."

Igor hung up without speaking again.

Chapter Ten

Most of the passengers had already boarded the plane for Boston when Liz spotted Dexter and Amanda hurrying along the moving walkway to the flight gate. Dexter held an oversize panda, presumably because Amanda's arms were already filled with a scruffy teddy bear and a neon-yellow stuffed rabbit. An Easter gift that had been unexpectedly successful, Liz guessed, eyeing the creature's virulent pink satin ears with disbelief.

Even from a distance of fifty yards or so, she could see that Amanda was hopping with excitement, and that Dexter was smiling down at her, the hard lines of his jaw softened into tenderness, every angle of his body speaking of love and the urge to protect. When they reached the end of the walkway, he clutched the panda in his teeth, freeing a hand to help his daughter onto firm ground.

In that moment, Liz knew—without logic, but with utter, unshakable conviction—that Dexter was no killer. Evan's dying words might mean a multitude of different things, but she would never accept that Evan had intended to accuse his employer of murder. She had decided days ago that Dexter would never kill a woman to rid himself of the threat of a paternity suit. Today, witnessing the agony of Evan's death, she had lost her mental bearings for a while. She had spent the past two hours wondering why she was waiting to board a plane with a man who could well be a murderer. Now she realized that Evan's stumbling words had temporarily distorted her understanding of Dexter's character. Watching him with his daughter, she knew that her instincts were a safer guide to the truth than a dying man's semiconscious ramblings.

"Time to board?" Dexter asked as he approached.

"Yes, it's a DC-10. We're all together. Nonsmoking." She glanced toward the suddenly silent child. "Hi, Amanda. Would you like me to hold one of your animals?"

"No, thank you, Ms. Meacham. I can hold them myself." Her response was exquisitely polite—and totally lacking in warmth.

"Please call me Liz. 'Ms. Meacham' makes me feel like your teacher."

"You're nothing like any of my teachers," Amanda said positively.

Liz decided not to explore the precise meaning of that statement. Dexter, she noted, was looking faintly amused by his daughter's covert hostility. She wondered why. "We'd better get moving," she said brightly. "We don't want the plane to leave without us."

"I like going to Grandma's house." Amanda threw down the words more as a challenge than as a statement. Eyeing Liz with a hint of speculation, she added, "Grandpa's fun, too. We go fishing. Only him and me."

"How nice for you," Liz said and smiled, somehow refraining from pointing out that "fun" was just about the last word she would have used to describe the dour, fastidious Mr. Rand, Sr. Dexter's prim and proper parents, with their old-fashioned, aristocratic attitudes, had been one of the greater tribulations of her brief marriage.

Amanda took the window seat, Dexter squeezed his long legs into the cramped center position, and Liz took the aisle. "Sorry," she apologized. "None of my credit cards would stand first-class fares. You're flying as *Mr. Meacham*, by the way."

"Good idea. It might throw the journalistic hounds off the scent for a while."

"Not to mention the police."

"I'm not sure that we can avoid the police," Dexter said. "I told my housekeeper where we're going. I didn't want to create the impression that we were running away."

"I thought running away was exactly what we were doing."

He grinned. "Good grief, no! Just beating a strategic retreat."

"Translated into plain English, that sounds to me a heck of a lot like running away."

"Who's running away, Daddy?" Amanda's childish treble floated with appalling clarity across the hum of the engines and the clatter of the meal carts. "Is it Ms. Meacham?"

"Nobody's running away," Dexter replied. "Not literally. Here, have a lollipop." He pulled the candy out of a plastic bag tucked into his briefcase. "My emergency kit," he murmured to Liz. "Before Amanda was born, I wondered why parents ever gave their children candy or cookies. Then I wised up to the real world."

"Why is Ms. Meacham coming to Boston?" Amanda asked, licking her lollipop.

"Because I asked her to. I want her company."

Amanda digested this information in silence. "Is she going with you to Washington?"

This time her comment was overtly unfriendly, and Liz wondered what had prompted the change in Amanda's attitude. When they'd first met a couple of nights ago, the child had been more than ready to be friendly.

"I hope Liz will come with me." Dexter didn't rebuke his daughter for her rudeness, but he gave subtle emphasis to his use of Liz's name. "You know, Liz is a very good friend of mine, and I hope she'll be a friend of yours, too, one day."

Amanda scowled. Without replying, she leaned down and pulled a coloring book out of her carry-on bag. Dexter watched her for a second or two, then turned back to face Liz and spoke softly. "Her best friend at school took her aside yesterday and gave her a long lecture, during which she apparently pointed out that stepmothers are always mean and wicked. Amanda has converted overnight from wanting me to marry again into wanting me to remain single forever."

Liz spoke quickly. "She certainly has no reason to view me as a threat."

He hesitated for an instant. "We've spent a lot of time together the past few days, you and I. Naturally, she doesn't understand why."

Amanda thrust her picture under Dexter's nose. "Look, Daddy," she said. "What color shall I do the house?"

After that, Dexter devoted most of his attention to entertaining his daughter, and the tedium of the four-hour flight was interrupted only when the flight attendant arrived to serve cocktails and dinner. Liz normally avoided meals on planes, but realizing she had eaten nothing all day, she chose something optimistically called chicken cacciatore. Dexter and Amanda chose beef bourguignonne. The attendant seemed to have considerable difficulty in deciding what each tray contained, which wasn't surprising, since both the beef and the chicken were smothered in an identical dark red sauce. Happily, Liz discovered she was too hungry to care which dinner she got.

Darkness had long since descended when Dexter finally drove the rental car into the maple-lined driveway of the centuries-old Rand family home. Amanda, wedged between Liz and her father on the front seat of the car, fought a valiant battle against dozing off. With a visible effort, she would straighten up and demand attention every time Dexter addressed a remark to Liz.

Strangely enough, Liz found this typical childlike need for attention and reassurance more endearing than the polite self-possession Amanda had displayed on the first occasion they met. A couple of times she had to restrain herself from putting an arm around the child and saying, "It's okay. Relax. I'm not going to take him from you. I couldn't, even if I tried."

Dexter's parents caused an even stranger reaction within Liz. Either time and a grandchild had mellowed them out of all recognition, or her perspective was vastly different from the tension-filled days of her marriage.

They greeted her with the polite, formal reserve she expected. Her reaction to their cool courtesy, however, was neither irritation nor a burning sense of her own inadequacy. It was merely relief. One of the advantages of centuries of selective breeding, she reflected wryly, was that proper Bostonians seemed to have a repertoire of polite conversation for every occasion. Meeting a divorced former daughter-in-law, who had recently shared an apartment with their son's murdered-possible-mistress, seemed to present no special problems.

"How are you, Elizabeth? You look very well. I hope the flight wasn't too tiresome. I asked the housekeeper to put you in the blue bedroom. I'm sure you will find it comfortable."

Liz had nothing to do except mumble platitudes—a soothing end to a traumatic day.

By contrast, their welcome to Amanda showed just how far off the mark Liz had always been in assuming that neither Mr. nor Mrs. Rand was capable of deep emotion. They welcomed their granddaughter with a brief kiss on the cheek rather than the exuberant hugs and kisses traditional in some families, but love shone in their eyes, and their voices were warm with the intensity of their feelings.

What was more, Amanda clearly understood that she was the apple of her grandparents' eyes, and basked in the glow of their devotion. The adults shared coffee and liqueurs, while a maid brought in a tray of hot chocolate and cookies especially for Amanda. Curled up between Mr. and Mrs. Rand on the sofa, she displayed her drawings with the entirely accurate expectation that they would be rapturously received. Leonardo da Vinci could not have had his early sketches examined with more attention or greater enthusiasm, Liz reflected in silent amusement. If only Mr. Rand's colleagues at the bank could see him oohing and aahing over Amanda's purple house, their impression of his personality might undergo a radical change.

Amanda's artistic treasures had finally been laid to one side as she drooped more and more wearily against her grandmother's shoulder. "We'll talk tomorrow," Mr. Rand said to Dexter. "No, my boy, don't hurry your brandy. Stay here with Elizabeth. I'm sure you need some time to yourselves right now."

"Thanks. I'll just get Amanda to bed—"

"Indeed you won't." Mrs. Rand rose gracefully to her feet, demonstrating that it was possible to interrupt with every appearance of perfect manners. "Amanda and I have a special story to read tonight. We've been saving it since last time she was here, haven't we, dear?"

"Yes. It's called *The Secret Garden*, and now I'm big enough to read it to Grandma."

"If I may, I'll come along and listen, too." Mr. Rand put his brandy snifter on the tray. "I seem to remember that was always one of my favorite stories."

Mrs. Rand looked across at her son. "You'll show Elizabeth where the blue room is, Dexter?"

"Of course. Good night, Mother."

The masculine Rands exchanged handshakes. Mrs. Rand gave her son a brief peck on the cheek, but Liz noticed, as she wouldn't have done nine years earlier, that the older woman's eyes were bright with unshed tears. "I'm glad to have you home, Dexter," she murmured. "If there's any way we can help..."

"You've helped already," he said. "Just being with you and Dad puts things into better perspective." Hunkering down, he held Amanda close. "Sleep tight, poppet. I'll see you in the morning."

She clung to his neck for a few moments, then turned quite happily to take her grandmother's hand. "Good night, Ms. Meacham," she said pointedly.

There was no doubt about it, Liz thought ruefully. The Rand family genes got to work early, teaching little junior Rands how to annihilate their enemies with politeness. On the brink of returning an equally cool good-night, she astonished herself by bending down and gathering Amanda into a swift hug.

"My name's Liz," she said softly. "It would be awfully nice if you could call me that. Sleep tight, Amanda. Give Rabbit a kiss from me."

Amanda didn't return Liz's hug, but neither did she reject it, which seemed a step in the right direction. Although why she felt this pressing need to be accepted by Dexter's daughter, Liz couldn't quite decide.

When Amanda and her grandparents left the room, a silence descended that was less than comfortable. "What I want more than anything in the world is a shower," Liz said.

"Me, too. I'll show you to your room."

"You don't have to bother. Just give me directions."

"The second door on the right as you go up the staircase. There's a connecting bathroom."

"Fine. Well, thanks for everything, Dexter. I'll see you in the morning."

"I should be thanking you," he said quietly. "But you're right. We'll do better if we talk in the morning. You must be exhausted, and by coming here, we've bought ourselves some time to relax.''

"Yes. It was a pretty miserable day." She didn't move, and neither did Dexter. "Well," she said at last. "I guess I'd better be on my way. Second room on the right, wasn't it?"

"Yes." Dexter was noted as a brilliant conversationalist. At the moment, however, he seemed to be having as much difficulty as Liz in finding anything coherent, let alone brilliant, to say.

"Um . . . good night," she managed finally.

"Er . . . Sleep well."

His voice sounded as tense as she felt—which was like a tightly tuned guitar string, waiting to be strummed. Unfortunately, this sort of tension had become very familiar to Liz over the past few days. She felt it anytime she was with Dexter, but when they were alone together, it became almost unbearable. Her body screamed out the message that if she stepped forward into Dexter's arms, her tension would be wonderfully, blissfully, released. Her mind, meanwhile, sent out frantic reminders about what had happened the last time she allowed her physical desires to control her response to her former husband.

For once in her life, Liz got smart. Without trying to explain her actions, she turned abruptly on her heel and hurried from the room. Too many more minutes of staring at Dexter, and she might have done something totally crazy. Like telling him what was on her mind. And at that precise moment it surely wasn't murder.

NO BATH, not even after a grueling competition, had ever felt so good. Liz shampooed her hair and scrubbed every inch of her body with imported English lavender soap. She couldn't expunge the morning's horrific memories, but the hot water helped to rinse away at least some of her guilt at leaving Denver. Evan had been long past mortal help when she and Dexter abandoned him, and yet she was having difficulty in smothering the sharp prick of her conscience. She had been the last person to see Evan alive. Therefore she felt an obligation to report everything she had heard and seen to the police. Somewhere in her childhood civics classes she had obviously absorbed the lesson that policemen were good guys, and anybody who evaded them was bad. Liz felt bad, as if she deserved to be arrested.

She stepped out of the claw-footed tub, which was no decorator touch but had been there, she was sure, since "modern" plumbing was installed in the Rand mansion at the turn of the century. She wrapped her damp hair in a hand towel and her body in a bath towel, which was fluffy, but not overlarge. Yawning, she pushed open the door and stepped into her bedroom.

Dexter, clad in a T-shirt and faded jeans, sat on the bed. Her bed. "We need to talk," he said. His voice sounded low and oddly thick.

She tightened the towel above her breasts, although it was already so tight that breathing seemed difficult. "Now? This minute? I thought we decided everything could wait until the morning."

"Not this." He stood up and came toward her. "Precisely what happened that day in Frankfurt?" he asked.

"In Frankfurt? At the Olympics?" She was so astonished that she forgot to hold onto her towel. He caught it for her and handed her the ends, but not before his gaze had made a swift, burning assessment of everything the towel was supposed to conceal.

"Thank you," she said, her voice husky.

"You're welcome." His gaze rose slowly from the swell of her breasts to the curve of her lips, and stayed there. Fire exploded in her veins and raced throughout her body.

Don't look at me! she wanted to shout. But another part of her yearned to throw the towel to the floor and yell, *Yes, look at me! Look at what you've been missing for the last nine years!*

In the end, it seemed simplest not to say anything. Besides, she needed all her concentration. Her fingers were trembling so much that she couldn't complete the simple task of tucking one end of the towel into the other.

"Here, let me," he said. His hands, cool against the blazing heat of her skin, traced the swell of her breasts and then slowly, with infinite care, tucked in the ends of the towel together. "What happened that night in Frankfurt?" he asked quietly.

Defiance shaped her reply. "I messed up," she said, the old defensive mechanisms rushing into action. "I threw away a first-place standing and robbed America of its guaranteed gold. Didn't you read the newspapers?"

"I'm all grown-up, Liz, and I've learned not to believe everything I read."

"You were there. You saw for yourself."

"I don't think I saw the truth."

She turned away, shaking with the pain of remembering. "It doesn't matter now. It's a long time ago. I was winning at the end of the short program. I skated terribly in the final segment of the contest. I lost. There's nothing else to say."

His hands were on her shoulders, his callused thumbs circling in a hypnotic massage. "I always blamed Alison," he said. "I assumed that somehow she messed up your concentration. But it wasn't Alison, was it? It was Susan. If it had been Alison, you'd have talked to me afterward."

She drew in a long, sharp breath. "Yes," she agreed, her voice scarcely more than a whisper. "It was Susan." Honesty compelled her to add, "And it was me, too. In the last resort, Susan didn't have the power to make me lose. It was entirely my own fault. Champions like Pieter Ullmann can block absolutely everything out of their minds except what they need to do to win. Alison had that same capacity, although her artistic skills were never quite strong enough to take her to the absolute top. My problem was the opposite. Technique and artistry weren't hard for me, but my coach warned me that my mental discipline was never up to scratch. I always allowed my feelings to affect my skating."

"That's why you were so damn brilliant," Dexter said, an odd hint of anger in his voice. "Your coach was wrong to try to train the emotion out of you. When you had a really good day, you weren't just a superb skater, you were fire and passion captured on ice."

She twisted in his arms, suddenly needing to see his face. "I didn't know you were so impressed by my skating," she said.

He gazed down at her, eyes hooded. "I never once saw the end of your long program, because I couldn't stand the emotional tension you generated. That was why I had to choose my seat so damn carefully, so that you wouldn't notice when I stopped watching."

"Why didn't you ever tell me any of this before?"

His shoulders lifted in a self-mocking shrug. "I was young. I was intimidated by your talent."

"Intimidated! You? Good grief, Dexter, you were the most arrogant, self-assured man I'd ever met—"

"In my own area of expertise, maybe. You showed me that there was a whole creative side to the universe that I'd never even suspected. A lot of the time when I was with you I felt hopelessly...inadequate."

"And I felt inadequate because I couldn't be controlled and efficient like you." She wanted to laugh, or perhaps to cry, with the frustration of so many months when they had totally failed to understand each other. "Why didn't you tell me what you felt?" she asked.

"Because I was a fool. And because I was a combat pilot, working in a brutally masculine environment, testing supersonic jet fighters. I'd spent years being trained not to express my feelings. It needed to be that way, or we'd have gone to pieces every time a test plane showed up with problems. Nerves over my wife's skating performance didn't fit too well with my macho self-image. How the hell could I talk to you about the way I felt, when I couldn't even admit the truth to myself?''

She felt a wave of regret, not for her lost Olympic medal, a loss she'd long since learned to live with, but for the foolishness of two people who'd thrown away a marriage because they were too scared to admit that they were less than totally competent, less than a hundred percent perfect. She smiled sadly. ''Wouldn't it be nice if there was some way to prevent people getting married until they're mature enough to handle it?''

His answering smile was wry. ''Heck, half of us would never pass the test.'' He ran his hand slowly down her side, shaping the narrowness of her waist and the delicate flare of her hips. ''I wish I'd known you were pregnant,'' he said.

''Alison was the only person I told. I was so sure you'd be angry. I didn't want you to be tied in to a marriage that you regretted.''

He didn't answer her directly. ''I saw Alison hand you a glass of something to drink, right before you went out on the ice. You know, all these years I assumed she'd put some sort of drug in it.''

''Dexter, she gave me Gatorade! And I took maybe two sips maximum! Why in the world did you suspect Alison of doing something so horrible?''

''Because she was jealous of you—''

''You mean, you thought she was jealous of me.''

''No, I haven't changed my opinion about Alison. I may not have assessed my other relationships too clearly, but I always understood Alison. She hated the fact that you skated so much better than she did. You were her twin—''

"But not an identical twin," Liz protested. "We were no more alike than any other set of sisters who happened to be the same age. It's not surprising our ability levels were different."

"Believe me, Alison didn't see it that way. She envied your talent."

Liz looked away. "She's dead now, so we can never resolve this disagreement. Besides, that night in Frankfurt, she had nothing to do with what happened. I'd pulled a tendon in my ankle during practice and I was pumped full of Novocain and painkillers. That was a big part of the problem. But it was Susan who destroyed my concentration, not Alison. Although in the last resort I don't blame anyone but myself. I should never have let Susan get to me."

"What did she say, Liz?"

"Does it matter? I accepted a while ago that she was so far removed from the world of competitive skating that I truly don't think she understood the damage she caused by talking about my failing marriage an hour before I was due to go out on the ice. The whole incident's over, Dexter. We have no reason to discuss it."

"It's not over," Dexter said. "How can it be over, when what she said affected our lives for the past nine years? Tell me, Liz. I need to know."

She stared abstractedly into the distance, seeing the cavernous entrance to the ice rink as if it were yesterday. "Susan told me she was in love with you," she replied slowly. "That was no surprise. Everyone on base knew she'd been in love with you for years."

"And that threw you enough to destroy your concentration?"

"No. But she pointed out that her father was your commanding officer, and that she was the perfect wife for you."

"I'd known her for five years," Dexter interjected impatiently. "Didn't it occur to you that if I'd wanted to marry her, I could have done that years before I ever met you?''

Liz lifted her eyes to meet his. ''She told me that you finally realized you should have married her, not me. That you bitterly regretted our marriage, and that our life-styles were totally incompatible. Given the fact that you and I couldn't be in the same room without starting to fight, what she said seemed to make a lot of sense.''

''Given the fact that we couldn't be in the same room without tearing each other's clothes off and making passionate love, what she said made no sense at all.''

Liz's mouth twisted painfully. ''I didn't know our sexual relationship was anything special—''

''Dear God, Liz, you can't have been that naive!''

''Whatever you felt for me, it seemed pretty easily transferable. You married Susan a month after our divorce was final.''

''Because I was so damn torn apart, I didn't care anymore! I wanted peace and quiet and calm and stability. And...''

''And?''

''I'm ashamed to admit it, but I wanted you to think I didn't give a damn. I didn't want you to know that I was bleeding inside and grieving for what we'd shared. No siree, I wasn't going to have people feeling sorry for me. Hell, if I married Susan fast enough, everybody would think I'd had another woman lined up and waiting all along, and that suited me just fine.'' He flushed slightly. ''You deserved better. For that matter, so did Susan. She wasn't vindictive, you know. Just entirely, totally without imagination. She thought you were an unsuitable wife for me. She saw how tempestuous our marriage was. She concluded that I would be happier married to her. She told you her conclusion. Logically, as far as she was concerned.''

''Unfortunately, the rest of the world isn't made up of imitation Mr. Spocks.''

"Thank God for that!" His hands skimmed back up her body to rest on her shoulder. "You're shivering," he said.

"This bath towel's damp. It doesn't make the best cover."

"Then take it off."

"No!" Her mouth spoke the word with suitable vehemence, but her treacherous body was already leaning toward him in silent longing. Dear God, but she wanted him to make love to her!

He cupped her face in his hands and brushed a thumb tenderly across her mouth. "I want to love you," he said huskily. "I've been aching to feel myself inside you every minute of the past three days. But I'm not falling into the old, destructive patterns again. If you say no, Liz, I'm going to accept what you say. I had my fill of playing caveman when we were married."

He bent his head and kissed her, a long kiss, full of hunger and adult need. "Come to bed with me, Liz," he said, when the embrace finally ended. "Come willingly. Let me know that for once you want me with your heart and mind, as well as your body."

It was a simple request, but one she wouldn't have been able to fulfill nine years earlier. Now, however, she was many years wiser, as well as older. Her gaze never leaving Dexter's face, she let her arms drop to her sides. The towel slipped down her body and fell into a soft heap at her feet.

"I want you in all the ways there are," she said huskily. "All the ways a woman can want a man. Make love to me, Dex. Remind me of what I've been missing."

For all the passion they had shared during their brief marriage, it was the first time Liz had ever admitted she wanted Dex before she was so fully aroused that she had no choice but to beg for completion. He had obviously not been prepared for her openness, and for a moment she felt him go still, as if he couldn't quite believe what he had heard. Then, with a small, incredulous sigh, he reached out and pulled her into his arms, crushing her mouth beneath his and holding her tight against his hips.

"You feel so right in my arms," he murmured. "God, how did I ever let you go?" His fingers stroked over her breasts, dancing a trail of fire down to her thighs.

"With difficulty. Like me letting you go." Her hands reached for the zipper of his jeans. With an incoherent groan, he took her fingers and guided them in a swift downward movement, opening her hand over himself as he stepped out of the jeans. His lips reclaimed hers with something akin to desperation, and his tongue thrust into her mouth, sparking a thousand pleasure points deep within her.

She clung to him, her body molten, but her mind sharp and clear with the knowledge that she wanted to be held by this man, that she wanted him to caress her, and that his possession would be total only because she willingly gave herself to him.

Dexter swept her into his arms, carrying her to the bed in a gesture familiar from a hundred previous occasions. But this time her response was different from everything she had experienced before. This time she was mature enough to recognize that he didn't take her to bed as an act of domination, so she didn't cling to him in anguished resentment that her body had once again taken charge of her will.

Instead she curled against his chest, reveling in the sensation of hard muscles rippling beneath her cheek. As soon as they reached the bed, she pulled his head down to her mouth, actively seeking the pleasures of his kiss. At last, after nine years of growing up, she realized that Dexter was not the conqueror and herself the conquered. They were equal partners, each wholly dependent on the other for fulfillment.

"I want you so much," she whispered, her fingers tangling in his dark, springy hair. The wonderment in his eyes made her realize how rarely in the past she had consciously expressed her needs.

"Show me how you want me," he commanded, his voice hoarse.

"Like this." She arched her hips upward in explicit invitation. His answering penetration was swift, deep and total. She felt his possession in every cell of her body, and his name sprang in a reflexive cry to her lips.

"Liz," he groaned. "Liz, my love, never go away again. Don't leave me."

How could she risk a second relationship with Dex? On the other hand, how could she ever leave him? For a moment Liz was filled with panic. To stay with Dex opened her to the chance of endless pain, but to leave him again would be to condemn herself to a future of bitter regret. Then the icy coldness of her worry vanished, unable to survive in the burning heat of her passion. Her body shook with the rapturous beginnings of climax, and her thoughts spiraled away into darkness.

Clinging to him, murmuring his name, Liz surrendered herself to the ecstasy of ultimate union with the man she loved.

Chapter Eleven

It was still pitch-dark when Liz awoke out of a bone-deep sleep. Fear clutched at her throat and chilled her limbs. She rolled over onto her back, staring up at the ghostly glow of the high ceiling, deriving comfort from the warm feeling of Dexter's legs intertwined with her own. Whatever caused her to wake had been terrifying.

She listened carefully to the late-night sounds of the house. All she heard was the rustle of the May breeze in the bushes, the sigh of Dexter's breathing, and the creak of two-hundred-year-old wood settling a fraction of an inch deeper into the ground. Nothing very scary. Nothing to bring her panting and sweating out of a deep sleep.

Slowly the realization dawned that it had been her own dreams that had jerked her so abruptly into consciousness. Liz closed her eyes, trying to return to the drowsy state in which dreams could be remembered. A memory teased at the corner of her mind, and she frowned in fierce concentration. Evan. It had been something about Evan. Something he had said just before he died.

Suddenly, with the brilliance of a spotlight shining behind a flimsy curtain, she realized precisely what it was that had brought her awake. She leaned over and shook Dexter's shoulder. With the instincts of a longtime combat pilot, he sat up, instantly awake and alert.

"What is it?"

"Evan—when he was dying. He said some things, and I didn't tell you. Dex, I'm scared."

He didn't waste time inquiring why she hadn't told him earlier, or even why Evan's remarks had suddenly become urgent at four in the morning. He folded his pillows into a backrest. "What did Evan say that's worrying you?"

"He said somebody would have to kill me."

"What? And you've only just now decided to mention this? For God's sake, Liz, who's going to kill you? Or didn't Evan mention that trivial detail?"

"He just said *they*. And he said several other things at the same time," Liz added defensively.

"They must have been damned exciting if you forgot you were slated as the next murder victim!"

"Not exciting. Frightening. I guess my brain overloaded and stopped processing information logically. At the time I convinced myself he hadn't recognized me—"

"You think that's possible?" Dexter interjected. "You think somebody else may be at risk rather than you?"

"No, I don't. My subconscious obviously treated his words more seriously than the rest of me. Once I fell asleep, and my mind had time to sort out its impressions, I guess my subconscious decided that Evan had definitely meant me, and that I was at risk."

"Did he speak to you by name? Give any sign that he'd recognized you?"

"He called me Liz a couple of times. And remember, he'd phoned my office asking me to come around to the house, so he was expecting to see me. Presumably when he went to the door and let in the murderer, he thought it was me. So all in all, it seems like Evan knew exactly who he was speaking to, and tried to warn me."

Dexter took her hands and pulled her against his chest, stroking her hair with gentle fingers. "I won't let it happen, Liz. I swear to you, I won't let it happen. Now we know you're at risk, there are all sorts of things we can do to protect you."

Rationally she knew that even Dexter couldn't stop a truly determined killer, otherwise presidents and princes would never be assassinated, but the passionate concern in his voice soothed the ache of her fear. Hope replaced the knot of dread that lay coiled in waiting at the pit of her stomach. "Should we call the police?" she asked.

"I have a better idea than that; we can contact the FBI. I'll explain more later. First I need to know what else Evan said before he died."

She looked up at him, without moving from the warm circle of his arms. Even in the darkness, the angles of his face seemed hard, uncompromising—and starkly honest. Nestled against his chest, her body still soft with the imprint of his lovemaking, it was difficult to remember that yesterday, however briefly, she had suspected him of murder.

"What else did Evan say?" She organized her thoughts. "Well, he admitted that he'd been in love with Karen."

Dexter didn't seem surprised. "I wondered if the baby was his," he said quietly. "Once or twice, Evan let slip remarks that indicated he cared about Karen. I never noticed them at the time, only in retrospect, when my twenty-twenty hindsight vision started to operate."

"Why didn't you say anything to the police?"

He shrugged. "I didn't have anything constructive to say. There were already enough groundless suspicions bubbling in the police cauldron without adding mine to the stew. I pointed out to Rodriguez that Evan was solely responsible for personnel records in my Colorado office, and that was as far as I could go."

"You think Evan deliberately lost Karen's file?"

"I suspected it all along."

"But why?"

"Evan screens every applicant for employment. He checks all the references. He would be the first person to know if Karen's records didn't quite tie together. Either he recommended her for hiring, knowing her references didn't check out. Or, more likely, he became suspicious later on, double-checked and then destroyed the file, knowing her records wouldn't stand up to scrutiny."

"It fits," Liz admitted. "He said that he'd been a fool, and that he'd done it all for her. The odd thing is, Dex, I still don't believe Evan was the father of Karen's baby."

This time, Dexter appeared startled. "Did he actually say that? For a dying man, he seems to have said an awful lot."

"That's just it. He only mumbled a few half sentences, and all the rest is conjecture on my part. But he did make specific reference to another man. It was almost as if discovering Karen was pregnant had finally made him accept the truth. 'He is so beautiful and so dangerous.' Those were the last words Evan spoke before he died."

Dexter smiled grimly. "Well, that takes us a giant step farther forward in unraveling the puzzle. Now we know there was a mystery man in Karen's life who exerted a great deal of influence over her. We knew that four days ago."

"We also know that somebody must have wanted to introduce Karen onto your staff really badly, to go to all the trouble of compromising Evan Howard."

"You're right. Which makes me more convinced than ever that those security leaks from my Washington office were somehow engineered from Denver by Karen."

"But she had no clearance to handle secret documents, did she?"

"None. She didn't need it as my administrative coordinator. She handled party political matters, not government material. But the reality is that people become lax about security, particularly with colleagues they know well. By the time Karen made her sixth or seventh trip to my DC office, she might have been able to gain access to a supposedly off-limits area. She was probably trained to find ways of doing just that."

Liz shivered, her fear returning with renewed intensity. "But I don't understand what this has to do with me! Why am I going to be killed? Dexter, for heaven's sake, what connection have I got with secret documents missing from your office? I sell *picante* sauce, for heaven's sake, not missiles!"

"Blueprints for part of a fighter jet," he corrected absently. "That's what went missing." He fell silent for a moment. "I wonder if we've been approaching this whole situation from totally the wrong direction," he said at last. "We've been trying to work out ways your roommates might be connected to each other. We've been trying to find out details about Karen's hidden past. Let's look at the puzzle differently. Let's assume *you* are the center of what's going on, not an inconvenient intruder who keeps bobbing up at the edges."

Liz resisted the urge to break into wild, frustrated laughter. "But Dexter, I am an intruder! How can I be at the center of something when I've not the faintest idea in the world what's going on?"

He looked at her, his expression coolly assessing, but his eyes conveying warmth and support. "If you're intended as the next murder victim, you don't need to know what's going on. Maybe your death is the crux of the plot. Whatever that plot is."

She refused to give way to the hysteria that threatened to engulf her. Wrapping her arms around her waist, she fought against a wave of sickness by forcing herself to respond logically. "We already know of four people who've been killed. Three of my roommates and Evan Howard. At the same time, your office has been traced as the source for some top-secret blueprints that have turned up on the international arms market. Do I have it right so far?"

"You're making a link between two separate sets of events, but I think the link's justified. We're also guessing that Karen and Evan were at least marginally involved in the theft of top-secret papers from my office."

"But none of this *leads* anywhere!" Liz exclaimed. "So let's say, for argument's sake, that I'm the next victim on the list. What happens then? Does it become easier to steal more secrets? No! Does it protect the master criminal? No! I've no idea who he is! I couldn't reveal a thing about him, because I don't know anything. So someone who knows nothing about anything at all is going to die. Big deal."

"Perhaps they're afraid you might discover who the murderer is?"

"Then they could as logically kill you or Rodriguez. Why me?" Liz jumped out of bed and began pacing. "Maybe Evan didn't recognize me, after all. Maybe I'm not going to be killed. I think we've got this all wrong, Dex."

"Unless," he commented slowly, "unless they want a specific person to be accused of your murder."

Liz's head jerked up and she stopped her pacing. "You?"

"Don't you get the feeling that somebody out there is working very hard to set me up?"

Liz gave a small, scared laugh. "I'm real anxious to frustrate them, Dex. Tell me how."

Dexter stared silently into the darkness for several seconds. His decision reached, he flung back the bedclothes and reached for his jeans. "We'll do what I suggested in the first place. We'll get the FBI to take you into protective custody."

"They'll agree to do that?"

"If I tell them they must," he said, with unconscious arrogance. "Whether or not I'm being set up, you seem to be on line as the next victim. I'll contact Harry Cooper at the FBI...." His voice died away. "Damn! We're not at home. I can't contact him from here, except by calling the Bureau and leaving a message with the switchboard operator. Maybe I'm becoming paranoid, but I don't want to do that.'' He pulled on his T-shirt, then resumed. ''Would you be willing to come to Washington with me on the early flight? Most of the emergency safe houses are in the DC area, so you'd be flying to the right place. If we take the first flight out from Logan, we can be talking to Harry in his office by nine o'clock.''

''If I have to fly to Washington in order to stay alive, I vote in favor,'' Liz said dryly. ''I've decided recently that I'm amazingly interested in staying alive.''

He walked around the bed and kissed her hard on the lips. ''You'd better believe I'm not going to let you die,'' he said. ''We have nine years of catching up to do. Last night just made me hungry for more.''

Hungry for what? Liz wondered. For more sex, or a deeper, more meaningful relationship? From prudence or cowardice, she chose not to inquire.

DEXTER'S PARENTS ACCEPTED their son's departure with the same equanimity with which they had greeted his unexpected arrival the night before. Amanda, however, was hopping mad that her father and Liz were once again taking off together.

''I went into your room this morning and you weren't there,'' she told her father accusingly.

''I expect I was in the shower.''

''You were in *her* room.'' Amanda pointed her finger accusingly. ''I saw you come out. You like her better than me.''

Liz felt herself blushing, but felt obligated to make some sort of explanation. ''Your daddy doesn't love you less, just because he and I are friends,'' Liz said, bending down so that she was at eye level with Amanda.

The child glared at her. ''I hate you!'' she said and burst into tears.

With less patience that she had ever seen him demonstrate, Dexter took out his handkerchief and dried his daughter's eyes. "Amanda, you're being silly," he said crisply. "You're also being extremely rude to someone who would like to be your friend."

"I want to come to Washington with you!"

"Honey, you can't. I'm sorry. Grandma and Grandpa have agreed to bring you down at the weekend. I'll look forward to seeing you then. In the meantime, please try not to believe all the stories your friends tell you. Stepmothers are often wonderful people, who make the children in their families very happy."

Amanda buried her nose in her grandmother's skirts, ignoring her father's outstretched hand.

"Don't worry, Dexter," Mrs. Rand said with her usual patrician calm. "Amanda will soon settle down with us, and we'll see you on Saturday morning at National, if you'll come to pick us up. We'll take the usual flight."

"Of course. I'll be there."

Liz was concerned about Amanda's escalating dislike for her, but she had little time to mull over the problem. Dexter plied her with questions all the way to the airport, making her recount Evan's dying words in painstaking detail, and then analyzing every possible meaning that they could come up with for the enigmatic phrases. By the time their plane landed in Washington, Liz felt that her brain had been sucked dry, and the only firm conclusion she and Dexter had reached was that some beautiful and dangerous man, clearly not Evan, must be the father of Karen's baby.

"How do we define beautiful and dangerous?" Dexter queried ruefully. "That airline steward we interviewed was damn good-looking in a meaty kind of way, but do you think he could be termed dangerous?"

"Lethally boring," Liz commented. "And the kind of bedmate who likes to find out if you can do it suspended from the chandelier. But I doubt if that's what Evan meant.''

"With all his international travel, an airline steward might be able to set up the contacts to make a sale of stolen documents, though. It's a possibility, however remote.''

"He didn't seem bright enough," Liz said.

"How do we know that wasn't a brilliant facade?" Dexter's face showed a hint of weariness. "Damn, but I have the feeling we're running awfully hard just to remain in the same place.''

The morning didn't improve. Murphy's Law was in full operation, and when they arrived at the FBI building they learned that Agent Harry Cooper was in Seattle until the next day. "Probably checking on Brian for me," Dexter commented ruefully to Liz.

Drawing on all the clout he could muster as a United States senator, Dexter asked to see the director of the Bureau. The director, he was informed with icy politeness, was giving a briefing at the White House and then was flying by Air Force One direct to Texas. The receptionist, conveying the impression that she was granting an undeserved audience with a divine being, suggested that a deputy chief would be able to speak with the senator at three-thirty that afternoon. "He will have to cancel another appointment in order to see you, Senator," she added reprovingly. "A very important appointment.''

"My business with the director does happen to be a matter of vital national security," Dexter said, his own voice biting.

The receptionist looked offended. "National security is what the Bureau deals in, Senator. All our business is of the highest importance.''

"You're losing your touch," Liz said teasingly as they emerged from the FBI building. "A few years ago, she'd have been eating out of your hand.''

"A few years ago I wasn't old and impatient—and you weren't in danger of being murdered."

His clipped words caused a chill to ripple along Liz's spine. Her steps faltered and she almost slipped. Dexter reached out, steadying her, and she quickly regained her balance. In an unthinking, reflex reaction, she glanced around to see if anybody had noticed her clumsiness.

A thin, middle-aged man, fifteen yards or so to their rear, was pocketing something that looked suspiciously like a camera. She groaned. "Damn! Dex, I think there's a reporter on our tail."

Dexter swung around in the direction she had indicated, reaching the reporter in a few athletic strides. Liz could see that his body was stiff with frustration. "I don't want anyone to know I'm in Washington," he said to the man, his voice low and hard. "I'd appreciate it if you'd not publish any of those pictures you've just taken."

The reporter's expression was difficult to read, but Liz could have sworn she saw fright, as much as anything else. How strange, she reflected. Fear wasn't an emotion she associated with photojournalists on the prowl.

"I'm free-lance," the man jerked out. "I can't afford to waste a morning's work."

Dexter pushed a bundle of notes into the man's hand, his mouth twisting with distaste. "Here. That's enough to buy the whole damn camera. I'd like the film, please."

The reporter stared blankly at Dexter, and Liz gained a fleeting impression that, like a cornered animal, the man was poised between fight and flight. With a sudden nervous gesture, he pulled the camera out of his pocket and flipped open the back. He unrolled the film and waved it back and forth in the weak sunlight.

"There," he said. "Now you know for sure I'm not gonna publish these anywhere." He thrust the ruined film into Dexter's hands, snapped the camera closed, and took off at a brisk walk toward the nearby subway.

"Unpleasant little reptile," Dexter remarked. "What next?"

"Don't you need to go to your office?"

"Would you mind waiting there with me until it's time for our appointment with the deputy director?"

"If you like. Or I could check into a hotel—"

"No hotels," he said flatly. "Look, we've decided there's a good chance that someone's going to try to kill you, and then frame me. The best way to protect both of us is to make sure you're always in a group of at least three people. That way I can't be framed, so presumably you won't be killed."

"I hate to cast doubts on such a comforting theory, but what if we're only half right? What if somebody wants to kill me and doesn't care about setting you up? Then your scenario doesn't work."

"Yes, it does," he said, directing her toward his offices on Capitol Hill. "If you're never without three or four people around you, then you can't get killed."

"Unless the three or four people are all in this crazy plot together."

"Liz, after those blueprints went missing, the employees in my DC office were checked out so carefully that we almost know the last time each of them went to the bathroom. I suppose I can just imagine the possibility that one of them might have slipped through the screening net, but three? Take my word for it, the people in my DC office are clean."

"Don't you ever go to the movies, Dex? It's always the guy who's Mr. Clean personified that ends up being the villain in chief."

"Liz, honey, this isn't the movies. This is real life."

Liz, honey. The words sounded sweet, and Liz allowed herself to relax. After all, she only had to survive until three-thirty that afternoon, and then her problems would be over. Despite all the horror stories in the press about

government incompetence, Liz retained an optimistic faith
in the ability of the FBI to protect U.S. citizens. The deputy director would listen to her story, wave his magic wand
and whisk her away to a safe house. The very name of the
place suggested that once there, the risk of being murdered
would vanish. While she stayed safe in her safe house,
Dexter and Agent Harry Cooper would then busy themselves with the investigation, and before long, some master criminal would be revealed.

A niggling doubt surfaced as Liz contemplated the fact
that she had no idea who the master criminal might be, and
even less idea of what he was up to. She banished the doubt
to a far corner of her mind. What was the FBI for, if not for
flushing out master criminals and uncovering dastardly
plots?

Whether Dexter shared her sudden lightheartedness, or
whether he disguised his true feelings in order not to depress her, Liz wasn't sure. Superficially, however, their
mood as they entered his suite of offices was surprisingly
carefree. Dexter made brief introductions, and then took
Liz into his private office, asking a secretary and two research assistants to join them.

While Dexter busied himself reviewing a forthcoming
speech on Air Force overspending, Liz quietly retreated to
a corner of the room and made herself useful by tidying the
small library of books and softcover publications dealing
with Colorado. She was in the midst of arranging a taste-
ful display of travel magazines trumpeting the beauties of
the Rocky Mountains, when the phone rang. It was the
sixth or seventh call put through to Dexter already, and Liz
had no idea why she suddenly straightened from her magazines, her mouth dry with irrational fear.

One of the research assistants picked up the phone. "A
personal call for you on line three, Senator."

Dexter took the phone and listened in silence for about
a minute. Without placing his hand over the mouthpiece,

he looked at his three staff members and nodded politely toward the door. "I'm sorry, this call may take a few minutes. Would you mind leaving me?"

Liz stepped forward. "Dexter, no! Remember what we agreed."

He looked in her direction, but Liz had the feeling he scarcely saw her. He turned back toward his assistants without acknowledging her in any way. "Would you start work on those amendments, please? Right away."

The young man and the two women trooped obediently from the room. Liz hurried forward and leaned against the desk. "Dexter, for God's sake, what is it?"

He spoke into the phone as if he had no awareness of her existence. "I am alone now."

The voice at the other end of the line echoed in the sudden, suffocating silence of the office. "Amanda has a message for you, Senator. She says please cancel your appointment with the deputy director of the FBI."

A child gave an anguished cry. "Daddy, where are you?"

"Don't leave your office, Senator, and keep Ms. Meacham with you. We'll be in touch."

The line went dead.

Chapter Twelve

Dexter returned the phone to the cradle with infinite care. "I was mad at her," he said. "When we left Boston this morning, Amanda knew I was mad at her."

Liz swallowed hard over the horror that had lodged like a physical object in her throat. She reached out and touched him very gently on the back of his hand. He was ice-cold.

"We have to call your parents, Dex. Maybe...maybe Amanda's at home with them. Maybe the call was just some horrible, sick joke."

"You know it wasn't." He pressed a hand against his eyes, as if willing himself to think rationally. "My parents' number is in the Rolodex," he said, and she realized his mind had temporarily blanked out. He couldn't remember his own parents' phone number.

She searched swiftly through the card index, then dialed with shaking hands. It was a personal line, and Mrs. Rand answered the phone with a bright "Hello."

"This is Liz. Liz Meacham. We've run into a bit of a problem here." She refrained from any further explanation, not wanting to worry Dexter's parents, if by any chance the threatening phone call turned out to be a hoax. "Could you please hold on for a moment while I pass you over to Dex?"

She put the phone into Dexter's hand, and he gripped it so tightly that his entire fist went white.

"Where's Amanda?" he asked without any preliminaries.

"Heaven's, you sound fierce," Mrs. Rand replied cheerily. "Amanda's on her way. Your secretary didn't expect to be in Washington until five at the earliest."

"My secretary? You sent Amanda here, to Washington? With my secretary?"

"Well, that's what you asked us to do! And I must say, Dexter dear, your father and I don't agree with giving in to Amanda like this, just because she had a temper tantrum this morning. With all that journalistic fuss over Evan Howard's death, she'd have been much better off staying with us until the weekend. Have you seen the papers this morning—?"

"My secretary came to your house to collect Amanda? Is that what happened, Mother?"

"But of course it is. You should know, for goodness' sake, she was following your instructions. Judy came, that nice young woman from your Washington office that I always speak to." Mrs. Rand's voice was no longer cheery, but choked with the beginnings of fear. "She gave me your note, Judy I mean, and said that she and Amanda would have to hurry to catch the next flight. I packed her suitcase.... Dexter, dear heaven, has the plane crashed or something?"

"No, Mother. Nothing's crashed." Liz could see the monumental effort with which Dexter pulled himself together. The veins stood out on his forehead as he gritted his teeth, using sheer force of will to lower his voice into a semblance of its normal tone. "I'm glad Judy decided to try for the earlier plane. I'm sorry, Mother, I didn't realize she and Amanda had already left Boston. I didn't mean to alarm you."

"But Dexter, you *have* alarmed me! Two minutes ago you didn't seem to know what I was talking about. Are you sure everything's just as it should be?"

"Of course, everything's fine."

"Dexter, you sound—strange. Promise me nothing's happened to Amanda. Did we do the right thing in allowing her to go with your secretary?"

The vein in Dexter's forehead throbbed, but by some miracle of control he kept his voice steady. "Yes, Mother, please don't worry. You did exactly what I wanted. Liz and I—" He swallowed hard. "Liz and I both felt that Amanda was getting far too upset about our relationship. It seemed better to have her here with us."

"I've never understood this modern obsession with having one's children approve of one's adult relationships." Mrs. Rand spoke with some of her normal tartness, and Dexter's grip on the phone relaxed marginally.

"Mother, I have three separate people making urgent hand signals at me. I must go. Will you and Dad still come down to DC this weekend?"

"Probably not. Just make sure you bring Amanda to stay with us as soon as school's finally out. In fact, we were thinking of taking her on vacation to—"

"Mother, I'm now fielding four sets of hand signals. I'll talk to you and Dad later. Bye now."

He hung up the phone, his face drained of every trace of color. "I couldn't tell her," he said. "She and my father wouldn't understand. They'd think it was just a question of paying the ransom, and I don't believe money is what these kidnappers are after. My parents would want to contact the police, and I know Amanda will die as soon as we do that."

It didn't seem like a good idea to allow Dexter to focus his attention on the frightening unknown of what Amanda's kidnappers planned to do. Liz decided to direct his thoughts to the few areas where they might be able to come up with answers. "Is Judy really your secretary?" she asked.

"Yes, one of them."

"Is she in the office today?"

Dexter blinked, focusing his thoughts on the mundane question with obvious difficulty. "I believe I saw her as we came in."

He depressed a button on his intercom and a pleasant voice answered, "Yes, Senator?"

"Judy, have you ever met my mother? In person, I mean?"

"Why no, Senator. Although we've spoken several times over the phone, when she's been trying to track you down."

"Thank you. And I guess you've never met my father, either?"

"No, Senator. He attended a Christmas party once, but I had the flu and didn't get to meet him."

"Thanks, Judy. By the way, screen all my calls, will you? I only want to take personal ones." Dexter flipped off the intercom and leaned back in his chair. "They knew exactly whose name to use," he said bitterly. "I suppose we have Karen to thank for that."

"They took a big risk, though, didn't they? Assuming your mother wouldn't recognize the difference between the impersonator and the real Judy?"

"Not much of a risk. Judy has a pleasant, medium-pitched voice, and as close to a standard American accent as you can get. How distinctive would that be? She introduces herself as my secretary, produces a note from me—"

"And how did they get that, do you suppose?"

He shrugged. "Easily, if they have access to samples of my writing. Not to mention a supply of stationery probably stolen by Karen. Provided the handwriting was close to mine, it would pass muster. My mother isn't likely to submit the damn note to a graphologist before letting Amanda go."

Something prickled at the back of Liz's mind. *Graphologist*. Why did that word make her uncomfortable? The connection clicked into place. *Pieter Ullmann*. His defense on the blood-doping charges would rest largely on the evidence of a graphologist. Odd that the irrelevant connection should have flashed into her mind at such a tense time.

Dexter's fist crashed onto the desk, sending papers flying. "Damn it, Liz, I can't just sit here waiting! I'll go mad. Why don't they tell me what they want me to do? God knows, I'm willing!"

"Perhaps we should ask one of your secretaries to cancel our appointment with the deputy director of the FBI? Maybe they're waiting to hear that you've obeyed that instruction before they give you the next one."

Dexter closed his eyes for a second. "Thank God you're here, Liz. At least one of us is thinking like a sane human being." He pressed his intercom again. "Judy, please contact the FBI urgently and tell them that I won't be able to keep my appointment with the deputy director at three-thirty this afternoon. Make all the necessary apologies, won't you?"

"Certainly, Senator. Should I give any special reason?"

Dexter's mouth tightened. "You could say an unexpected emergency."

"I'll call right away, Senator."

Liz walked over to the window and stared down at the crowds hurrying toward the Capitol building. The day was warm, and the men had doffed their jackets, while the women mostly wore bright summer dresses, their arms bare to the sun. The beautiful spring day didn't seem a good moment for contemplating the end of life, either her own or Amanda's, but Liz was very much afraid that her death was the next item on someone's agenda. And by canceling her appointment with the deputy director, she had lost her best chance of safety.

In his inevitable concern for his daughter, Dexter didn't seem to have registered the significance of the demand that Liz should remain in the office. She hoped that the kidnappers simply wanted to prevent her from making contact with law enforcement officials. She feared that they wanted to keep tabs on her for some infinitely more gruesome reason.

Far beneath her, a family grouped itself on a flight of marble steps, posing for a picture. Even at this distance, she could see that the two children were prancing around in excitement, and the parents were attempting to keep them still with fond exasperation. Amanda should be prancing like that, Liz thought. Instead, she was probably bound and gagged in a dark room.... Shuddering, she snapped her mind closed on the unbearable images.

She sensed Dexter come up behind her. "Liz, I'm sorry," he said, putting his arms around her waist. "I went to pieces for a while, but I'm back together again now."

She turned in the circle of his arms, and saw that he spoke the truth. His face was still a stark white, but his eyes were sharply focused and fierce with intelligence. His fear for Amanda had been leashed by his habitual iron control.

"No father could hear that his daughter had been kidnapped and carry on as if nothing had happened," she said. "I understood."

"I've only just realized that it was your safety I put at risk by canceling our appointment with the deputy director. I had absolutely no right to ask you to make that sacrifice."

"You didn't ask," she reminded him. "I suggested that you should make the call."

"And I'm truly grateful, Liz." He drew in a deep breath. "If it'll make you feel any better, I think the kidnappers have already made their first mistake."

She looked up eagerly. "What's that?"

"If they hoped that keeping me in suspense would soften me up, they've miscalculated. Badly. My first reaction to that phone call was as a parent. Whatever they'd asked me to do to get back Amanda, I'd have done it. Now I'm reacting with my head as well as my heart. We may not have much time, Liz, so the first thing I want you to do is memorize a phone number." He picked up a pen and scrawled a series of eleven digits across the back of her hand. "That's what you might call a high-powered emergency number," he said. "Dial it anytime, and you can summon pretty much whatever help you need."

"Why don't you call it now and ask for a commando squad to rescue Amanda?"

"They have some highly trained specialists available at the other end of that number, but they're not miracle workers. We have no idea where Amanda is. Where would a commando squad start looking? It's much better if we wait for the next phone call, so that we at least have a chance to find out what's at stake in this hideous game."

She cleared her throat. "Dexter, in view of your position in the Senate... Have you considered...? I mean, what are you going to do if they ask for another top-secret weapons blueprint in exchange for Amanda?"

He was silent for a while. "I'm going to pray a lot," he said at last. "And then try to fool them. I have convincing fakes—blueprints and specifications—for all the systems currently being considered by our committee. Agent Cooper insisted on getting them when we first tried to track down the source of the leak in my office. All the plans and papers have been produced by government experts and should fool anybody except a top-notch weapons specialist. The errors had to be pointed out to me, and I've had a lot of intensive technical training. With luck, I should be able to get Amanda back before her kidnappers realize they've been cheated."

Liz had no idea how realistic Dexter's hopes were, although she derived some reassurance from the knowledge that he was talking about expert fakes, prepared at leisure, not some botched job rushed through in response to the crisis of Amanda's kidnapping. And it wasn't certain, of course, that the kidnappers wanted blueprints. They might yet astonish both Dexter and Liz by demanding a straightforward cash payment.

The phone rang before she could say anything. "A personal call for you on line three," Judy announced. "Do you want to take it, Senator? The caller wouldn't give her name."

Liz and Dexter exchanged glances. *A woman?* Dexter picked up the phone, his deliberate movements showing the strain placed on his control, she thought. "Put her through, please."

"Dexter, darling, this is Jeanette." He recognized the low, husky and stunningly sexy voice immediately. "I wasn't sure whether you were in Denver or DC this weekend. I'm going sailing, and I wondered if you were up for a little rest and recreation."

"I'll have to take a rain check this weekend. But thanks, anyway, Jeanette. I'll look forward to seeing you soon." Dexter hung up the phone.

"I think you just ruined a beautiful friendship," Liz said, trying to lower the level of tension and disappointment. "I'd guess that's the last time Jeanette's going to offer you the full facilities of her boat."

"We're just good friends," Dexter replied impatiently. "Hell, I wish they'd call!"

"Just good friends," Liz repeated, the phrase triggering another memory. This seemed to be her day for making odd connections. "Dexter, do you remember that reporter we met outside the FBI building? In retrospect, does it occur to you that he looked a heck of a lot more like a private detective than an aggressive photojournalist?"

"You may be right, although how a P.I. fits into this—" The phone rang again and he snatched up the receiver.

"A personal call for you on line three, Senator. The caller preferred not to give her name."

Dexter's shoulders slumped. "Put her through," he said wearily.

"Good afternoon, Senator." The voice was crisp, businesslike, and strangely flattened, as if it echoed through some sort of synthesizer. "Please depress the red button on the right of your phone, thus scrambling our conversation and making it impossible to trace."

Dexter pressed the button. "I have done what you asked."

"Please wait a moment, Senator, while I check the accuracy of your statement."

The pause lasted about thirty seconds. "I am delighted to see that you are prepared to cooperate, Senator. It bodes well for our future negotiations."

"I want my daughter back. Where is she?"

"Your daughter is well and reasonably happy, although she misses your company. She will continue to be well if you follow some simple instructions. Please listen carefully, Senator, since I don't plan to repeat this information. Within the next half hour, your office will receive a delivery from the Golden Slipper Boutique. The delivery will be made by an employee of the store and will consist of evening clothes and accessories for Elizabeth Meacham. You will pay cash on delivery for these purchases. We know that you, Senator, keep a spare tuxedo in your office. You and Ms. Meacham will dress for the evening in the clothes I have indicated. At six o'clock, having said a cheerful goodnight to any of your staffers still lingering in the office, you will summon a cab. You and Ms. Meacham will drive directly to the French Embassy, where a reception for the new ambassador from Chad is being given. Your office, I'm sure, received an invitation. You will be contacted again later this evening."

The voice stopped abruptly and was followed by an echoing silence.

"Amanda!" Dexter yelled the name desperately. "Amanda! Let me talk to my daughter!"

The silence of the phone was absolute. Dexter dropped the receiver into the cradle and turned to look at Liz. "I wish they'd let Amanda speak to me." Despite all his efforts, his voice shook.

"Next time they probably will. Dexter, she'll be all right. They need to keep her well, so that they have something to bargain with. The kidnappers know you aren't going to do a deal unless you have proof that she's alive and unharmed." The platitudes seemed unavoidable, even though they were patently false. She wished that Dexter were a little bit less clear-sighted, a little bit better at the art of self-deception. Kneeling beside him, she clasped his hands and pulled them gently against her breasts. "What in the world do all those bizarre instructions mean, do you think?"

Once again her ploy worked. The practical question brought his emotions back under a semblance of control. "Probably no more than a test to see if we're willing to follow their directions."

"And are we? Is it smart to go partying at the French Embassy because some brutal kidnappers told us to?"

"Yes," he said. "It's smart, because it's the only way we're going to get more instructions." His face became remote, harder than ever. "Liz, I wish I could pretend that I'm offering you a choice, but I'm not. I need you at this reception."

"I'm willing to come with you."

He freed his hands from her clasp, so that he could frame her face. His thumbs stroked a gentle caress across her lips. "Liz, I truly believe that you would be more at risk if you tried to contact the police than if you come with me. But my beliefs may not be a reliable guide at the moment. I have tunnel vision, and Amanda is at the end of the tunnel."

"I wouldn't expect it to be any other way."

His expression didn't soften at all. He bent his head and took her mouth in a quick, hard kiss. "I love you, Liz," he said. "I love you like hell."

A tap at the door was followed by the appearance of a young woman's head, poking uncertainly around the corner. "Sorry to interrupt, Senator, but a delivery boy is here from the Golden Slipper Boutique. He says you're expecting him, and that you owe him six hundred and ninety-three dollars."

"I'll be right out," Dexter said. "Thanks, Bobbie."

LIZ EXPERIENCED a definite sense of unreality as she showered in the small bathroom attached to Dexter's office, then dressed herself for the reception. The gown the kidnappers had sent from the Golden Slipper was black, sleek, low cut and elegant. The price tag hanging from the zipper indicated $495 in discreet gold figures. A bargain for some society matrons, perhaps, Liz thought, but for herself, whose clothes usually came from a discount warehouse, there was an undeniable pleasure in the soft swish of heavy silk against the new designer underwear that had come with the gown.

Putting on her makeup, she wondered if French aristocrats on their way to the guillotine had felt something like she did now: a curious mixture of anticipation, defiance and a fear too great to be acknowledged. Why did it seem so important that she should look good for the delectation of a bunch of kidnappers? She could find no answer. But as she twisted the final pin into her long blond hair, she knew that tonight of all nights, she was determined to look her best.

She stepped into high-heeled, diamanté-buckled evening shoes, and pushed her wallet and a few cosmetics into the matching purse also thoughtfully provided by the kid-nappers. A final glance into the mirror revealed a sophis-ticated, attractive woman whom Liz scarcely recognized. With a twinge of sadness, Liz realized that this particular style of dress reminded her of her sister Alison. Alison had loved the dramatic combination of black and silver, choosing the combination for most of her skating outfits.

Liz couldn't allow herself the luxury of such bittersweet, distant memories. At the moment she had more pressing matters to worry about. Like finding Amanda. And keep-ing herself alive.

THE FRENCH EMBASSY was located opposite Georgetown University Hospital. During the cab ride from his office, Dexter tried to warn Liz of what was in store for her but, lacking any experience of the Washington cocktail party circuit, she was still unprepared for the barrage of atten-tion that was directed toward her.

Washington's inner power elite throve on gossip. A scandal involving one of their own provided meat and drink for the endless round of formal functions that had to be endured. A double murder involving a popular senator rated almost a ten on Washington's ecstasy scale.

"The French ambassador ought to send you a personal thank-you note," Liz muttered after a particularly bruis-ing encounter. "You've obviously made his night. Do you think *anyone* remembers this reception is supposed to be in honor of the ambassador from Chad?"

"Nobody," Dexter replied promptly. "Probably not even the ambassador from Chad."

"When do you think we can leave?"

His expression became momentarily bleak. "I don't know. Can you hold out for another half hour?"

She took some champagne from the tray of a passing waiter. "Another glass or two of this, and I might even make forty minutes."

"Miss Meacham, I believe?" The voice was soft, insinuating, and Liz felt the blood freeze in her veins. Somehow she forced herself to turn around and face her questioner.

"I'm Elizabeth Meacham, yes."

The woman was pushing sixty, with teeth and skin yellowed by smoking. "It's a pleasure to welcome you to our nation's capital, Miss Meacham. I'm sure it was wise of you to take a holiday from Colorado. Do you and the senator have any statement you'd like to make for my column?"

Liz expelled her breath in a rush that left her limp. A journalist. The woman was a darned journalist! Liz wasn't sure whether to scream with frustration or laugh with relief. She was still trying to make up her mind when Dexter intervened.

"If I give you an exclusive, Betty, will you go away and leave us in peace?"

The reporter's eyes gleamed. "You betcha."

"Miss Meacham and I recently became engaged and are planning our wedding shortly. There, you owe me one, lady. Coming at this particular time, that announcement is going to make your column the talk of the town tomorrow morning."

"You and Miss Meacham were married before, and the marriage only lasted nine months. Any reason to expect a longer relationship this time?"

"Don't push your luck, Betty. You can say, quote: 'The senator commented that this time he was older and wiser. A hell of a lot older and hopefully a hell of a lot wiser.' End quote." Dexter turned and looked down at Liz, his eyes darkening as if he meant every word he said. "Off the record, our marriage is going to work this time, because we're even more in love. At least, I am."

Although she knew he'd only invented the story in order to get rid of the reporter, Liz's whole body responded to the lie. She felt the heat rise in a deep flush from the pit of her stomach, and her cheeks flamed. With seeming indifference to Betty's avid eyes and flapping ears, Dexter carried Liz's hands to his mouth and dropped the lightest kisses against her knuckles. "You're always beautiful," he said huskily, "but tonight you're positively stunning. I love you, Liz."

Her heart hammered wildly in her chest. When he looked at her like that, she couldn't quite convince herself that this was all a charade. She was so lost in the fantasy world Dexter had created that she jumped when Betty's voice intruded. "Too much sentiment makes me nauseous," she said. "I'll see you two lovebirds later. Like you said, Senator, I owe you one."

They lingered another half hour at the reception, but no one approached them with cryptic messages or whispered instructions. The crowd had thinned to a mere handful of guests when Liz and Dexter finally took their leave.

"Your limousine, monsieur?" the doorman asked.

"We'd like a cab, please," Dexter responded.

The doorman whistled one up, accepting Dexter's tip with the smoothness of vast experience. "Your destination, monsieur? I will tell the driver."

Dexter and Liz exchanged helpless glances. "To my apartment, I guess," he said. "Tell him The Fountains, in Chevy Chase."

"Certainly, monsieur." The cab door was slammed, and Liz leaned back against the tattered leather of the seat, trying to think of something she could say that might make Dexter feel better.

"Perhaps they couldn't approach us because there were too many people around."

"They could have made the opportunity if they'd wanted to. Betty Stone managed to get us alone, and we weren't even cooperating with her."

Liz developed a sudden fascination with the beading of her purse. "Couldn't you think of any other way to be rid of Betty? Is that why you told her we were getting married again?''

"No. I was a low, underhand conniving schemer. I told her we were engaged because I hoped it might—'' He broke off as the cab swerved violently to the right, cresting the sidewalk but continuing to move.

"What the devil?'' Dexter demanded, just as an ambulance with lights flashing and siren howling roared out of the Georgetown hospital driveway and catapulted in front of the cab. The cabdriver braked immediately and swung around in his seat, leveling an extremely menacing gun straight at Liz's head.

"Either of you move and she gets it,'' he said.

The two doors closest to the sidewalk were wrenched open. "He has a gun!'' Liz screamed in warning.

It was all she said. A leather-gloved hand was clamped over her mouth and she was hauled from the cab. For a crucial second she failed to struggle, thinking that her abductor might be intent upon rescuing her from the gun-toting cabbie. In the two seconds it took to realize her mistake, all chance to scream and attract attention had been lost. With one hand still clamped over her mouth, her captor pulled her arms behind her back with brutal efficiency and bundled her face first onto the floor of the ambulance. The driver didn't even wait for the doors to be slammed behind her before he released the brake and set the ambulance shooting forward into the narrow Georgetown street.

The fist pressing her down to the ground relaxed its pressure. "You can sit up now, *dorogoya*.''

She lifted her head, too stunned to move the rest of her body. "Mikhail?'' she whispered. *"Mikhail?''*

He smiled the warm, familiar smile she knew so well. "Hello, Lizushka. Welcome to Washington.''

Chapter Thirteen

He couldn't do a damn thing, because they had him covered by two guns: the cabbie's .45 Magnum and the 9-millimeter Soviet Makarov pistol aimed square between his eyes by the squat, balding man who'd just climbed into the front passenger seat.

Dexter silently cursed his helplessness. Dear God! Now they—whoever they were—had not only Amanda, but Liz, as well! He writhed under the knowledge that he had brought Liz into this danger. He was the one who'd insisted they follow instructions and attend the reception at the embassy. He was the one who'd insisted on canceling their appointment at the FBI.

The sick knot of guilt in Dexter's guts hardened into a bitter determination to frustrate his opponents or die trying. And right at this moment, he reflected grimly, it looked as if he was going to die for sure.

The gunman in the passenger seat steadied his aim with brisk professionalism. Not a good sign. "Good evening, Senator Rand. My name is Igor. It is certainly my pleasure to meet you."

Dexter stared ahead in stony silence.

Igor sighed. "It would help your situation, Senator, if you would cooperate. The driver of this cab is about to put his gun away and resume driving. We do not wish to attract the attention of a cruising police vehicle by remaining parked. You will clasp your hands behind your neck, please. If you do not, you will be shot in the knee.''

Igor meant what he said, Dexter was sure of it, and a broken kneecap would make escape virtually impossible. Without breaking his silence, Dexter did as Igor instructed. He stared out of the front window, not deigning to meet the eyes of either of his captors. With a despairing lurch of his stomach, he saw the ambulance containing Liz hurtle off into the darkness, its emergency beacons flashing. An old trick for hurrying from the scene of a crime, but nonetheless damnably effective, he reflected wryly.

Schooling his features into blankness, Dexter held his hands unmoving behind his neck. He carried no concealed weapons, and therefore cherished no hope of outshooting his captors. Any attempt at escape would have to wait.

Igor gave a curt nod to the cabbie, who returned his .45 to the inside pocket of his jacket and immediately set the cab in motion. Dexter had hoped Igor might try to frisk him, but the man was obviously too seasoned a veteran to attempt something so dangerous. Igor knew—unfortunately—that in the close confines of the cab, it would be easy for Dexter to grab Igor's gun and turn the tables on his attackers.

"We are taking you to a house in the country," Igor announced. His tone of voice suggested that Dexter should be appreciative of this rare treat. "Miss Meacham will be joining us there."

Dexter tried to show no reaction to this piece of news. He willed himself to remain silent, but lost the battle.

"Where's Amanda?" he asked, the words torn from him. "What have you done with my daughter?" By a superhuman effort, he managed to bite back the need to ask anything more about Liz. It might give him some infinitesimal advantage, if Igor and his crew thought him indifferent to Liz's fate.

"Amanda is already at home with her grandparents, Senator Rand. When we arrive at our destination, I will permit you to make a phone call confirming her safety. You may dial the number yourself, so that you will know there are no tricks, and you may ask any questions that come into your head to ensure that she is indeed at home and unharmed."

"How can I believe you? Why would you—?" Dexter cut off his question. Since he expected nothing but lies in answer, he wouldn't demean himself by asking.

"Ah! You wish, perhaps, to know why we have released your daughter? The answer is simple. We took her to demonstrate our power. We have released her as a gesture of goodwill, Senator Rand. We want you to see that cooperating with us is not a difficult business. It was never part of our plan to harm your daughter. We Russians are sentimental about little children."

"May I lower my hands?" Dexter asked curtly. "My arms ache."

Igor curled his finger around the trigger of the gun. "No, Senator Rand. You may not lower your hands."

Dexter leaned back against the seat and stared out of the cab window. He recognized exactly where they were. Ironically, for all the good it would do him, they were driving past Langley, headquarters of the CIA in suburban Virginia. Now that he had time to reflect on his situation, he found the fact that he wasn't blindfolded deeply depressing. He could think of several reasons why his captors wouldn't have bothered with a blindfold. All of them were unpleasant.

The roads were relatively clear of traffic as they drove through Tyson's Corner, but the cabdriver seemed in no hurry, or perhaps he was avoiding the risk of a ticket for speeding. Their journey continued through Reston until, after about an hour, the cab stopped outside a pleasant-looking house in a semirural setting. Dexter recognized the area as one much favored for weekend trysts by Washington's "in" crowd.

Igor's method of removing his prisoner from the cab once again demonstrated his experience. At a nod from Igor, the driver, .45 in hand, pulled Dexter from the cab with sufficient force to send him sprawling on the gravel driveway. With a foot in the small of Dexter's back, the driver expertly searched him for weapons.

"He's clean, boss."

Igor exited from the cab and grunted. "Stand up, if you please, Senator Rand. I would remind you that the more quickly you walk into the house and demonstrate some signs of cooperation, the more quickly you will be permitted to telephone your daughter."

They knew precisely which carrot to dangle in front of his nose, Dexter reflected. Unfortunately, the knowledge that he was being manipulated didn't prevent the ploy from working. At this moment, he wanted to hear Amanda's voice with an intensity that overrode all other considerations.

The cabbie dug the .45 into the base of his spine. Unresisting—not that he could have resisted in any way that would have left him alive, he reflected—Dexter allowed himself to be led up to the front door and into the comfortably furnished living room.

"Sit," Igor commanded.

He sat down on the cream leather sofa the man indicated. Later, he cautioned himself. Later you can try the heroics. "I'm ready to phone my daughter," he said, his tone curt.

Igor smiled, displaying a gold tooth. "I see you are a practical man, Senator, who believes in dealing with first things first. I am glad that my superiors, in selecting you for our purposes, did not underestimate your common sense." Igor gestured with his gun to indicate a phone on the glass-topped coffee table. "Please feel free to call your parents' home, Senator."

Dexter picked up the phone and examined it carefully, pulling off the base and unscrewing the mouthpiece. It looked like standard phone-company issue. He could see no sign that it had been tampered with, and Agent Cooper had recently given him a refresher course in methods of bugging and otherwise distorting normal phone service. Dexter screwed the phone together again.

"I want to dial Information," he said curtly.

"Please, Senator, be my guest. You are welcome to test for yourself that this is simply a normal phone. You do realize, of course, what will happen to your daughter, should you attempt to communicate with anybody we deem... undesirable."

"I want to check that the phone isn't rigged to go through to one certain number, manned by your personnel, whatever digits I dial."

"I repeat, Senator. Feel free."

Dexter called Information in New York, and asked for the number of an old friend from his Air Force academy days. The woman responding sounded bored enough to be the genuine phone-company article. He even heard her gum snap as she connected him to the computer, which provided the correct number.

Feeling more confident that the phone hadn't been rigged, he then dialed his parents' home. His father answered with a crisp "Hello."

"Hi, Dad, this is Dex. Sorry to bother you at this hour, but is Amanda there?"

"Yes, she is, but she's on her way to bed. What in the world's gotten into you, Dexter? Dragging her off to Washington, and then turning around and telling your secretary to bring her back again to us! The poor child's exhausted from all that useless flying."

Dexter gripped the phone and willed himself to stay calm. "Let me talk to Amanda, Dad. And could you save the lectures until tomorrow? One way and another, this has been a helluva day."

"Here's Amanda," Mr. Rand said, his tone still disapproving. "It seems she wants to talk to you."

"Hi, Daddy! Why didn't you come to see me when I was in your secretary's apartment? Judy was pretty nice, but I didn't like being there with her. She told me you were too busy to come and see me."

Dexter drew in a long, shaky breath. "Hello, sweetheart, it's great to hear your voice. I'm sorry we missed each other today. Was Judy—? What did Judy give you for lunch?"

"Hot dogs, and she let me have two slices of chocolate cake." Amanda sounded less than interested in Judy. "Why didn't you come to see me, Dad? Why did I have to fly to Washington if you're too busy to come and see me? I felt sick on the plane coming back to Boston, and my ears popped."

"Judy and I had a bit of a mix-up in our communications, sweetheart. I didn't actually know you'd arrived in Washington. I'll explain to you what happened another time. In fact, I didn't really want you to leave Grandma and Grandpa's house, so if anyone else comes to get you, anyone at all, you just stay put with Gran and Gramps, okay?"

"Okay. When are you coming to see me?"

"I don't know exactly, sweetheart, but soon, very soon."

"I miss you, Dad." A small pause. "Is Ms. Meacham with you?"

"Not at the moment." He needed every ounce of discipline he possessed to keep the urgency from his voice and the panic from his expression. "Amanda, promise me you'll stick close to your grandparents, will you? That's very important."

"Okay. Grandpa and I are going fishing tomorrow. And Grandma says I have to go to bed now. It's eleven o'clock and a ridic—ridikolus hour for me to be up."

"Yes, it is late." Dexter's voice thickened. "Good night, Amanda. I love you lots and lots."

"I love you, too." She yawned. "Good night, Dad. Take care."

"I will," Dexter said, holding the receiver long after his daughter had hung up.

"Satisfied, Senator?" Igor asked. "Your daughter, as you heard, is well and happy."

Dexter played back the conversation in his mind. Amanda's chatter had been entirely natural. If there had been kidnappers in the room, coercing her to reply, Dexter knew he would have heard the fear and constraint in her voice. And his father would have been even less capable of pretending cheerfulness than Amanda. There was no way, he decided, that either of them could have been under any sort of duress. Whatever hideous payment Igor might try to exact in exchange for his generosity, Amanda was temporarily safe.

Dexter shifted his position on the sofa and looked straight into Igor's eyes. "Okay," he said. "My daughter's home with her grandparents, and she hasn't been harmed. What do I have to pay to keep her safe?"

As she pulled herself off the floor of the jolting ambulance, Liz felt no fear. For a crucial few moments, she was aware of nothing save an overwhelming sense of betrayal. "Why, Mikhail?" she asked. "Why are you doing this?"

"Doing what, *dorogoya*?" His warm smile had not changed at all, giving her an unearthly feeling that somehow she must have misunderstood, that somehow she wasn't in danger, that somehow Mikhail was still the same friendly brother-in-law she had known and liked for years.

She shook her head, trying to clear her mind of its dangerous fuzziness. "Mikhail! You've kidnapped me, for God's sake!"

His eyes twinkled in what she now realized was a sickening parody of brotherly teasing. "God, Lizushka, has nothing at all to do with my actions. I follow the orders of my government."

Bile rose in her throat. "Your defection...it wasn't genuine, was it?"

"I am Russian. I will always be Russian. Only you Americans, in your arrogance, would believe that I wished to change my nationality. My defection was a carefully planned move, approved by the leaders of the KGB."

"But why, Mikhail? Why didn't you stay in the Soviet Union? Nobody in America begged you to defect!"

"My government saw an opportunity," Mikhail said. "I willingly took it."

"For your government? The same government that holds your mother hostage—?" Light suddenly dawned in Liz's fuddled brain. "Was that it?" she asked. "Did they promise to get your mother an exit visa if you helped them? Oh Mikhail, you should have known better. They'll never honor their promises, and you'll be in their service forever."

"My mother," he murmured mockingly. "Ah yes, my dear old mother, pining for her exit visa. You are so easy to deceive, Liz, that it almost becomes boring. There is no mother. I haven't seen the woman who bore me since the day she left me on the orphanage steps in Leningrad. What's more, I have no desire to see the old bag, if she still lives. The staff tell me she was an extremely inefficient whore, who was forever getting pregnant. I was the third bastard of hers that the state had to take care of. And who knows how many abortions the workers of Leningrad paid for on her behalf?"

"I thought that the great and glorious Soviet state had abolished whores," Liz said caustically.

"Only high-paid ones," he said. "And with the current political climate, who knows, even the high-priced ones may soon reappear. We like to feel that our motherland has all the amenities of her capitalist rivals."

Despite the fact that the gun in his hand had never once wavered, Liz couldn't bring herself to believe that her images of Mikhail were so totally false. "What about Karen?" she asked. "Was her baby—? Mikhail, was it yours?"

He shrugged. "Probably."

"Did you—kill her?"

"But of course. It was always our plan to compromise Dexter Rand through Karen. Her death was the catalyst designed to set all the other ingredients of our plan bubbling. My dear Liz, please stop bouncing around. You are making the driver nervous. And you know how sensitive I am to other people's nerves."

"On the contrary. It's obvious I know nothing at all about you."

"*Dorogoya*, you have seen me regularly for the last four years."

"Seen you through blinders, I think."

"Not at all. I am the man who enjoys spending Saturday nights drinking vodka and eating caviar with you."

"But you were living a lie, Mikhail!"

"What is truth? Part of me is that man you spent time with in Colorado Springs."

"It's the other parts of you that I'm worried about. What's going on Mikhail? Why have I been kidnapped? How are you hoping to set up Dexter?"

"So you did at least work out that much."

"If you're planing to use me as leverage against Dexter, you're wasting your time."

"Lizushka, I never waste my time. That is how I clawed my way out of the orphanage."

"I would say you've been wasting your time for the past four years. How does it help the Soviet Union to have you train Americans like Pieter Ullmann to become Olympic winners? It was a Russian who got beaten into second place."

Mikhail was silent, and enlightenment dawned. "That was a mistake, wasn't it?" Liz breathed. "Pieter was never supposed to win! You assumed you'd be able to psych him out, to tempt him into breaking training at some crucial point. You didn't realize how rock-bottom determined he was to win the gold."

Mikhail's eyes glittered in the dimness of the ambulance interior, but he said nothing.

"That business about blood doping was all nonsense, wasn't it?" Liz persisted. "Were you so angry with Pieter that you and Karen plotted to get his gold taken away from him?"

"Pieter's been a womanizing fool since he was sixteen!" Mikhail burst out. "How was I to know that where skating is concerned, he is pure dedication and hard work?"

"Two hours watching him on the ice should have given you a hint," Liz taunted. "Maybe you're not quite such an expert judge of character as you think, Mikhail. Your masters can't have been too pleased with you recently. I doubt if they sprang you from the Soviet Union so that you could produce winners for the United States."

Mikhail leaned forward and backhanded her hard across the mouth. She tasted blood, but refused to cry out. He thrust her onto the stretcher bed, propping her against the wall of the ambulance.

"Whatever my mistakes with Pieter, I have read your character well, Lizushka. You share in abundance the two fatal flaws of all Americans: you believe your friends tell you the truth, and you have hope for the future."

"Those aren't flaws, Mikhail, they're strengths."

"You are naive, *dorogoya*. Perhaps it is better so. Perhaps you will be lucky enough to die without suffering the anguish of knowing your death approaches. Even now, even at this moment, I can see that you somehow expect the cavalry to come riding to your rescue. Isn't that how Hollywood promises it will be? In the United States, innocent maidens are never run over by the train."

"If it's naive to believe that good guys win in the end, Mikhail, then I'm proud to be naive. Whatever you're plotting against Dexter Rand, it isn't going to work out."

"There is one small flaw in your reasoning, Lizushka. I believe *I* am the good guy and that my cause is just. I also know that the plan we have for subjugating the senator to our will is foolproof. Dexter Rand will be our man by the end of this night, take my word for it."

"You're wrong!"

"We shall see, Lizushka. Now, we are nearly at our destination and I say only this. Prepare yourself for a shock, little sister. I think you will find that we have a most amusing surprise awaiting you."

When they let her out of the ambulance, Liz saw that they were in the driveway of a typical two-story, upper-income suburban house. Whether they had driven into Maryland or Virginia, she had no idea. Of Dexter there was no sign.

Mikhail had bound her wrists together with surgical strapping tape, and he held his hand tightly over her mouth as they walked up the gravel path to the house. His gun poked into the small of her back, so she didn't even consider screaming, but some absurd, lingering hope of rescue caused her to sneak surreptitious glances to the left and right as she was propelled toward the back door.

There were other houses in the neighborhood, she saw, although they were relatively far away and screened behind trees and bushes. But even if she could somehow make a break for it, she knew she couldn't assume those houses represented safety. The chances were good that they contained enemies rather than friends. Mikhail said something in Russian to the ambulance driver, a young man shaped like a gorilla, carrying a submachine gun that seemed to grow like an extension from his right arm.

Sandwiched between the two men, Liz was taken in through a back door and conducted down a brightly lighted staircase to the basement. Liz barely had time to register that it was furnished in typical suburban style—complete with a Ping-Pong table in the center of the large room—before Mikhail bent forward and murmured in her ear.

"The moment has arrived," he said softly. "There is somebody who has been waiting most anxiously to see you, *dorogoya*."

Liz's heart pounded with sudden, suffocating force and her lungs felt squeezed tight by lack of air. "Who is it?" she asked. "Who wants to see me?"

A rustle of silk whispered behind a Victorian-style screen in the far corner of the room, and Liz's head jerked in that direction, like a puppet's pulled by a string. A slender, fair-haired woman, wearing a scarlet silk robe and a pair of high-heeled black shoes identical to Liz's own, stepped out from behind the screen. Her blue-gray eyes were fringed by long lashes, and her naturally pink lips formed a striking contrast with her pale, almost translucent, complexion.

The pounding of Liz's heart intensified. She felt giddy, nauseous, disoriented. The fear she had held at bay for so long rose up in her throat and emerged in a single giant scream. She gazed at the woman in hypnotized horror. Except for the red silk robe, she was looking at a mirror image of herself.

At the sound of Liz's scream, Mikhail clapped his hand back over her mouth with bruising force, but the woman merely smiled—a cruel, mocking smile that held no hint of sympathy.

"Hello, Lizzie," she said. "It's been a long time, babe."

Chapter Fourteen

The nausea wouldn't go away, neither would the dizzying sense of unreality. Liz clutched at her stomach. "Alison?" she whispered. *"Alison?"*

The woman smiled. "That's who I am, sweetie. Although not for long."

"Wh-what have you done to your hair? And your nose is different." Liz realized belatedly that she was hardly addressing the major issue. "I thought . . . we all thought you were dead."

"You were intended to, sweetie."

"But how could you let us all believe you'd been killed? Good God, Alison, Mom had a stroke when she heard about the plane crash! She's been a helpless invalid ever since, and all over something that never really happened!"

A faint trace of color stained Alison's cheekbones. "Mother had high blood pressure for years, so she was probably headed for a stroke anyway, whatever happened. Besides, she isn't miserable. How can she be, when she doesn't know what's going on? And the Soviet government helps to pay for the best nursing care. I'll bet she's happier than half the people who haven't had a stroke."

Liz stared at her sister in stupefied silence. Alison, she realized in wonderment, truly believed what she was saying. Even as a child, Alison had always been capable of twisting the truth to fit her own personal needs. Apparently that character trait hadn't altered. Liz clenched her fists in an effort to keep herself from screaming.

"What's going on?" she asked tightly. "Why have you suddenly decided to come back from the dead? And why have you changed your hair and your nose to look like me?"

"That, sweetie, should be obvious even to you. Alison Kerachev isn't coming back from the dead. Elizabeth Meacham is merely going to be played by a different person."

"I see." Liz, in fact, saw a hell of a lot more than she wanted to. Like the fact that she was shortly going to be dead. Two Elizabeth Meachams obviously wouldn't fit into anybody's scheme of things. She swung around and sought out Mikhail, who was viewing the encounter from a corner of the room, an amused, proprietary smile flashing occasionally as he looked from one newly identical sister to the other.

"Somebody's gone to a lot of trouble to change Alison's appearance," Liz said. "We both know your government doesn't spend money just to keep its citizens happy, so what's going on, Mikhail?"

"You will know in good time, *dorogoya*."

"Don't call me that!" The endearment lacerated Liz's nerves, and she struggled to regain control of herself. "Something important's at stake here, that much is clear. It must have taken months of surgery and a great deal of money to make so many changes in the way Alison looks."

Alison strolled over to link her arm through Mikhail's. "There wasn't that much to change, sweetie. We weren't identical twins, you and I, but the plastic surgeons tell me our bone structure is remarkably similar. I had to have my nose bobbed, and they did a bit of work on my jaw, which was damn painful and definitely isn't an improvement. I have to tint my hair, because yours has more red in it than mine, but that's easy enough to do, except for the fact that I hate the color. Fortunately our eyes have always been amazingly alike, and they're the most difficult feature to change."

Liz's gaze traveled over her sister's body. "You're thinner. At least in most places."

Alison grinned mockingly, running her hands over her breasts. "You like my new boobs, sweetie? Best quality silicone implants, courtesy of the toiling Soviet masses." She jiggled her bosom with evident satisfaction. "Yes, these almost make up for all the months I spent on a starvation diet, trying to keep pace with your weight loss. Every time Mikhail sent us a new picture and a new set of statistics, you'd lost another couple of pounds and another few inches. What the hell's been going on in your life?"

"My roommates were getting murdered," Liz said dryly. "I have this weird aversion to coming home and finding my friends splattered over the sidewalk. If affects my appetite."

Alison shrugged. "They weren't friends, only acquaintances. Besides, you're so damned stars-and-stripes patriotic, you ought to be glad they're dead. They were all spying for the Soviet Union. Karen didn't even exist except as a creation of the KGB. She was smuggled into the country two years ago, direct from her Siberian training camp."

Liz didn't dispute her sister's statements. There seemed little point. Alison's definitions of patriotism and friendship seemed to have nothing in common with Liz's. "I'm a market-research specialist with a medium-sized Mexican-food company," she said. "What interest could the Soviet government possibly have in me? Why in the world would they spend all this money to replace a junior manager at Peperito's?"

"Nobody cares about your job at Peperito's," Mikhail said curtly. "We are replacing you in your role as the former wife of Dexter Rand. It is the illustrious senator who interests our government."

For a few moments, Liz was shocked enough to forget to be frightened. "You think Dexter won't notice the substitution?" she asked incredulously. "He'll know Alison isn't me, the second she walks into the room."

Alison glanced toward her husband. "I do hope she isn't correct, sweetie."

Tight-lipped, Mikhail replied. "It's unfortunate that your sister has spent so much time with the senator over the past week. Our plans required her to be thrown again into his orbit, which is why she was persuaded to share an apartment with Karen Zeit. However, we didn't anticipate—"

"We?" Alison queried softly.

"I didn't anticipate such an occurrence," Mikhail admitted, scowling at his wife. "Based on your information and the many conversations Liz had with me, it seemed her hatred for Dexter was too great to be overcome, whatever the circumstance. Even so, I am sure he will not detect the substitution."

"And if he does?" Alison persisted.

"In the last resort it doesn't matter—provided the realization doesn't come for a week or two. You know as well as I do that the senator will be forced to comply with our wishes, if he wants to remain alive. Our plan is foolproof."

"But you already kidnapped Amanda!" Liz said. "If the KGB want to force Dexter to do something—anything— you have the perfect method of control!"

"Not at all, sweetie." Alison turned away from a narrow wall mirror where she had been admiring her silhouette. "Kidnapping Amanda gives us only limited control. Either we return her and so lose our hold over Dexter, or we kill her. In which case, once again we have no hold over Dexter. Taking Amanda was nothing more than a device for getting the two of you to the French Embassy, and keeping you away from the FBI."

"You would kidnap a child just to get Dexter and me to the French Embassy?"

"Of course. Why not?"

"Why is Dexter so important to you?" she asked Mikhail. "There must be at least twenty or thirty senators with more political clout than him."

Alison smiled pityingly. "Shall I give her a lesson in world politics, Mikhail?"

"If you wish. Although time marches on, and I see no necessity for explanations."

"That's your Russian background, sweetie. You never think the toiling masses need to know anything. Personally, I'm all in favor of freedom of information."

Mikhail laughed bitterly. "You're not in favor of anything unless it puts power or money into your pocket."

"Are you complaining, sweetie? I've directed quite a lot of those useful commodities your way since we were married, so I suggest you shut up." Alison bestowed a mocking kiss on Mikhail's cheek and walked without haste across the rec room.

She stopped when a few inches still separated her from Liz. For the first time in years, the two sisters were within touching distance. Liz's heart constricted painfully as she looked into her sister's blue-gray eyes and read there the certainty of her own death. The pain wasn't only for her imminent end. She wanted to live—desperately—but at this moment her most profound regret was that Alison could so readily conspire to abet her own sister's murder.

"Why?" Liz asked. "Why are you doing this, Alison? What did I or anyone in our family ever do to make you so full of hate for us?"

Alison gave an odd, defiant little shrug. "How could you understand? You have no idea what it's like to be constantly second best. The apple of Daddy's eye, as long as Lizzie wasn't around to enchant him. Pretty, but not quite as pretty as Lizzie. Smart, but not quite as smart as good old Lizzie. A world-class skater, but not quite as good as the ethereal, passionate Lizzie.''

"You're wrong, Alison. Our parents never measured out their love according to how worthy we were. They loved us because we were their children, not because we were pretty or smart, or because we won medals for skating."

Alison totally ignored Liz's remarks. "For a while, I could train harder and win more competitions than you," she said. "But eventually your natural talent showed through. You won the U.S. championship, I bombed out. Then I barely made it into the first round of the Olympics, whereas you were expected to win. And then, to crown it all, there was Dexter—"

"Dexter? What on earth has he got to do with our relationship? You'd fallen in love with Mikhail long before I even knew Dexter."

Alison's mouth twisted into a thin, bitter line. "You never realized how I felt about Dexter, did you? I met him when we first went over to Germany, weeks before you even heard his name. The only snag was, I couldn't get him interested in me, however hard I tried. Finally I persuaded him to come to the rink and watch me skate. Only you were already out on the ice practicing when we arrived. I remember the music that was playing. It was Ravel's *Bolero*, and you were going through a routine that was so erotic that even the cleaners had stopped to watch. So what happened? The same damned thing that always happened to me when you were around. He forgot about me. Dexter saw you and stopped dead in his tracks. The music ended. You looked up. You opened your innocent little eyes wide, smiled your cute, naive little smile, and two minutes later he was at your side, asking you out to dinner."

"Alison, you know my marriage to Dexter was nothing to envy! It was already broken past repair by the time you married Mikhail and left for Moscow."

"And I worked damned hard at breaking it, sweetie. With a little help from Susan, who was almost as naive and gullible as you in her own way."

Liz felt her confused emotions coalesce into a hard ball of pride. She lifted her head. "No, Alison. You didn't destroy my marriage to Dex. You didn't have that power. Nobody has the power to destroy a marriage except the couple themselves."

"Well, if you say so, sweetie, but I sure think I helped things along a little. And now I'm going to have the power to do a whole bunch of exciting things where Dexter's concerned. You see, Lizzie, I'm going to make sure that Dexter's votes in the Senate, all go the way the Soviet government wants them to go."

"You're crazy!" Liz breathed. "Even if Dexter thought you were me, he wouldn't vote according to my instructions. Don't you understand anything at all about his character?"

"Sweetie, I know everything about Dexter Rand. As soon as he became a senator, the KGB started to compile a dossier on him. Right from the first, he was targeted as the senator they most wanted to neutralize."

"But why?" All Liz's frustration and bewilderment sounded in her question. "I would have thought the KGB had much bigger problems to worry about than the junior senator from an underpopulated state like Colorado."

"You still don't understand, do you, Lizzie? It's Dexter's expertise in weapons technology that's so worrying. Not only is his vote always technically sound, but other senators recognize his mastery of military hardware and follow his lead. Since Dexter took over the Appropriations Committee, Congress hasn't funded a single useless weapons system, and Dexter's managed to swing financial

218 *Free Fall*

backing for three breakthrough defensive systems that would never have left the drawing board if not for his support,"

So that was it, Liz thought, recognizing the ring of truth in her sister's voice. It was Dexter's years of practical experience in the Air Force, coupled with his outstanding technological training, that made him so dangerous as a senator—and such a valuable target for the KGB. "I still don't see where you come into this, Alison. Do your spy masters plan to have you curl up beside him in bed and seduce him into voting your way? 'Darling Dexter, I love you so much, please vote no on the Phantom X-32 jet fighter aircraft?' Even the KGB can't be dumb enough to think that would work."

Mikhail stepped forward. "Enough," he said. "There is no reason for this conversation to continue. Take off your clothes, Liz. Your sister needs to wear them."

Liz sat down. "Go to hell, Mikhail."

She had known resistance would be useless, but she was tired of surrendering so tamely to her own inevitable destruction. When Mikhail dragged her back onto her feet, she kicked him hard on the shins. His response was a swift, brutal punch to the ribs that knocked the air out of her lungs. As a skater, she had fallen often enough to be quite familiar with physical pain, but she couldn't control her instinctive gag reflex, and for several seconds she fought to draw every breath. When she opened her eyes again, the driver from the ambulance was holding her hands immobile in front of her, and Mikhail was unzipping her gown at the back.

Mikhail gave another Russian command to the driver, who at long last put down his submachine gun. Silently he found the end of the strapping tape and ripped it off Liz's wrist, so that Mikhail could take off the black gown. Once her wrists were free, she struggled to resist being undressed, but achieved nothing except to slow down the process slightly and to receive several stinging slaps from Mikhail and the ambulance driver.

Alison lit a cigarette and puffed on it nervously as Liz's slip was removed and handed to her. Still smoking, she shrugged out of the red silk robe and into the long black slip.

"The damn thing's too tight," she muttered around her cigarette. "Hell, Mikhail, she lost even more weight."

"I think not. Calm down, Allie. You chose the outfit in the first place, remember? You wear the same size as Liz in everything except for the shoes, and you're already wearing the identical pair of shoes." He smoothed the slip over his wife's hips and handed her the dress. "Perfect," he said, closing the zipper.

"She's split the damn seams. Dexter'll notice for sure if he touches me. Why did you let her wriggle around like a stuck pig in a thunderstorm?"

"Split seams are no problem. The senator will expect Liz to have struggled. Here, take her purse. There is makeup inside, and a perfume spray. Do you want me to hold her face still so that you can copy her exact style of makeup?"

Alison grimaced. "Just the eyes. I don't want to go upstairs wearing fresh lipstick and powder."

Liz shivered and bent to pick up her sister's robe. The very thought of being touched by Mikhail—or Alison—made her physically ill. The ambulance driver gestured menacingly with his gun, which he'd picked up again, but he didn't prevent her from slipping into the robe. It smelled of cigarette smoke and Alison's perfume, but Liz felt marginally less vulnerable when Mikhail and his sidekick weren't staring straight at her bra and stockings. Mikhail waited for her to tie the belt, then caught hold of her face and turned it toward Alison. Liz closed her eyes, willing the nausea to go away.

"Very good," Mikhail said softly. "With eyes shut it is easier for Allie to copy your eye shadow."

Liz didn't struggle. When Mikhail finally released her, she turned one final time to look at her sister—the sister who was now a mirror-perfect image of herself. She knew that at any moment she would start to feel fear, but right now, all she felt was anger and sick revulsion, mingled with shame that a member of her own family could contemplate such treachery.

"Alison, don't do this," she pleaded. "Don't betray your own country."

Alison didn't reply at once, and Mikhail jumped in. "Russia is Alison's country now," he said. "Russia has given her power and wealth and a useful task to perform. She owes no loyalty to America, merely because an accident of birth decreed that she would be born here."

"She wasn't just born here. She spent the first nineteen years of her life benefiting from the opportunities that America provid—"

"Try not to sound like such a naive fool, Lizzie, dearest." Alison stubbed out her cigarette. "I'll see you around, little sister. Your ex-husband is upstairs, and I don't want to keep him waiting."

IGOR'S SMILE showed no sign of strain. Positively exuding cordiality, he chuckled at Dexter's grim question. "You are required to pay nothing, Senator Rand. We ask merely for a little cooperation."

"Kidnapping Amanda and abducting Elizabeth Meacham at gunpoint isn't likely to inspire me with feelings of goodwill."

"But Senator, how can you be so unreasonable? Amanda is safely at home with her grandparents. And, as a further gesture of our extreme benevolence, I have somebody else waiting to see you. She comes now." Igor clicked his fingers to the cabdriver, who walked over to the door and pulled it open.

"Dexter!"

At the heartrending cry, he stood up and turned around, just in time to see Liz being half dragged, half carried into the living room. Her arms were held by two men: the cabbie, and another man whom Dexter vaguely recognized but couldn't quite place.

Fighting down his immediate, instinctive impulse to rush to Liz's side, Dexter struggled to remain in control of his reflexes. If he kept his cool, there was a slight chance he might be able to find some weakness in Igor's position that would enable him to bargain for Liz's safety. But if he once allowed himself to start reacting emotionally, it would be all over. Except in the movies, unarmed combat provided no defense against three expert gunmen. If he gave in to his emotions and started throwing punches, he might—with luck—win Liz twenty seconds of freedom before the bullets exploded in her body.

Liz was obviously not doing too well. *Poor kid,* he thought. He could hear the choked little sounds emerging from her throat as she bravely attempted to silence her sobs, and when her two captors finally released her arms, she ran across the room and collapsed helplessly against his chest, repeating his name in an endless, desperate litany.

Overwhelmed by a primitive masculine urge to hold her tight and pour out meaningless words of love and comfort, Dexter strained to remain alert and rational. He couldn't afford to let Igor guess how desperate he felt about Liz. Dexter knew Igor's type of old, and he had no doubt that the man was capable of ordering Liz's fingernails pulled out one by one if that seemed the quickest or surest way to manipulate him. Willing Liz to understand his coldness, he brushed a hand over her hair in a friendly, but somewhat impersonal gesture of reassurance. He tried to imagine how his father would behave with an over-wrought, but distant, relative and modeled his own behaviour accordingly.

"Liz, my dear, you must calm down. Hysterics aren't going to help anybody." *That was it,* he told himself on an inner sigh of relief. Just the right mixture of mild affection, tolerance and exasperation. About a hundred light-years away from what he was really feeling.

"Oh Dex, I'm so frightened!"

Her words were little more than a squeak of panic, and something deep within him stiffened in surprise. Why was Liz behaving like this? Of all the women in the world, she was surely the one least likely to crumple into his arms and reveal her fears. He would have expected her to come into the room fighting and spitting out defiance to her captors. What the devil had they been doing to her to provoke such an atypical response?

With gentle hands he pried her away from his chest, so that he could look at her more closely. "What's happened?" he asked softly. "Are you hurt?"

"They hit me," she whispered.

Alarm prickled down Dexter's spine. The antennae that had so often warned him of danger in his fighter-pilot days quivered into alertness. Why was Igor allowing Liz to sob out her ill-treatment in his arms? Why did he have this odd sensation of breathless expectancy—as if everybody in the room were waiting for him to show some reaction to this encounter with Liz?

To buy himself some time, he drew her back into his arms and dropped a light kiss on her forehead before reaching up to stroke her hair again. To his surprise, she wriggled within his clasp and turned up her mouth, asking for a kiss.

It was an invitation even Superman could not have found the strength to refuse. Dexter bent his head and touched his lips to Liz's soft, delicate mouth. She clung to him, her lips parting eagerly, her tongue seeking his. He responded automatically, his mind reeling, waiting for the flame—the inevitable, mind-blowing flame—that always burst into life when he and Liz exchanged kisses. Nothing. His body didn't harden, his pulse didn't quicken. Nothing.

Dexter slowly raised his head from the kiss, breathing deeply, and simultaneously casting a quick, surreptitious glance around the room. He became aware of three things: Liz smelled of cigarette smoke and a heavy, unfamiliar perfume: Igor was looking like a cat who'd swallowed the cream and the canary; and the man who had dragged Liz into the room two minutes earlier was Mikhail Kerachev.

Mikhail Kerachev. Alison's husband. Alison, who was dead. Liz's brother-in-law.

Dexter rapidly concluded that he would stake his life on the fact that the woman in his arms was not Liz.

Chapter Fifteen

Mikhail pulled roughly at the woman in Dexter's arms, dragging her away with such force that she tumbled to the floor with a bone-jarring crunch. Dexter had trained enough men in unarmed combat to know that Mikhail's roughness hadn't been faked. Looking down at the whimpering woman, he realized he was in the bizarre position of having to pretend concern for her well-being, when every atom in his body was screaming with concern for the real Liz.

He knelt beside the woman, wondering what subtle signals he had picked up to warm him so quickly that she was a fake. A ringer for Liz, maybe, but definitely not the real thing. He examined her covertly for telltale differences. He'd be damned if he could spot any, except perhaps for the eyes. The blue-gray shade was identical to Liz's. The sweeping lashes had the same upward curve and thickness, the eyebrows the same delicate arch. But the mind and soul looking out from the window of these eyes bore no relationship to Liz's passionate, generous nature. This woman was calculating every tear and every whimper—and as far as Dexter was concerned, her calculation showed.

"Liz, my dear, come and sit on the sofa." Turning to Igor, he spoke stiffly, as he would have done if he'd really felt compelled to ask for a favor on Liz's behalf. "She needs water. And can you instruct your minions to behave with a little less brutality?''

"But certainly. Comrade Mikhail, you have heard the senator. Please refrain from exercising your temper on his ladylove."

"She is not my ladylove," Dexter said swiftly. *Too swiftly?* he wondered. He tried once again to adjust his voice to the controlled, strained tones he would have used if Liz had really been curled at his side, nursing her bruises. "If you think I have any special feelings for Liz, you're wrong. She is merely my former wife. You of all people should know that any relationship between us ceased to exist long ago. We hadn't seen one another in nine years until you precipitated our reunion by killing Karen Zeit."

"The reality of your relationship with Ms. Meacham is of little interest to us, Senator Rand. As is so often the case, truth is irrelevant. The appearance of truth is all that concerns us."

"Is that what this is all about?" Dexter asked. "Is there some specific lie you're expecting me to palm off as truth?"

"Such a quick wit," Igor murmured admiringly. "We shall deal well together, Comrade Senator."

"That seems unlikely. And I am not your comrade."

"Not yet, Senator. But wait. You have not heard the terms of my proposition. I hope you will agree they are heavily weighted in your favor—given the circumstances in which you find yourself."

"Just state your terms," Dexter said wearily.

"You will change your *Yea* vote on the F-19B fighter aircraft to a *Nay*. Furthermore, you will campaign actively against the plane in the Senate and in the United States as a whole. The vote is already skintight because—fortunately—most people do not have your expertise in military matters. If you switch your vote and speak against the project, the F-19B will not go into production."

"Which will be very convenient for your government," Dexter said softly. "That plane is the best airborne defensive weapon ever to leave the drawing board."

"Indeed. I acknowledge the truth of your statement. In return for this considerable favor, you, Senator, will be allowed to live. In fact, you will be allowed to live precisely as before, with perfect freedom to vote as you please on most other Senate issues."

"Most other issues?" Dexter queried cynically. "Just how many times will I be required to sell my vote in exchange for my so-called freedom?"

Igor smiled tightly. "Only on military matters, Senator. Whenever a vote comes before your Defense Appropriations Committee, you will wait for instructions as to how you are to cast your vote. Otherwise, feel free to follow the dictates of your conscience."

"How generous you and your government are."

"Indeed, I am glad you appreciate our generosity. Do you agree to our terms, Senator Rand?"

"Yes," Dexter said instantly. "I agree."

The woman seated next to him on the sofa drew in a sharp breath, but Igor simply laughed. "Now, now, Senator. We are not fools, and I must tell you that your prompt agreement fails to carry conviction. As a responsible representative of my government, I have to ensure that you do not pretend to agree with us merely to buy your freedom."

Dexter's body tensed. "We should speak bluntly, Igor. I'll tell you frankly that I don't see any way you can force my cooperation, if you allow me to leave here alive."

"You are wrong, Senator. We have a guaranteed method of ensuring your cooperation. Quite simply, Ms. Meacham will die if you do not vote as we have requested. What is more to the point, you will be accused of her murder."

"Dexter, don't let them kill me!" The woman on the sofa clung to his arm, sobbing pitifully.

If anything at all had been needed to clinch Dexter's conviction that this woman was not Liz, her hysterical reaction was it. Careful to conceal his disgust, he bent over her, whispering false words of consolation and encouragement. When he straightened again, he looked at Igor with a scorn he had no need to fake. "If I vote in favor of funding the F-19B, killing Elizabeth Meacham won't change anything. The plane will still go into production, whether or not I'm accused of her murder. True, I'll have to bear the weight of Liz's death on my conscience, but the aims of your government won't be advanced by one millimeter."

"Alas, Senator, it seems that you gravely underestimate the wisdom of our planning. The circumstances of your trial will seal the fate of the F-19B."

"Even if I am found guilty, how does that invalidate my vote on a piece of military hardware?"

Igor's laugh was triumphant. "Because the FBI and the CIA in a rare moment of cooperation will uncover documentary evidence proving that Ms. Meacham is a Soviet spy, and that she has been working in collusion for many years with her friend Karen Zeit and her brother-in-law Comrade Mikhail Kerachev. We plan to take a series of most compromising photographs tonight, featuring you and Ms. Meacham. This house is already known to the FBI as a trysting place for personnel of the Soviet Embassy. We will have all the documents we need to make it appear that Ms. Meacham has blackmailed you successfully for some months."

"How can you hope to prove that, when it's totally untrue?"

Mikhail walked across the room to stand beside Igor. "In several interesting ways, Senator. For example, the military blueprints missing from your office. The FBI has been searching for some weeks without success to find the culprit. We have proof that you yourself were the person responsible for their theft."

"Karen Zeit stole those documents, I'll stake my life on it."

Mikhail smiled. "The evidence shows otherwise, Senator."

"What's more," Igor interjected smoothly, "the evidence also shows that Elizabeth Meacham coerced your favorable vote on the F-19B and that you then murdered her in desperation to escape from the toils of her blackmail. Tell me, Senator, do you doubt, in such circumstances, that the Senate will reconsider its vote on the new aircraft? I think we can safely guarantee that the Senate will eventually vote against the plane. The only question for you to decide is whether they vote against it before or after Ms. Meacham is killed and you are accused of her murder."

Dexter bought himself time to think by comforting the woman who was once again huddled in his arms. Her capacity for producing crocodile tears was truly remarkable, he reflected. He'd only ever known two women capable of turning on a flood of tears at whim. One was a famous movie actress, now gray-haired and over fifty. The other had been Liz's sister Alison. If Alison hadn't been reported as dead, he would be suspecting... In fact, he was suspecting...

With falsely tender hands, Dexter framed the woman's face and used his thumbs to brush away her tears. The blue-gray eyes stared up at him with barely concealed calculation. *Yes,* he thought grimly. Plane crash or no plane crash, the woman he held in his arms was undoubtedly Alison. Even after nine years, he'd recognize that look of mingled sexual invitation and cold self-interest anywhere.

Igor gave one of his characteristic grunts. "I await your answer with interest, Senator."

Dexter forced himself to stroke his hand soothingly down Alison's back, while his brain raced at a feverish pace, weighing options and calculating odds. "Don't worry, darling, I'll get us out of this mess somehow," he whispered. "You can trust me."

"Oh Dexter, darling, please save me!"

Her lines had a distinctly hackneyed ring to them, Dexter decided cynically. Obviously exile in Moscow hadn't prevented Alison from watching the current crop of corny American TV shows. He nuzzled her hair. "We'll find some way to escape," he murmured. "You'll see, dearest."

Alison gave a pretty little sigh that ended on a delicate little sob. "Oh Dexter, you're so brave."

Barely concealing his distaste as she insinuated her fingers between the pearl studs of his evening shirt and stroked his chest, Dexter looked up at Igor. "If I promise to vote as you wish on the F-19B, how do I know Liz will be safe? How do I know you won't kill her as soon as I walk out of here?"

Igor seemed to recognize the first hint of real concession in Dexter's attitude, and couldn't quite conceal the triumphant twitch of muscles in his cheek. The outcome of this elaborate plot had perhaps not been as certain in his own mind as he liked to pretend.

"Senator Rand, how many times do I have to repeat that we are all of us here men of goodwill? Ms. Meacham will be safe, for the simple reason that we wish for your continued cooperation in halting the insane arms race between our two countries. You are a man of peace. My government is a government of peace. In working with us, you will make the world a better place for everybody. Your vote against the F-19B is valuable to us, yes, but it is nowhere near as valuable to us as a continuing voice in the Senate that reliably reflects our views."

That was undoubtedly true, Dexter reflected. A senator whose vote could be counted on in all matters related to the defense and the military would be a tremendous asset to the Soviet government. But he didn't want to seem to compromise too early, even though he was almost eaten up with the desire to get out of the house so that he could initiate a search for Liz. God damn it, he'd call out the whole U.S. Army if need be, but he'd find her!

Dexter removed Alison's straying fingers from inside his shirt, and kissed her knuckles with what he hoped was a reasonable facsimile of tender sorrow. Still holding Alison's hands, he turned again to the Russian. "Somehow, Igor, your goodwill doesn't strike me as a very reliable form of protection for my ex-wife."

"Senator, our government wishes you to be happy. We don't wish to kill Ms. Meacham unless your actions make her death absolutely necessary. Indeed, we hope that one day soon we may read in the newspapers that Washington society has turned out in force to dance at your wedding to Ms. Meacham."

His wedding to Liz! Like a drumroll underscoring the moment of revelation, Dexter heard the thunderous beat of his heart. Igor, he was sure, had unwittingly revealed the purpose behind the substitution of Alison for Liz. They wanted him to marry her! If Alison became Mrs. Dexter Rand, the KGB would have pulled off the enormous coup of planting one of their agents in the innermost circles of Washington power.

Resisting the impulse to punch her squarely in the jaw, he gazed down at Alison. Soulfully she gazed back up, the picture of suffering womanhood. Her role was obviously to play the terrified victim to the hilt, so that Dexter would be convinced that "Liz's" life was in danger and would comply with Igor's demands.

It was symptomatic of the limitations of KGB planning, Dexter thought, that they could seriously believe he wouldn't detect the substitution of Alison for Liz. Although, looking at the perfect duplicate the KGB had created, he was forced to admit that a month earlier he might have been deceived. If Liz hadn't come to him the night of Karen's death . . . if their old attraction hadn't instantly flared…if they hadn't spent long hours making love until every cell of her body seemed imprinted on his soul…

But none of that helped one goddamned bit with his major problem, which was how to get out of here in time to rescue Liz. If he could convince Igor that he was safely "turned," there was a chance that Liz could be saved. Dexter wouldn't allow himself to calculate just how slim the odds of saving the real Liz actually were. Some calculations were better not made, if he wanted to preserve his sanity.

Why the blazes didn't Alison stop sniffling? Didn't she understand anything about the way her twin would behave? "Hush, sweetheart," he murmured. "We'll find a way to come out of this in one piece, I promise you."

She lifted her face, eyes glistening jewellike with tears. How the hell did she cry so much without smudging her mascara? he wondered.

"Oh Dexter, how can you save me? You'll never vote against your conscience, I know you won't. You're not that kind of a man, or I wouldn't love you."

The urge to sock her one was getting stronger by the moment. "The F-19B is just a plane," he said, gritting his teeth. "I place more value on human life than on a weapons system. Especially your life, Liz."

Would that do it? he asked himself. Acting wasn't one of his major skills. Did he sound convincingly like a man preparing to compromise his lifelong beliefs to save the woman he loved? He glared at Igor. "But don't think I'm going to vote the way you tell me ever again!" The last wriggle of a man in a noose. Had he pitched his voice more or less right?

Igor grunted with satisfaction, but Mikhail looked uneasy. He muttered something in Russian to Igor, who dismissed his comment with a curt reply and an impatient wave of the hand. Mikhail was obviously more worried than his boss about Dexter's relatively swift surrender.

Dexter decided it might be smart to voice a few more doubts.

"I'm still not sure you'll keep Liz safe," he said, draping an arm around Alison's shoulder. "I think you may be stringing me along. What's going to happen to Mikhail, for example? According to your scheme, he's going to be identified as a spy if I don't vote the way you want. Does that mean Mikhail's volunteering to spend the rest of his life in an American jail? That seems unlikely."

"Very unlikely," Mikhail agreed. "But it won't happen, Senator. I leave tomorrow—" He glanced at his watch and corrected himself. "I leave today for Stockholm, and from there I fly immediately to Moscow. My time of exile in America is over. I shall soon be back among my own people, training Russian skaters for the next Olympics."

Igor spoke. "You see, Comrade Senator, we have thought of everything. So may we have your agreement that you will vote *Nay* on the F-19B fighter project?"

Dexter allowed his temper to snap. "Yes, you have my agreement, damn it! You've left me no choice. And I've told you before, I'm not your blasted comrade!"

Igor smiled. Very gently. "But Senator, that is exactly what you have just become."

He crossed to the sofa and hauled Alison roughly to her feet. "And now, Comrade Senator, we come to the most interesting part of the evening. The photographs. Would you start undressing your former wife, please?"

THE AMBULANCE DRIVER turned guard looked bored out of his mind but attentive. Gun clasped firmly in hand, he had stationed himself midway between the chair Liz was tied to and the stairs leading out of the basement. Liz had needed about two and a half seconds to decide that appealing to his better nature was unlikely to produce very positive results. Wisely, she had kept silent.

She had reached several other equally gloomy conclusions, among them one that even if she miraculously managed to overpower the guard, she still wouldn't have a snowball's chance in hell of making it out of the house alive. But since she seemed destined to die anyway, she damn well intended to die escaping, not tied to a chair.

A noise overhead—a sound almost like furniture being moved—caught the guard's attention for a couple of minutes. Liz scooted her chair a vital six inches closer to the wall, the carpet muffling the telltale scraping noises. Her goal was the nail head she had seen sticking out of the paneling. If she could just pierce the surgical tape that kept her hands strapped uselessly behind her back, she would be one step closer to a successful escape.

She poked the nail through the tape and began sawing away, keeping her upper body still so that the guard wouldn't realize what she was doing.

She had a couple of advantages, Liz thought, flexing her wrists within the layers of tape. The guard didn't expect her to try to escape, and he didn't know that she was an expert in self-defense—not the stylized self-defense of karate and judo schools, but the real-life self-defense she had been taught by a women's group in New York. Liz had gone to the class after being mugged and almost raped on a New York subway. If she could somehow get the guard to come up close without arousing his suspicion, Liz thought— hoped—prayed—she would have a chance of overpowering him.

From his frequent glances toward the ceiling, it was obvious that the guard's interests lay on the floor above, where the action—whatever that might be—was actually taking place. For a man with a body like King Kong and a trigger-happy finger, playing keeper to a mere woman presumably wasn't much fun.

Her hands were free! A sizable chunk of skin had been left on the nail, but at least she was now potentially mobile. Liz turned an involuntary crow of triumph into a passable imitation of a sob and huddled pathetically in her chair. The guard glanced indifferently toward her, then went back to stroking his gun.

How the devil was she going to get him to come closer? Displaying several inches of thigh wasn't likely to do it. The guy looked as if his bedmate of choice would be a Sherman tank. Liz waited until his gaze wandered toward the door, then toppled her chair with as much of a crash as she could muster on the carpeted floor. For good measure, she added a strangled shriek that she hoped sounded feminine and flustered. She was careful not to scream too loudly. She didn't want to attract the attention of whoever was moving around overhead.

Blood drumming in her skull, she lay on her side, coiled and ready to spring. She watched the guard stride across the room, his body language hinting at irritation rather than suspicion. With a carelessness that Liz prayed might save her life, he allowed the submachine gun to dangle by his side. He came closer. Liz held her breath. His stance suggested he might be in the habit of relying on his size for protection. If so, he might not know it, but he was extremely vulnerable.

Go for his eyes. The instruction from her defense class remained with her, although Liz wasn't sure she'd be able to carry it out.

Your life depends on it, she told herself. *No wimping out, kiddo. This isn't a trial run. This is for real.*

Muttering angrily, the guard bent over her. She launched herself upward from the balls of her feet, butting her head into his stomach with the full force of her weight. Before he could catch his breath, she stomped on his instep with the steel-shafted heel of her shoe, simultaneously sticking her fingers straight into his eyes. He gave a scream of pain even as he raised his gun. He was too late. Liz lowered her fist in a chop that knocked the weapon from his hand. They both dived for it, but she succeeded in grabbing it. She brought the barrel crashing down on his head. It connected with a sickening thud of metal pounding against bone.

The guard keeled over and lay in a crumpled heap on the floor. Liz stuffed a fist into her mouth. She wanted to cry. She wanted to throw up. She wanted to lean against the wall, shaking and shivering.

But she didn't have time for any of that. Tugging the broad silk belt of Alison's robe from her waist, she tied it around the guard's mouth in a makeshift gag. Panting and puffing, she pulled his wrists behind his back and strapped them together as best she could with the tape left over from the roll he and Mikhail had used on her. Right now the guard looked out for the count, but for all she knew, he might revive in five or ten minutes.

"Sleep well, buster," she murmured, wiping her sweaty palms on the sides of Alison's robe.

The stairway was obviously useless as an escape route. Liz had no doubt she would encounter armed opposition long before she reached the upstairs hallway. However, from what little she had been able to see, the house was a typical upper-income suburban home. Which meant that the narrow door in the far corner of the basement was worth exploring. Chances were good that it led into some sort of furnace or utility room.

Tucking the submachine gun under her arm, Liz ran to the corner and pulled open the door. A utility room lay concealed behind the paneling. Never had a bare concrete floor, a dusty furnace and miscellaneous wispy cobwebs looked so attractive. Smiling, she stepped into the little room.

As soon as the door to the rec room closed behind her, darkness descended. Her heart rapidly sliding into her shoes, Liz fumbled for a light switch. Such complete darkness must mean that the room had no windows. *No windows.* And therefore no way out.

When the naked overhead bulb flicked into life, she hesitated, almost afraid to walk around the tiny eight-by-ten space. What would she do if the basement was entirely below ground level? *You'll start digging, that's what,* Liz told herself grimly.

It took her less than a minute to confirm her worst fears: the furnace room lacked any form of window, even a tiny, single pane.

Liz slumped against the plasterboard wall and stared blindly at the furnace. As if to mock her earlier optimistic thoughts, she saw a small gardening trowel, minus its handle, nestled at the base of the hot-water heater. To dig her way out? She gave a bitter laugh. She had no idea where Alison and Mikhail had gone, but she doubted if she had more than thirty minutes before somebody would come back to check on her. Even if she had two hours—an impossible dream—she couldn't dig her way out of the basement in two hours.

But maybe she could find a hiding place and outwait her captors. Maybe she could squeeze between the furnace and the water heater. Or clamber onto the top of the appliances to reach the ceiling. The acoustical tiles would be easy to remove.

Anything, any hope, was better than surrendering meekly to the fate Mikhail and Alison had in store for her. With renewed energy, she resumed her inspection of the utility room.

She found the grating tucked into an odd position behind the furnace. At this time of year the furnace wasn't operating, so she had only marginal difficulty in squeezing behind the furnace to examine her find more carefully. Clamping down hard on her rising excitement, she peered through the iron latticework at the murky hole behind. She couldn't see all the way to the end, but had the definite impression that there was a faint lessening of the darkness toward the end of the crawl space. A window? *Dear God, let it be a window.*

The grating should have been easy to remove, but rust had welded it stuck and she struggled for almost ten minutes, using the trowel as a lever, before she managed to pry it loose.

Sweating, filthy and triumphant, she rested the grating on top of the furnace, tossed the submachine gun onto the rocky concrete floor of the crawl space, and then heaved herself inside. By lying flat on her stomach and stretching out her hand as far as it would go, she was able to reach the grating and pull it into place behind her.

Surely the crawl space must lead somewhere outside? Wasn't that what they were for—to provide access to water pipes and telephone lines? Liz closed her eyes, willing herself not to hope too fiercely. Squatting, because the rough concrete floor was too painful to crawl on, she waddled and wobbled along the ten feet of dark tunnel. High-heeled evening shoes and a silk robe definitely didn't make the most convenient escape outfit ever invented, she realized.

She was steeling herself for disappointment, so when she found the window she stared at it stupidly, wasting several precious seconds in blank contemplation. It was encrusted with grime and dust, so she scraped at it with the heel of her shoe, trying to detect some sign of an alarm system. As far as she could tell, there wasn't an electronic beam or even an old-fashioned electric wire anywhere in sight.

They can't have been careless enough to leave this entrance to the house unprotected, Liz warned herself. *When you smash this window, all hell's going to break loose.*

But waiting wasn't going to disconnect the alarm system, if there was one. And every minute she delayed made the prospect of pursuit more likely. Drawing in a deep breath, Liz plunged the heel of her sandal through the glass.

Silence. No bells clanged, no sirens hooted, but she knew that meant nothing. Some of the most sophisticated alarm

systems flashed silent warnings in every room. In a frenzy
of fear, she slashed at the glass with the butt of the gun,
indifferent to the shards of glass splattering against her
wrists and arms. When the wooden frame was denuded of
glass, she pulled herself through, ignoring the ripping of
glass fragments on her breast and stomach and legs.

She emerged into a shallow window well, which was
slimy with leaf mold and garden debris. Liz peered cautiously over the rim of the well and allowed the night breeze
to caress her face with the promise of freedom. She smiled
wryly. Cobwebs, crawl spaces, leaf mold, chilly night air.
This was her night for finding strange things beautiful.

Body tense, ears straining, she gazed rapidly from one
side of the house to the other. She could see most of the
front driveway, and it seemed empty. The ambulance must
have been driven into the garage, out of sight of any inquisitive neighbors. Abandoning the gun as too heavy to
carry, Liz used her upper-body strength to pull herself out
of the window well.

She was on her feet, kicking off her high-heeled shoes
and running across the damp grass before her conscious
mind could scream caution. She ran away from the lighted
driveway, away from the front of the house. Like any other
frightened night creature, she sought the safety of darkness, and angled through the trees and bushes as she dashed
toward the road. At any moment she expected to hear the
hue and cry of pursuit. At any moment she expected to hear
the hateful softness of Mikhail's laugh. *Dorogoya.* She
would never be able to hear that word again without shuddering.

She was on the road now, running along the grass bank
at the side. Still no sound of pursuers, only the rasp of her
own breath in her lungs and the distant bark of a dog.

The lights of a house loomed ahead. Was it safe to knock
on the door and beg for help? Her feet had almost turned

into the driveway, when some primitive survival instinct flared to life, reminding her that she had no way of knowing who owned these houses. The owners were as likely to be enemies as friends.

Over the relentless thrumming of blood in her ears, she heard the unmistakable sounds of a car approaching. Instinct once again took over, sending her scurrying for the protection of a clump of shrubbery, thick with spring foliage. Now that she had stopped running, she had time to notice that her teeth were chattering, even though she didn't feel cold. Oh God, she didn't want to die! Not before she had a chance to see Mikhail and Alison in jail. Not before she had a chance to tell Dex how much she loved him.

It wasn't a car she had heard, but a small pizza delivery truck, and it turned into the driveway right next to where Liz was crouching. After her experience with the ambulance, she was no longer trusting enough to believe that a truck saying Poppa Pellini Delivers on its side panels necessarily meant that the truck contained pizzas. Squirming as deeply as she could into the protection of the bushes, she watched the truck draw to a halt.

A young girl in a gingham uniform climbed out of the truck, cardboard carton in hand. If she carried a bomb, Liz could only think it smelled a lot like pepperoni. The girl walked across the grass toward the front door, leaving the engine running and the radio blaring a hit from the top twenty.

Swifter than thought, Liz left the protection of the bushes and ran toward the delivery truck. She threw herself into the driver's seat and let off the hand brake. The truck moved forward. The Fates were on her side, Liz thought, glancing down. It had automatic transmission.

Without a twinge of remorse for having entered the ranks of car thieves and other felons, Liz stepped on the accelerator. Ignoring the anguished shouts of the delivery girl, she gunned the truck out of the driveway.

First she was going to rescue Dexter. Then she was going to eat some stolen pizza.

Chapter Sixteen

Liz found the all-night convenience store about ten minutes down the road at the first intersection she came to. It was obviously a hangout for local teenagers and, despite the fact that it was almost one in the morning, the place was quite crowded.

Liz jumped down down from the truck and headed for the phone. A stack of cracker boxes inside one of the windows turned the glass into a shadowy mirror, and for the first time in hours, she became aware of how she looked—and how little she was wearing.

But there was no time to worry about the red silk robe, now tattered, smeared with leaf mold and flapping beltless in the nighttime breeze; no time to worry about the fact that she wore nothing underneath the robe except a lace teddy, a fancy garter belt and shredded stockings. There was certainly no time to worry about what her face and hair must look like, daubed with dust and festooned with cobwebs.

Pulling the robe firmly around her waist, Liz strode into the convenience store with all the dignity a shoeless, mud-spattered woman could hope to muster.

By some miracle, the phone was not only in working order, but nobody was using it. Ignoring the openmouthed stares of two teenagers, who obviously felt somewhat resentful that their dyed-feather mohawks and safety-pinned ears couldn't begin to compete with Liz's bizarre outfit, she picked up the phone and reached for some change—only to realize that she had no money. Her body beaded with cold sweat, she wondered if Dexter and Amanda were about to lose their lives for the sake of a quarter. Shaking, she turned to the teenagers.

"Could you please loan me a quarter?" she asked. "I have a really important call to make. Somebody's life is at stake."

His gaze pitying, one of the youngsters reached into his pocket and flipped her a quarter. "You oughta give him up, lady. Ain't no good thinking he'll stop knocking you around, because he won't."

"Thank you. It's not what you think, but I'm really grateful." She dropped the coin into the slot and dialed the FBI emergency number. Her fingers shook so badly that it was a miracle she managed to dial correctly.

The thirty seconds before an FBI operator came on the line seemed endless. The moment the call connected, Liz started speaking.

"I'm calling on behalf of Senator Dexter Rand of the United States Senate," she said. She knew her voice sounded squeaky and uncertain, but she drew in a steadying breath and continued with all the firmness she could muster. "I have a special emergency number I need to reach, and only the FBI can put the call through."

"What number's that, Miss?" The FBI operator sounded bored and irritated, as if she'd already handled more than her share of crank calls that night.

Liz repeated the eleven digits Dexter had compelled her to learn, and sensed an immediate change in the attitude of the woman at the other end of the phone. "I'm connecting you now," the woman said briskly. "Hold on, please. The connection will take about thirty-five seconds."

Precisely thirty-two seconds later, Liz was talking to the commander-in-chief of Washington's Special Forces.

ALISON, clad only in a black satin slip, pretended to cringe and sob as Mikhail positioned her in yet another seductive pose on the cream leather sofa. Dexter wondered how many more tears the woman could shed before his temper frayed completely. Not very many, he suspected. He glanced at his watch. One-thirty a.m. Three hours since he and Liz had been captured. Time to get the hell out of here.

"Enough of these damn fool photographs," he said, picking up Alison's dress and tossing it to her. For once the role he was playing and the reality of his feelings coincided. "Igor, you've made your point. These pictures link me to Elizabeth Meacham. They strengthen the circumstantial evidence of the case you're constructing against me. But nothing you photograph here tonight will compel me to vote against the F-19B. You're going to have to trust my word that I'll vote against the plane, just like I'll have to trust you to set Liz free. It's a standoff, Igor. If both of us acknowledge that fact, maybe we can all go home."

Igor grunted, but whatever reply he might have made was lost as a huge gorilla of a man burst into the room, shielding his bruised and puffy eyes against the overhead lights that had been turned on for the photographs. Waving his arms—seemingly to display a grubby red silk belt—the man burst into a stream of impassioned, apologetic speech in Russian.

Taking advantage of Igor's momentary distraction, Dexter edged toward the arched doorway that connected the living room to the dining room. The overhead light switch was fixed to the connecting wall right by this arch. And the heavy table lamp that provided the only other source of light in the room rested on a nearby coffee table. If he were very lucky he might be able to flip the overhead switch and, in a continuation of the same movement, throw the table lamp at one of his captors. His chosen victim would almost certainly be knocked out, since Dexter's aim was outstanding. And the resulting darkness would pro-

vide him with a valuable few moments' head start, if he
wanted to make a dash for freedom.

The temptation to go out fighting was great, and yet cool
logic warned him that this wasn't a situation that war-
ranted physical action. Pretending to accept Igor's demands was probably a safer, more certain way to extricate
himself from Igor's clutches. Unfortunately, for a man of
Dexter's training, pretending meekness required more self-
discipline than anything else.

Igor and Mikhail were obviously furious at whatever
news the newcomer had brought. Shooting a quick glance
at Alison, Dexter saw that she, too, was so perturbed that
she had temporarily forgotten her role as Liz. She sat on the
edge of the sofa, eyes flashing in cold fury as Igor hurled
questions at the gorilla man. There was no doubt in Dexter's mind that she understood every word Igor and Mikhail were saying.

If he was going to make a run for it, the dining room
would provide his only possible escape route. Dexter turned
unobtrusively to scan the room behind him. A very swift
survey was sufficient to tell him that it didn't present a realistic prospect of success. Both doors opened onto the
main hallway, and he would undoubtedly be caught long
before he reached the front entrance.

Dexter allowed himself one more regretful glance around
the shadowy dining room. A slight movement caught his
eye, and he froze into absolute stillness. Someone was
crouched there, half-hidden by the bulk of the china cabinet. His heart leaped.

A black-clad man, face masked with greasepaint, rose
slowly to his feet, fingers pressed against his mouth in an
urgent signal for Dexter to keep quiet.

"What is going on over there?" Igor demanded suddenly. "What are you doing by the door, Senator Rand?"

"Keeping out of your way," Dexter replied easily, shoving his hands into the pockets of his pants and lounging

carelessly against the wall. "Seems like you and your friend Mikhail are seriously upset about something."

Igor hesitated. "A minor administrative matter only," he said coldly. "There has been some small mistake in regard to Comrade Mikhail's airplane ticket for Stockholm."

Right, Dexter thought. *That's why gorilla man looks ready to shoot himself, and the rest of you look mad enough to hand him the gun.* Aloud, he merely said, "A mistake in the ticket, eh? It's amazing how no government seems able to get its clerical system working efficiently, isn't it?"

"I admit that our bureaucracy has not yet attained the degree of socialist efficiency we might wish." Igor sounded considerably more mellow. He was too seasoned a campaigner to allow Dexter more than a glimpse of his anger. "Mikhail, why don't you and Yuri go back downstairs to the basement and search for the missing ticket? I'm sure Yuri has simply mislaid it somewhere."

"Very well, if you think it worthwhile. Personally, I think he must have dropped it outside the house." Mikhail took Yuri's arm and propelled him with considerable force toward the basement stairs. Casting a glance toward the sofa, he said, "Lizushka, my sweet, do you not wish to put on your dress? The Comrade Senator will not be able to take advantage of your charming body tonight. That pleasure must await the vote on the F-19B."

Alison flashed her husband a look of sheer venom, but recalled to a realization of her role, she stood up and struggled into the dress, a fresh set of tears flowing down her cheeks. Dexter thought the woman deserved an entry in the Guinness Book of World Records. Most Crocodile Tears Ever Shed in One Continuous Session.

Mikhail and Yuri disappeared from view. Dexter sincerely hoped they would walk straight into the arms of a pair of waiting commandos. He was becoming more and more optimistic that somehow Liz had managed to escape. How else had the commandos known where to come?

Pretending to refasten the studs on his shirt, he risked another quick look into the dining room. The single black-clad figure had now become four. Dexter let his hand creep up toward the light switch. One of the blackened faces dipped in a brief, authoritative nod of approval.

In a single swift move, Dexter flipped off the overhead switch and leaned forward to grab the table lamp, jerking the cord from the wall socket. In the last moment of light, he took aim at Igor, then threw the lamp with all the force he could muster. He heard the satisfying clunk of lamp hitting flesh, a split second before the four black shadows erupted into the room.

ALISON FINALLY STOPPED CRYING when one of the commandos walked over and slipped her wrists into a pair of handcuffs. "What the *hell* do you think you're doing?" she demanded.

"Arresting you. I have to warn you that anything you say may be taken down and used in evidence at your trial—"

Panic swept over Alison's lovely features. "I don't know what you're thinking of," she said, her voice husky. She looked with desperate appeal toward Dexter, who was talking softly and animatedly to another of the commandos. "Dexter, darling," she called. "Darling, please tell this silly man he's making a dreadful mistake."

Dexter turned slowly, allowing every ounce of his scorn to show. "Why would I do that, Alison? I hope they lock you in jail and throw away the key."

She paled. "A-Alison? Y-you knew I wasn't Liz? All the time?"

"Not all the time. You had me fooled for about five seconds."

"But we're identical!"

Dexter smiled coldly. "You're nothing like Liz. You never have been and you never will be. Liz would no more have sat on that sofa weeping and wailing than she would have flown. Somebody should have told you that silicone implants and a nose job can't change a person's character."

"But you can't let me go to prison!"

"Watch me. You were perfectly willing to have your sister killed. Thank your lucky stars you're in America, and nobody's going to let me be alone with you in a quiet corner of the jail. Otherwise you'd need another nose job."

Alison was weeping again. This time her tears might even have been real. A commando entered the living room. "Ms. Meacham has just arrived, Senator, if you'd like to meet her outside."

Dexter left the room without a backward glance.

He saw Liz as soon as he stepped out of the front door. Spotlighted in the beam of a police floodlight, her entire face shone with joy as he walked toward her.

"Dex!" She ran into his arms, and he held her tight, feeling the softness that was Liz, the warmth and the passion that seemed to flow from every pore of her skin. He stroked his hands up and down her spine, trying to reabsorb the essence of her into his soul.

"The KGB are such fools," he said, lovingly plucking a dead leaf and a wisp of cobweb from her hair. "Imagine thinking I wouldn't know the difference between you and Alison."

She insinuated her fingers underneath his shirt. Wherever she touched, he felt a little explosion of desire. "How could you possibly tell us apart?" she asked. "They made her look just like me."

"They couldn't capture the magic," he said softly, only half teasing. "When she kissed me, I felt empty. My heart didn't start pounding, and my skin didn't feel as if it was on fire."

"Is that how you feel when we kiss?" Liz lifted her face, blue-gray eyes dark with wonder. "I thought it was only me who felt like that."

He hadn't realized how much he loved the eloquence of her eyes until he had seen the coldness of Alison's. "I think that's how I feel," he said solemnly. "But Igor had me captive in there so damn long I've almost forgotten. Can we test it and see?"

She raised her mouth eagerly to meet his. Their lips joined in an explosion of need and pent-up anxiety. She tasted warm and passionate, generous and sexy. She tasted of Liz. She tasted of love. His heart started to pound. His skin felt as if it were on fire. He knew that if they remained together for the next sixty years, she would still retain the power to stimulate and entrance him. He wondered why in the world they had wasted so much time apart.

The spotlight mounted on one of the trucks swung around to focus on the squad of commandos escorting Igor, Mikhail, Alison and four other men to the waiting vans. Liz and Dexter didn't even notice.

She put up her hand to touch his cheek. He caught her fingers, and kissed every spot where he could see a cut or a graze. "Did they tell you Amanda is safe?" he asked. "She's been back home with my parents since early this evening."

She nodded. "The commander told me. I'm so glad for you, Dex. My biggest nightmare was that they'd kill her before the Special Forces could get to wherever Mikhail and gang were hiding her."

"We'll fly home tomorrow and see her," he said.

"I'd like that. You won't feel completely secure until you've hugged her."

"Marry me, Liz," he said huskily. "Live with me and be my love. This time we'll get it right, I know we will."

She went very still. She was quiet for so long that he forced a laugh. "I hoped it wouldn't be such a difficult decision."

She looked up, her expression grave. "Dex, you don't have to feel obligated—"

"Obligated? You think I feel obligated? Are you crazy, woman?" He dragged her hard against his body, moving his hips aggressively so that she could feel the potency of his arousal. "Does that feel like a man who's *obligated*? Liz, where in the world did you get such a crazy notion? I love you. I want to marry you."

She looked away. "My twin sister's going to jail for treason," she said. "Sometimes...maybe...love isn't enough."

Dexter felt the relief start to seep into his veins. "Love is always enough," he said quietly. "Answer me one question, Liz. Do you love me?"

"Yes, but—"

"There are no buts. Your sister's choices are her responsibility, not yours. And if you're worried about the damage her actions will do to my career in the Senate, there'll be none. Alison and Mikhail will almost certainly be tried *in camera* and Igor, unfortunately, won't be tried at all. He's already shrieking for his lawyer and claiming diplomatic immunity. The most the State Department will be able to do is get him shipped back to Moscow."

The commander slammed the door on the second of the navy-blue unmarked vans, then gave the instruction for the small convoy to move out of the driveway. Two rows of faces peered over the bushes on either side of the property, as two sets of neighbors viewed the fascinating goings-on. Liz and Dexter didn't even hear the engines start up, much less notice that the vans were leaving.

"Even if you don't care about Alison and what she's done, there's still the problem of Amanda. She doesn't like me."

"Darling Liz, I love my daughter to distraction, but that doesn't give her the right to choose my wife."

"How about the right to choose her stepmother?"

"Liz, you're worrying about phantoms. The week before last, Amanda was all in favor of me getting married. Last week she was opposed. Next week she might be all in favor again. It's not that I'm dismissing the importance of her feelings, but she doesn't know what a stepmother is. I'm confident you can show her that stepmothers are wonderful."

"I'd like to try," Liz whispered. "I love you so much, Dex. I think maybe I never stopped loving you."

"I love you, too. Darling Liz, it's so good to have you back."

Liz was only vaguely aware of the commander of the Special Forces, the driver of the commander's car, and two rows of fascinated neighbors watching as Dexter swept her into his arms and demonstrated—with amazing thoroughness—that two human beings can kiss almost indefinitely without any need to come up for air. Then the outside world faded from her consciousness, and nothing was left except Dex: the taste of him in her mouth and the throb of him in her heart.

She returned to reality when the commander, a man not normally noted for his overflowing supply of sentimentality, finally tapped Dexter on the shoulder. "Senator, I'm getting chilly, even if you and Ms. Meacham seem to be doing a damn fine job of setting each other on fire. You might be interested to know that our headquarters contains a most comfortable suite of rooms." He cleared his throat. "With a king-size bed. We could drive you there now, if you and Ms. Meacham are ready to leave. Then you'd be on hand for tomorrow's debriefing."

Dexter grinned. "If your suite has a shower as well as a bed, it's a deal."

"A king-size shower," the commander replied. His men would never have believed it, but Liz could have sworn there was a distinct twinkle in his eye. "There's also a most accommodating Jacuzzi."

Liz looked up at Dexter, her mouth curving into a tiny smile. "The possibilities," she said, "seem almost endless."

Dexter lifted her hands and pressed the tips of her fingers to his lips. "Yes," he agreed. "They do."

❦ SILHOUETTE

Intrigue

COMING NEXT MONTH

HIS BROTHER'S KEEPER Gay Cameron

Trevor Steele didn't believe in deception, unless it could save Casey, a woman he swore not to touch, to kiss, to love…a woman his brother had married, and maligned. A woman who would have nothing to do with him, if she knew the truth.

SOMETHING BORROWED, SOMETHING BLUE
Adrianne Lee

After the Carlyle family lost its wedding heirloom that guaranteed bliss, all marriages failed. Now Lyssa set out to retrieve the necklace from the Rival family. Craig Rival almost trusted Lyssa—until the wedding necklace was stolen and his uncle's sudden death started to look like murder…

TIMEWALKER Aimée Thurlo

Benjamin Two Eagle was a courageous warrior who had been trapped in time, and Julia Stevens alone had the power to free him. He had been betrayed and would now see justice done. But although he had been released from one trap, did Julia now present an even more dangerous one?

THINGS REMEMBERED Kelsey Roberts

Danielle Baylor was determined to know the truth about her parents' deaths, but the closer she got to understanding, the closer Tyler Cantrell got to her. And the more Tyler held her in his arms, the more Dani was sure he held the key to unleash her secret demons…

COMING NEXT MONTH FROM

 SILHOUETTE

Sensation

A thrilling mix of passion, adventure and drama

EYEWITNESS Kathleen Creighton
LEFT AT THE ALTAR Justine Davis
FORGOTTEN VOWS?... Maggie Shayne
GABLE'S LADY Linda Turner

Special Edition

Satisfying romances packed with emotion

THE SULTAN'S WIVES Tracy Sinclair
A ROSE AND A WEDDING VOW Andrea Edwards
JAKE'S MOUNTAIN Christine Flynn
BABY MY BABY Trisha Alexander
SARA'S FATHER Jennifer Mikels
THE MOTHER OF HIS CHILD
Ann Howard White

Desire

Provocative, sensual love stories for the woman of today

WOMAN HATER Diana Palmer
ACCIDENTAL BRIDE Jackie Merritt
ONE STUBBORN COWBOY Barbara McMahon
THE PAUPER AND THE PREGNANT PRINCESS Nancy Martin
TEXAS HEAT Barbara McCauley
BEDAZZLED Rita Rainville

A years supply of Silhouette Desires — absolutely free!

Would you like to win a years supply of seductive and breathtaking romances? Well, you can and they're FREE! All you have to do is complete the word puzzle below and send it to us by 31st January 1996. The first 5 correct entries picked out of the bag after that date will win a years supply of Silhouette Desire novels (six books every month—worth over £150). What could be easier?

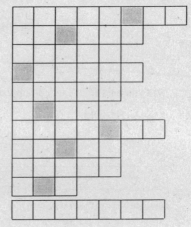

GMWIMSIN

NNSAUT

ACEHB

EMSMUR

ANCOE

DNSA

RTOISTU

THEOL

ATYCH

NSU

MYSTERY DESTINATION

Please turn over for details on how to enter

**How
to
enter**

Simply sort out the jumbled letters to make ten words all to do with being on holiday. Enter your answers in the grid, then unscramble the letters in the shaded squares to find out our mystery holiday destination.

After you have completed the word puzzle and found our mystery destination, don't forget to fill in your name and address in the space provided below and return this page in an envelope (you don't need a stamp). Competition ends 31st January 1996.

**Silhouette Desire Holiday Competition
FREEPOST**
P.O. Box 344
Croydon
Surrey
CR9 9EL

Are you a Reader Service Subscriber? Yes ❏   No ❏

Ms/Mrs/Miss/Mr _____

Address _____

_____

_____ Postcode _____

One application per household.

You may be mailed with other offers from other reputable companies as a result of this application. If you would prefer not to receive such offers, please tick box. ❏

COMP295
A